ST

SACHINCKO PARKER TUCKER

Linda
Stay alive
Sachincko P.
Tucker

ALABASTER BOOKS NORTH CAROLINA

This is a wonderful book of fiction. Some of the characters have actual Names known to the author, but with ficticious actions, locations, and time frames. Any resemblance to actual events or localities in connection to names used in this book is purely coincidental.

STICK OF IVORY

An Alabaster book
PUBLISHING HISTORY
Alabaster limited edition printed October 1998
Alabaster mass market edition / Feb 1999

Editor Sam Zahran

Printing by Rose Printing Company, Inc.

ISBN # 0-9667558-0-4

PRINTED IN THE UNITED STATES OF AMERICA

THANKING GOD THROUGH JESUS CHRIST

This book is dedicated in loving memory to my late precious Mother-in-Law Edna Tucker. Rest well, my sweet mother, you will live forever in my heart.

To my Mother Bishop Vernell Chestnutt without whom this would not have been possible. Thank you for all the financial support you gave me. I commend you for your tireless efforts and tough love you exhibited when I was a child. You made me believe in myself and gave me the fortitude to accomplish this odyssey. I love and thank you dearly!

STICK OF IVORY

PROLOGUE
1958

The August heat made the little girl's starched petticoats under her yellow and white nylon Sunday dress almost unbearable as she held tight to her mama's sweating fingers. She had sat through a whole hour of Sunday school with the other five-year-olds before the church service started, and now it was finally the end of the two-hour meeting. She hadn't fidgeted even once in Sunday school and only once in church, and that was almost right near the end when her slips started to itch her terribly in the still, blistering air inside the Bennet Union Baptist Church. One cocked eyebrow from her mama up in the choir stand in her long, black robe had put an end to that. Now they were on their way to the Dairy Queen to get her reward of a vanilla ice cream cone. As they walked around to the Colored side of the building, the little girl with her starchy slips still itching slid her fingers from her mama's and gave her thighs a good stiff scratch.

"Livia! Put your dress down," Mary Frazier whispered, looking down at the top of her little girl's wavy, jet black hair. Today, her hair was parted down the middle and braided into two very long, thick ropes. The ends were tied with twin yellow lace ribbons. The child gave her legs a few more quick, desperate scratches and let go of her slips. "Now come along," Mary said, holding out her hand for her daughter to grasp again. "That line at the window is getting longer and longer while we're just standing here."

Olivia's hand clasped the large fingers again, and her black patent leather Sunday shoes clicked away as she followed her mother to the back of the line. Blacks weren't allowed to go inside the air-conditioned ice cream parlor or sit on the white cast iron chairs and eat at the pretty white round tables. But the white lady at the small, round window was very nice to all the people she waited on; she always had a special smile for them. Sometimes the inside was extra busy, and occasionally a white person would go outside to the window and cut in front of everyone, but this nice white lady wouldn't have any of that: she sent them back into the parlor.

On their way home, the little girl happily licked away at her ice cream. Her mother, licking her own cone, smiled down at her. Mary knew it was difficult for her youngest child, the only girl, to be anything but the tomboy she was; after all, she did have four older brothers. But she'll do fine, Mary thought.

Just then, Mary looked up. Coming toward them, about twenty feet away, were two well-dressed white men in suits.

"Give me your hand, Livia," said Mary, reaching for it. As they neared the men and moved off the sidewalk to let them pass, she spoke: "Good afternoon to both you fine gentlemen, sir."

As the men passed, Mary and Olivia humbly kept their eyes to the ground and didn't anticipate any reply. Thus was life.

Mary had been taught compliancy by her mother, and she in turn taught her children to be subservient, but to a lesser degree. Times <u>were</u> getting better. But Mary wondered: If time had dealt even a semblance of humanity to the slaves or post-Civil War negroes, would she have been allowed to share an equal life with her white counterparts—or even a sidewalk . . . ?

CHAPTER ONE
1993

Saturday, August 8th, Sandy's sixteenth birthday, rolled in at 101 degrees before noon. Despite the heat, two of her closest friends kept the movie and pizza date which they had planned as a gift. Because of the heat, the girls waited until 6:00 p.m. to see the show. But it was just as hot when the three girls went into the movie as it had been at noon. Sandy had been dying to see this movie. For as long as she could remember, she had been fascinated by civil rights movies like the one she was about to see. The problem was that these issues in any form always left her feeling melancholy. She had been a lot younger when she saw Roots, and it affected her as much then as this movie would now.

When Sandy became a teenager, her mother, Olivia, said Sandy had developed "an attitude." She became quiet and moody when she had to be around adults. She didn't understand them and they didn't understand her, she thought. She used to love to read, but now she could care less, unless it was a book about slaves, and these only made her angry. She was always getting into trouble, so to fix that she became evasive and extra polite to grown ups.

A few years ago she went to see Janet Jackson in *Poetic Justice.* It was good, and Janet was her favorite. Everyone said they looked alike and she had taught herself to dance like her and sometimes she wore her hair like Janet wore hers in the video "If." like Janet in the movie, she learned to cuss like a sailor. She got so used to it that she let one slip out around her mother one day and got in big trouble. Most adults with the exception of her mother and some teachers only saw her quiet side. She spoke when she was spoken to and made polite, and short, conversation if forced.

Sandy was a beautiful girl, but it didn't phase her one way or the other. Standing 5' 6" and well-proportioned, she was thin but shapely. Her skin was medium caramel colored, and her hair was jet black and long. She wore a spiral, curly look, but on hot, hot days she wore a pony tail up high. She was not a troubled child. She had just begun to want to keep up with the crowd.

Sandy cherished the memories she had of herself as a child, five or six years old, sitting with her Grandmother Mary on the front porch of their home. While her grandmother sat knitting or crocheting, Sandy would sit on the floor beside her grandmother's rocking chair and play jack stones. She vividly remembered the scent of lilacs from that old-fashioned toilet water her grandmother wore. The fragrance seemed to encircle her.

Sometimes her grandmother told her a story or two; most of the time she reminisced about her slave ancestors. She heard a lot about Grandma Charlotte, her great, great grandmother, and that always made her jolly. But tales about mean white slave owners made her sad. The chair, rocking rhythmically, muffled the soft pat-pat of her jack stone ball. She couldn't hear the ball at all if grandmother was rocking fast and hard, and it seemed as though the harder she rocked, the faster she could knit, and she knitted fast when she was worried about something or someone. Other times she and her grandmother sat on the porch swing and ate raisins. At times like this, Sandy asked questions: "Why do white people hate other people, grandma?" "Will God still bless us when we hate them back?" "Grandma, everybody we know works for white people. Is this still slavery?"

Her grandmother would get a frown across her forehead and say, "Sandra, we are all God's children. People can be mean and all, no matter what color they are."

Sandy was convinced that whites owned everything and kept the black race under their thumbs. In first grade, she asked her grandmother why only four black teachers taught at her elementary school. Whatever her grandmother told her didn't satisfy her because she had drawn a conclusion of her own. By the time she was in second grade she was asking her Grandma Mary questions like: "Grandma, if you or me had a dog and we took away his flea collar, would you kick it and call it names because he got fleas?" Four months after the child turned seven, her grandmother died in her sleep. Sandy felt the loss as deeply as the older family members. And she never forgot the stories about Grandma Charlotte's life and loves.

Now, on her sixteenth birthday, here she was with her two oldest friends in the world, unable to share the thoughts that troubled her. Sandy wanted to be alone, to think for a while, so, even though they had all been starved for pizza, she tried to wiggle out of it. Before they crossed the street to the Pizza Palace, she stopped.

"I'm sleepy," she said. "I've got absolutely no appetite for pizza tonight. You all go on without me; I'm going home. Thanks. I had fun."

Julie, the smallest of the three girls, spun on her heels and faced Sandy. "What? Are you nuts or sumpin'? I saved my quarters for weeks to buy you this birthday pizza! What's your problem? I could've been at the beach this weekend but I stuck around for this. . . ."

Robin had been thinking that Sandy was extra quiet after the show. But not wanting pizza? "Hold it. Hold it!" said Robin, the smart mouth of the trio; "Sandy, that movie upset you, didn't it? Girlfriend, now that I think about it, these civil rights issues always get you down. Why did you let us take you? You could've seen something else. After all, Jesup does have two theaters now, remember?"

"No," Sandy said, looking down at her feet; "I really wanted to see it. You guys were great fun, but I guess that stuff will always get me down. I'm sorry!" She turned and ran toward home.

The girls knew that she was crying, but they didn't try to stop her; they understood. Julie looked up at Robin and exhaled, blowing her wispy bangs into disorder. "Ouch, I blew that, huh?" she shrieked. Julie might have been the smallest of the three, but she was surely the loudest. Without waiting for an answer, she went on. "Well, let's go get that juicy pizza!! She'll be okay. She got like this when we watched *Roots* on TV." The two ran across Main Street and into the pizza parlor.

By the time Sandy reached her bi-level white frame house, she felt a wee bit better. She climbed the three cement steps and sat in one of the four chairs occupying the porch. The porch swing was still where it always was, but gone was the rocker; it had served its purpose. It had rocked more babies in its time than you could shake a switch at! Sandy's mother let Sandy keep the rocker in her room now. Sandy's grandmother had passed the house and everything in it to her youngest child, Olivia. Grandmother had raised five children in this house. Sandy walked over to the swing and started swinging gently. Gone were the squeaks that used to tell her when Grandma Mary was on the porch with raisins to munch! Sandy's father, Richard, had oiled the springs and silenced the noise. That had upset her, but she never said anything about it. As she rocked back and forth in the swing, she looked out over the neighborhood.

Sandy had never lived anywhere else; her mother and father stayed in the house after they married and started their family, and that had suited grandmother just fine. She had never wanted her only daughter to leave home.

Sandy's dad was one of the town's four black police officers, and her mother was a second-grade teacher in one of the town's four elementary schools. The town had long ago been integrated, but the people still kept to their own kind. All their neighbors were black and most likely related in some way or another. The house directly across the street belonged to the Millers, one of the few families in Jesup not at all related to Sandy's family. Their house was an eyesore: it was a sprawling house that was never maintained, but Mr. Miller kept adding rooms to it. Nine kids and four adults lived there. The Miller yard was grassless, with fine, loose sand, like a beach; sometimes someone would rake it, but that was the exception. Several great white oak trees shaded the old house, and Mrs. Miller was the one most likely to be raking the debris in the yard. She was very pretty, despite the yearly pregnancies. She always had a smile on her lovely oval face, and her long black hair was forever neat in the hair net at the nape of her neck. Tonight Sandy could hear a baby crying and a man and a woman yelling at each other. Mr. Miller was probably fighting with one of Mrs. Miller's sisters, identical twins, who lived with them. The twins were twenty years old this year. Annette and Jeanette Smith shared everything. It was rumored they even shared Mr. Miller.

For a moment, Sandy lay back in the swing, closed her eyes, and tuned out all the noise. She heard nothing but the crickets singing and an occasional frog croaking in the distance. The breeze was tepid and caressing, and it felt good on her hot brow. Looking at her watch, Sandy decided to go in and let her mother know she was home. She didn't feel like conversation, so she planned to make it quick and get up to her room, fast. She silently thanked her Uncle Edward again for the small air conditioner he had installed two weeks ago in one of her bedroom windows as an early birthday gift. Stepping in the front door, she checked the lock behind her but left the porch light on because her father's car wasn't home yet. Her mother heard her come in and called out to her. Answering back, she walked into the kitchen.

"Hi, mom."

Olivia smiled and signaled her to sit down. "Want some iced tea?"

"No thanks," Sandy answered trying to keep it light. She didn't feel like trying to act happy right then and tried to get away as soon as she saw an opening, but her mother stopped her.

"Whoa! Where are you going? I haven't even asked you how you liked the movie."

Sandy already had one Nike on the bottom step but stopped and walked half way back to the kitchen.

"Mom, I don't feel like talking, but if you insist . . . ," Sandy said dryly. "Let me go wash my face. I'm hot." She sprinted up the gleaming hardwood stairs, holding on to the shellacked bannister all the way up. Olivia turned back to the dishes.

Olivia Tucker was a small woman, and there was a softness about her that was present in most Southern women. She was very content in her role as wife, mother of two, and teacher. Her family found her priceless. She was also a pretty woman with large dimples in each cheek that flashed when she talked. Her daughter looked a little like her, but their personalities were as different as night and day. She couldn't understand her daughter's sullenness.

She and her husband had made what they called a "functional" family life for their two children. They couldn't remedy the ills of society, but they were preparing their kids for them. Drying her hands on her crisp, white apron, she walked over to the stairs and called to her son to turn his boom box down. He had used his allowances to buy a new "Shai" and S. W. V. tape today, and he was trying them out. Olivia shook her head: her kids were blessed, she thought. She knew that Sandy would feel like this after that movie, but what could she do? She was always comparing her own childhood to Sandy's to show Sandy how different times were now and how fortunate she was. But Sandy didn't see it that way. She was very popular and had lots of friends, but over the summer she had become moody and, much to her mother's chagrin, couldn't shake it. Turning off the kitchen light, Olivia walked into the living room and turned a lamp on to wait for her daughter. She looked around the room. Most of the furniture that was there had been replaced with new pieces since her mother's death, with the exception of a few that she found irreplaceable. It was a pleasant room with walnut paneling replacing the faded rosebud wallpaper that she grew up with. The hardwood floors were waxed to a mirror shine, and area rugs like the braided one in the front of the old- fashioned flagstone fireplace gave the room a homey look. The mahogany coffee table and end tables were antiques. They had been willed to her mother by a former employer. The sofa and lounger were covered with a Tahitian cotton print, but her husband's easy chair was a solid gold that complemented the others. Tastefully decorating the walls in beautiful frames were pictures of her family and her husband's. A large Zenith console TV (a gift from her husband) adorned the space opposite the wall facing the door. Her brother Edward had sent the drapes and sheers all the way from Germany when he was there eight years ago. These were her pride and joy. They were heavy cream-colored lace sheers with paisley drapes over them. Olivia thought there were no better-looking windows anywhere in Jesup.

Just when Olivia decided that "If the mountain wouldn't come to Mohammed, then Mohammed would go to the mountain," Sandy came down the steps. She walked into the living room and flopped down into a chair. Olivia cut right to the chase.

"Sandy, I know what's bothering you. Do you want to talk about it?"

Yeah, right, Sandy thought. Fat chance. Looking at the blank TV screen, she effected her best 'Do I have a choice' look.

"Well?" Olivia said, after Sandy nodded but said nothing.

"'Well' nothing!" Sandy said. "Like you said, you already know."

Olivia did already know, and it was getting worse year by year. She frankly didn't know how anyone could help her daughter, and it made her a little frustrated.

"Sandy, why did you want to see that movie so bad when you knew how it would affect you? We are going to thrash this out tonight, and after that I don't want to hear it again, you hear?"

Sandy felt tears well up. Her mother was sweet but she expected a lot from her children.

She raised them with the same ethics her mother instilled in her. Sandy looked at her mother and searched for something to say.

"Mom, you're right. It is time for me to find something else to worry about." She tried to joke. "I had already decided to find something productive to occupy my time. It's just that I've been obsessed with this since I can remember, and the crazy thing is, I let myself get upset about something only God can change." She sat up straight in the chair. "Remember when I was little and used to pretend I was Bewitched and could twitch my nose and make things happen?" She laughed through her tears. "Well, I always pretended to go back to slave times to give Grandma Charlotte a silk dress and pretty shoes so that everyone, white and black, would love her and she wouldn't be a slave anymore."

Olivia remembered and smiled. "But, sweetheart," she said, no longer angry, "you were just a wee tiny girl at that time, and it was fun, right? Now you are too smart to worry about something you definitely can't change." She stressed the word *definitely* and looked her daughter right in the eyes. "Sandy, I think you let yourself get upset to keep from hating. So maybe it's good. But don't let yourself be consumed by it, honey."

Sandy acknowledged her mother's words, but she had to ask this next question, even if it prolonged this conversation they were having. Standing up, she walked over to the window and looked out. Olivia watched her daughter retreating and waited to hear her out. After a long while, Sandy spoke.

"Mama?" Olivia cocked her head: whenever one of her children called her "mama" they were in pain. Sandy turned back to face her mother. "Have you ever wondered what it must've felt like to have been a slave? Have you ever wondered what Charlotte felt? She was a slave, but she was also a woman. She had to look at those whites with all of their riches and comforts, while she was treated like a mangy dog. They gave her the bare necessities just to keep her alive because she was of value. I can just see her, Mom. They gave her no deodorant and then they said she stank. They had nothing back there in those days for the beauty and health of the black woman, so they called them 'dirty niggers.'" By now she had walked her way slowly toward her mother and sat down on the floor beside her chair. "Mom, if you took a white man and put him in a hut with dirt floors and no shoes and gave him only enough food to keep his body and soul together, what would you call that white man if you suddenly unchained him inside a store of clean black people?" She didn't wait for her mother to answer. "You'd call him 'dirty, stinkin,' thievin,' white trash.' Why? Because that's what you'd've reduced him to."

Olivia looked intently at her daughter and pushed a lock of hair out of her face. "Sandy," she began, "I've often thought that way, and I've let it get to me sometimes. But I had to realize that there is not one thing I could've done about it then, and I sure can't do anything about how they see black folks now. Honey," she paused, "you're beating a dead mule. Let it *go*."

Olivia bent over and kissed the top of Sandy's head and stood up; Sandy stood up too. She cupped her child's face in her hands and kissed her forehead again. Sandy nodded that she understood and tried to smile. She was anxious to go up the stairs to her room and close the door. She would have locked it, but the rule in the house forbade locking bedroom doors or walking into one before being invited in. The exception was getting permission from a grown up.

Once upstairs in her room, she sat on her bed and untied her shoe laces. It's early, she thought, but decided to go to bed anyway. She put on a big floppy T-shirt and got between the cool pecal sheets. She was determined to try to forget this thing after today. "Even if I die trying," she said to herself aloud. Mom is right, of course, she thought. Why do I continue to think about it? Even as she lay there thinking and talking to herself, her eyelids grew heavy, and sleep wasn't far away.

Sandy never heard her father come in from a tent revival in Savannah. She had been asleep about two hours when she heard a voice call her name. Thinking it was her mother, she sat up and tried to turn on the night lamp, but it wouldn't come on. That's when she noticed that the room was illuminated in an eerie blue glow. Rubbing her eyes to get the sleep out, she asked, "Who's there?" Was she still asleep? She wondered. She just slouched there because she couldn't keep her eyes open. She was about to nod over when she heard the voice again.

"Sandra! Sandra!" She sat ramrod straight this time. Nobody calls me that but my grandmother, Sandy thought. Then, the sweet smell of lilacs filled the room!

"Grandma Mary!?"

"Yes," the voice answered. "It's me Sandra. It's Grandma Mary."

"Grandma Mary," she said in a loud whisper to keep from shouting. Tears blinded her but she could still see her grandmother taking form. Soon her grandmother was sitting in her old rocking chair, right in the midst of the blue light. Sandy blinked to clear her eyes.

"Oh, Grandma! Is it . . . It's . . . It's really you!"

"Sandra, listen. I can only stay for a hot moment, so hang on to every word, Dear."

"You . . . you can't be real," Sandy interrupted. But Grandmother grew serious.

"Hush, honey, and listen to me! I have a special gift for you. But you must follow my instructions to the letter. The very thing you thought impossible has been granted to you, my special child. I've been here several times since I passed, and each time you had the same thing on your mind."

Sandy gasped. "You've been here before?"

"Yes, darlin', but you couldn't see me then because I was just checking on you. But listen," she insisted, putting a finger to her lips. "When you were an arm baby, I used to ask God to let me do something special for you one day, and, well, now He's answered my prayer. You used to tell me when you were in pre-school that you wished you could see my Granny Charlotte. Well, now you can, honey. You've been allowed to go back to see her. You've got two weeks to do what you need to do back there. But there are rules, Sandy, rules you must obey." Grandmother was talking fast now, and the tone of her voice frightened and excited Sandy at the same time. "First of all, you must tell no one, no one at all, or you forfeit everything! You will have the power to call anything you need right to your fingertips. Freed slaves and whites won't be able to see you, only those still in bondage. You will be able to pop in and out whenever you want. But here is the most important rule: You must finish your work in the past and be back here two weeks from tomorrow or . . . or you will be lost . . . Forever."

She was talking very fast now, and Sandy saw why. Her grandmother was fading away. "Don't go yet, Grandma! Wait!" Sandy called out in a desperate whisper. "How do I do this? Is there a charm . . . . "

Her grandmother's fading voice barely interrupted. "I've left it here for you, Sandra.

You're a smart girl. You'll figure everything out for yourself." Now, only a wisp of blue smoke was left in the light. "Never lose the amulet, my precious." Her voice called from far away now. "I love you."

Soon the room was dark again except for the thin light coming from the hallway at the bottom of Sandy's door. Sandy reached over and switched on her lamp.

"Whew," she whistled. Nervous, she spoke aloud to herself. "What a dream! I . . . whoa! What's that?" There was a white stick . . . or something . . . in the old rocker where she dreamt her Grandma Mary had appeared. She jumped over to the chair and picked up a stick, a small stick of ivory! "Damn!" she said, and put her hand over her mouth. "Oh, shit! I didn't mean to cuss! Look at this shit!"

The ivory was about the size of a nail polish bottle. It was cool to the touch. Still holding on to the ivory, bewildered, she turned off her lamp, said a quick prayer, and got back into bed. This calls for a plan, she thought. She lay there thinking, almost afraid to move. If this thing is real and I'm not dreaming, I'll have to use strategy. "Stop it!" she scolded herself aloud. This is one of those very real dreams and it'll be over in the morning. With this thought came the overpowering urge to close her eyes and sleep. In a moment, she was fast asleep, as if she were once again a baby, rocking in her Grandma Mary's arms.

The next morning, Sandy was the last one down for breakfast. She had awakened to find that she had in fact not had a dream—she did own the ivory. She stayed in the shower planning and came up with the perfect plan. Going down the stairs, she vowed that nothing would spoil this day. She had a list in her skirt pocket and the ivory in her bra. Her father had gone on to church early to meet with some elders about a new drug prevention program the police department was starting. Her mother was in the garden, working early to escape the August heat. Larry, her thirteen-year-old brother, stood alone in the kitchen when she got there. Testing her, the first thing he asked her was why her door had been locked when he came by to get her trash basket to empty it.

"How did you know it was locked, liar? Did you try to open it?" she asked, reaching for the cereal box. "I didn't hear you knock."

"Nope, I just checked to see if it was locked, that's all. But in case you forgot, *big* sister,"

Larry continued, stressing the word big (he never missed the opportunity to remind her that he had grown taller than her and was still growing) "you don't get any special favors today. *Yesterday* was your birthday!"

Larry was a replica of their father, tall and big-boned and with a very good face. They both had the kind of eyes and lashes most women would kill for. To go with that, they had generous mouths and nice thick hair. "So," her brother continued, "since I took out the trash for you this morning, *you* will do the dishes for me and we'll call it an even trade."

Sandy looked at him. He hadn't looked up from his job of dicing peaches over his cereal. But when he did he looked across the table and right into his sister's laughing eyes.

"Who died and left you boss, Mr. Testosterone? You never miss a turn to take out the trash for me when it's your turn to do the dishes. And forget blackmail, Leery Larry. My door wasn't locked this morning. Besides, little brother, you owe me one from last week anyway!"

She drained the last drop of her orange juice, put her bowl and glass into the sink, and left Larry staring after her as she flounced out the back door. Olivia was pruning her aster bush. Delicately, Sandy explained to her mother that she was having cramps. Her period. She'd rather stay home from church this afternoon and rest. Olivia understood and suggested that Sandy lie on a heating pad in her room for a while. Looking at her daughter's bobbing pony tail as Sandy walked away, she sensed that her daughter was lying to her. Then, with a sigh, she returned to the aster bush.

Sandy was about to climb the porch steps when Mrs. Julia, their next door neighbor, looked up. She had been snapping beans on her porch. "Well, well, if it ain't the birthday girl. How'd it go yestiday? Did ya like the scarves I gave ya?"

Sandy put on a smile. "Yes, Mrs. Julia, I loved them. Thank you."

But Mrs. Julia wasn't letting her go that easy. "Julie and Robin been by here a while ago," she said, peering around the gardenia bushes between the two yards. Julie was her granddaughter. Nobody could talk more than Mrs. Julia. Sandy remembered that when she was four years old she had decided to run away from home because Mrs. Julia talked to her too much. It was funny now. Her family laughed about that every time they told the story. Her dad would say, "I'm gonna send you to Mrs. Julia's porch if you don't behave."

Sandy was too close to the door now to stop. "Well, bye-bye Mrs. Julia. Have a good day," and she ducked her head and went in.

Sandy knew that her family ate supper early on Sundays, around four-thirty, like everyone else in the neighborhood. The noon services at Bennet Union Baptist Church would be over at 2:30. Good! She grabbed an apple off the table and dashed up the stairs. She would have two and a half hours to herself. She felt no qualms about the little blue lie she told her mother. She'd make it up to her, she thought.

Sandy fairly floated back to her room. She had planned this day so many times in her dreams. She had often written in her journal the dates, places, and names from all the old family stories so that she would never forget them. Now, with the charm from her Grandmother Mary, she knew just what she would do, to the letter, and she would execute it precisely. Just before she entered her room, she felt so good that she hugged herself, twirled around, and yelled "Yes!"

Once in her room, she locked her door. If she didn't, someone could push it open at a crucial moment. Besides, she had a legit reason: this old house had settled and left the door to her room warped. If she didn't lock it, sometimes it would not catch. Sandy put the ivory on the bed. Sitting Indian style in the middle of her bed, she polished her plans. She had to be razor sharp, and she would be. There was one thing she had to do, though. She had to make sure this wasn't just a figment of her imagination. If it was, she felt she would rather know now before she put all her hopes on the line. That, she thought, would kill her. So, holding the ivory, she began to chant. All of the stories, all of the names, all of the places that lived in her memory from her Grandma Mary's stories—all of them were as vivid as if she had lived them herself. For what seemed like an eternity, she chanted, "August 8, 1821, Savannah, Georgia," over and over.

But nothing happened.

She felt her eyes sting. She was going to cry, and then she felt it! The ivory was pulsating. It glowed in her fist. Her body felt strangely light and hollow. Just as she felt a spinning sensation, she opened her hand, dropped the ivory, and gasped. It all stopped!

"It works! It works!" she said, jumping up and down and screaming at the top of her lungs. She was spinning in circles. "Yes! Yes! Damnit, Yes!" She was still spinning when her mother knocked on the door.

"Sandy, unlock this door! Now, Sandy!"

Before her mother entered, Sandy remembered to put her ivory in her pocket. She unlocked the door for her mother but kept spinning and jumping and saying "yes, yes." Olivia, more bewildered than usual at her daughter's behavior, just stood there with Larry, wide-eyed, peering over her shoulders.

"Oh, Mom," Sandy shouted. She grabbed her mother and danced around with her before she planted a big, sloppy kiss on her cheek. "I love you, Mom." She let go of her mother and tried to stand up but was so dizzy she fell on the bed exhausted and just lay there trying to catch her breath. "Mom, don't ask," she said. "I'm just happy, OK?" She sat up and looked at her mother. She wanted to say something to them but pursed her lips as she remembered Grandma Mary's warning. She had to do everything in order. Jumping up from the bed, she ran right passed Larry still standing in the doorway. "Gotta go, folks," she said darting passed them. But Olivia and Larry wanted to know where. Going down the steps, Sandy shouted over her shoulder, "To the toolshed!" Clutching her pocket, she held on tight to the ivory, so tight it could have been a million dollars. At the back door, she jumped down the steps, her ponytail flying behind her.

CHAPTER TWO

Sandy had decided to drill a tiny hole through the ivory and to pass a fine but strong gold chain through it. But, for double protection, she also decided to cut a strand of strong fishing line to pass through the ivory, too. She would take no chance of losing this hunk of magic! She found the right size bit, put it on the drill, and made the hole. Sandy remembered the dizziness she felt when she tested the ivory. It would be my misfortune to lose it during the transition, she thought. Sometimes she was careless and forgetful, she admitted; even her father said so. "Scatterbrain," he'd tease her. She finished the job and sprinted for the house. Her parents and brother would be back from church soon.

In her room she put the chain, cord, and ivory around her neck. Soon it would be time for supper. She washed up and changed into a dress; she could hear her family downstairs now, so she went downstairs, carefully tucking her ivory inside the top of her dress. "Hey, daddy," she said, bending down to kiss her father's cheek.

Last night, he and his brother-in-law had returned late from the tent revival in Savannah, so he didn't get a lot of sleep, but the little he got was enough. In fact, he felt great. Today, Richard Tucker would work a half shift in the evening. Right now he was at ease, smiling and feeling like a king. His wife hated his often erratic work schedule, but she never complained about it. He knew his occasionally dangerous job disturbed his wife, but it paid the bills. Besides, Jesup was a nice quiet town where some still slept with unlocked doors.

Richard was a jovial man, and he loved his family dearly. He was big, but with not an inch of fat on him. His large, callused hands clearly showed that he did a lot of carpentry and yard work in his spare time. Because of the care that Richard and Olivia lavished on their home, the frame house seemed immaculate even at its worst. Every six years Richard and his brothers-in-law stripped the outside of the house and put on fresh, white paint. Richard could make practically anything from wood. He did all of the heavy yard work, even the redwood fence that divided the back of the yard was his handiwork. Some said that God had given him this talent because of his gentleness. If someone in Jesup needed something made from wood, he could make it. He would charge them only the cost of material, and often he would forego even that payment. "Awe, put it in the collection plate, if you will," he'd say.

Sandy loved the story about the bike. It seemed that one Christmas, when Richard was about fourteen, a very poor young boy wanted a bike just like the ones he knew his friends were getting. All of the other boys were talking about what colors theirs would be and how fast they would go. But everyone knew the poor boy wouldn't be getting a bike. Three weeks before Christmas, young Richard decided to do something about that. Day after day Richard worked in his granddaddy's barn. On Christmas eve, young Richard and his father went to the boy's house and knocked. When the door was opened, they presented the boy with a shiny red bicycle. Richard had used those three weeks to make his friend a bike. In the barn there had been an old bicycle that belonged to his uncle John. It had been broken up in an accident and was no longer workable, but Richard used parts from it and working parts from his old bike to make his friend a bike. The chain and the gear worked once they were washed and oiled with motor oil. The tires were good except for a hole in one of them, and he had fixed that with a patch. The handle bar, seat, tire shields, and frame supports were carved by Richard from wood.

Sandy loved him so much. "How was the revival last night, daddy?" she asked as she took her place at the table.

"Fine. Your uncle John stayed over last night, but by the time I got up he was gone. Oh, Livia, I almost forgot to tell you: John shouted last night at the revival. He stood up and shouted! I wish you could have seen the look on his face." Both Sandy and her mother clapped with joy. Uncle John had lost his wife and two sons in a house fire four years ago. Afterwards, he had become a very bitter man. But God was slowly delivering him, Olivia and Richard told their children. "Thought you were gonna have breakfast with me at 6:30, San?" her father asked.

Sandy flinched. She ached to tell her father and mother what had happened to her, but she knew she couldn't. She had always felt pangs of guilt whenever she kept things from her parents. This was different, she felt, but the guilt was still there.

"I'm sorry, dad. I was kind of tired," she said.

"I know," her father said reaching over and throwing a mock punch at her chin. "I knocked on your door twice and you didn't even rustle your sheets. Maybe next week, huh?" Sandy said OK and looked down at her hands.

Olivia brought out the pot roast and spoke to her husband. She sensed the uneasiness Sandy felt. "Richard, Sandy and I had a long talk last night, about what we've all talked about before, and she got up this morning much better!"

"Hey, that's great, Sandy!" her dad said, and reached over and caressed her cheek. Now she really felt like a heel. Why didn't everyone just leave well enough alone?

It seemed like an eternity before her mother finished putting food on the table and told her to go get her brother. Sandy could have called him from the bottom step, but she was glad to run up and get him. There was sure to be idle chit-chat during the meal but if she answered questions succinctly and didn't offer any news, she was sure that no one would notice how uneasy she felt.

The pot roast was succulent. Olivia served carrots, potatoes, and baby pearl onions with it. She also prepared creamy macaroni and cheese, buttery cornbread, and iced tea. It was during dessert that they had real conversation. Her dad was digging into his second slice of buttermilk chocolate cake before he said anything important. "Olivia, do you remember that old McPherson mansion that was turned into a museum over in Dade County?" Olivia acknowledged she did. "Well, it got robbed last night." Everyone looked up but Sandy. Larry's spoon was poised in mid-air, and Olivia froze with her napkin at her mouth. Before he went on he glanced briefly at his daughter. Richard cleared his throat and laughed. "That's some cake, ain't it, girl?"

Sandy's head snapped up. She tried to lighten the moment with a chuckle. "Oh, I'm sorry. I guess my mind was somewhere else, daddy. What did you say?"

"We were just talking about the McPherson museum being robbed last night." Richard was now looking at Olivia as he spoke. Forgotten was the moment. "I think it's just some dumb kids. The only things missing were some copper tubes and stuff like that. There isn't anything with a lot of value except that coin collection. It wasn't even touched." He shook his head. "Thing is, if these kids get caught they're going to do some time, and for what?" He shrugged and held his free palm up.

An event like the robbery caused excitement in their small town; it was different than the usual shoplifting and the occasional fight. Larry had to put in his two cents. "Weren't the guard dogs there?"

His daddy nodded and said, "But that dog ain't worth the food he's being fed. They should get a pit bull—their jaws lock when they bite."

Larry went on, excited. "I wonder if Mr. McPherson's ghost lives there?" His eyes were stretched wide.

But before he could say anything else, Sandy said, "Grow up, Leery Larry. I thought you outgrew ghosts with the tooth fairy and Santa Claus, or did you keep the ghost and the Easter bunny?" Sandy felt the sting of irony in her words after she spoke. Making fun of her brother about . . . a ghost! What would Grandmother Mary think?

"Alright, you two. That's enough," piped Olivia. "Let's clear this table, and, Larry, you'll dry the dishes for me tonight."

Larry didn't like that, and to make it worse, he mistook the expression on his sister's face for a smirk. "You mess with me and I'll tell daddy what you did this morning," he muttered to Sandy.

Olivia scolded him. "You, Mr. Larry, are going to get to that sink before I make you do the dishes alone! And before you even ask, the answer is 'No'! You can't bring that box down and play your tapes!"

Now, Larry was upset. "Why, maaaa?" he whined.

"Because it's Sunday; that's why!" And with that she put a dish towel in his hand.

Soon, Richard and Sandy sat on the porch and rocked lazily and enjoyed the gentle breeze that happened by. Sandy grew restless. "Daddy, I'm going to go up to my room for the rest of the evening. Tell mama, OK? She'll understand."

"OK, San. Just as well. I'm gonna see if I can't get your mother to take a walk with me when it gets a little cooler. Then, I'll be off to work." She hugged him.

"You're a doll, daddy." She always called him this when she needed a favor. "And, daddy, can I lock my door tonight? Remember, it doesn't close properly"

He smiled at her. "Go on, Sugar."

Sprinting for the stairs and past her mother she yelled, "Daddy said I could lock my door!"

Olivia frowned. 'Daddy' indeed, she thought. She yelled back, "Make sure you unlock it before you go to bed!"

Larry actually felt lucky tonight; he knew he should have been left to do the dishes alone, but his Mom was only making him dry them. In this way, he got his turn over with quickly. Tomorrow was his sister's day. When Olivia put the last dish in his hand to dry, he grinned and said, "Yes!" Olivia let the water drain from the sink and told Larry to go, but he wanted to talk.

"Mom, how come I have to spend the last two weeks in camp and San gets to run wild?"

Olivia put the towel on the rack and said, "Because you wanted to go, remember?" Larry shrugged.

"If you ask me," Larry said swinging his head in the direction of upstairs, "that female is weirder than most. Last school term all she did was wear make-up and chase boys. Now she only wants to read about slaves. Whatsup?

She didn't even get mad today when I borrowed a CD without asking her first. If you ask me . . . ."

Olivia clipped off the stove light and turned to her son.

"No one's asked you, so be quiet! Your sister is growing up, Larry, and sometimes growing girls chase boys. I think she's finally coming to terms with her feelings about slavery. It wouldn't hurt you, Mr. Larry, to take an interest in a book or two about slavery. Maybe you could ask Sandy to check out one of her favorite books for you at the library."

Larry had to have the last word. "I bet she's gettin' books at the library about boys! That's it!" Larry screeched as he followed his mother out of the kitchen. "She's gettin' books about boys!"

Olivia rolled her eyes and muttered something under her breath. Larry was always good for a laugh.

"Let's let Sandy handle her books and you worry about Larry for a change, OK?"

Once Sandy was in her room with her door locked, she calmed herself down. "OK," she spoke, "I'm in control." She pulled up the chain around her neck and pulled out the ivory and her list. She made notes to herself about what she hoped to accomplish. She continued to concentrate on what she now thought of as her mission. She felt apprehensive, but she knew this was normal; she sat Indian style again, in the middle of her bed, and gathered her thoughts.

Richard was in his recliner reading the evening paper when Olivia walked into the room and spoke. "I'm sorry I didn't take you up on that walk, but you either didn't go or that was the shortest walk you ever took. Which one is it?" Richard put the paper down and laughed. "Anything in the paper about the museum thieves?" she asked, sitting on the arm of his chair.

He nodded his head. "Forest Weller thinks its a bunch of kids, too. But what would a bunch of kids want with all that copper tubing and iron posts and stuff?"

"Well, look at it this way. If it's a bunch of kids, it can't get too serious, can it?" But Richard wasn't convinced. Olivia went on. "The last time kids in Jesup got in trouble was two years ago when we passed the new laws to keep them from buying cigarettes. Even then the little Pickett boy was the only one arrested, right?"

Richard sat absentmindedly stroking his chin. "That's just it," he said finally. "This thing stinks of the Picketts and if its them, that father of theirs is in the middle of it." He shook his finger at his wife and continued. "You mark my words. Those boys were born to be bad." But before he finished his sentence, he knew he was saying the wrong thing.

Olivia stood up, hands on hips and said, "Richard, no child is born bad. There is no such thing as a bad child. We make our kids what they are. Look at the Picketts, for example. They have ten kids in a house made for four. Mr. Pickett has been known to take those boys out drinking with him, and when they weren't drinking he was beating the tar out of them. Now what if you'd been raised that way?"

Richard tried never to argue with his wife about raising children. After all, she was the teacher, not him, and besides, he knew he could not win anyway.

Upstairs in her room, Sandy heard the muffled voices of her parents talking below. She knew it was time. Her heart beat faster and faster. She tightly palmed the ivory in her fist. Beginning to perspire, she shut her eyes and whispered over and over in a small voice, "August 8, 1821, Savannah, Georgia, Charlotte Worthinwood." Over and over she chanted. Suddenly, she recognized the heat in her fist. Then it spread to the rest of her body. The room was spinning, faster and faster. She felt heavy, then she felt hollow—then she felt nothing, absolutely nothing.

Sandy didn't know how long she was unconscious, but when she regained her senses she was lying on her side curled up on the ground. She was afraid to open her eyes, but she kept the ivory clinched in her fist. She noticed that her heart was beating calmly now as if she had awakened from a full night's sleep. It was then that she became aware of the noises around her and the smell of green tobacco, a smell she knew well from the tobacco barn she visited at her Godmother's in Kentucky one summer. Something that sounded like a frightened kitten forced her to open her eyes. "My God, I've made it! I've done it!"

There, sitting on the floor only a few feet away, was a young black woman, obviously a slave, frozen with fright at the sight of her. A shaky little hand clutched her throat, and her mouth formed a small, perfect circle. She was wearing a dirty burlap-looking turban on her head, and the chemise she wore was a tattered rag. But the girl was pretty, scrubby but pretty. She had nut brown skin that glowed with a golden hue.

The girl now completely ignored the dull metal disk that Sandy watched slide from her lap and spill onto the dirt floor. Quickly, Sandy stood up and stuffed the chain and ivory back down into her shirt. Sandy was nervous, but this girl looked as if she were in shock. Sandy tried to tell her that it was OK, but she only made it worse. Calmer now, Sandy didn't know what to do or to say.

"Shit," she muttered more to herself than to the girl. "I bet you just saw me appear out of thin air, didn't you?" By now the girl was praying and big beads of perspiration popped out on her forehead and nose. Sandy began to panic now, so she had to try one more time. "Listen," she started. "Touch my hand. I'm as real as you." But when she stuck out her hand, the girl jumped up, spun around and bolted out the barn door.

Alone, Sandy looked around her. This was a big tobacco barn, and it was now obvious that the girl had been eating. There were now flies buzzing around the fallen tin pan full of something that looked like oatmeal with fat in it. Just as Sandy finished her survey and started to leave the barn, she heard the girl coming back. She wasn't sure what to do—she heard a man's voice. Looking around for shelter, she hid behind a row of strung tobacco and stood petrified.

The two entered the barn. The girl spoke to the man in an accent so thick that Sandy could barely understand, but she knew that the girl was trying to convince him that she had indeed seen a ghost. "Bubba, yo no I don' lie. Dat ghos' was rat 'ere."

But Bubba wasn't convinced. "I ain't sayin' yo is lyin'. I thinks yo seen sompin else doe; mebbe a coon or sumpin. Now, if yo don' mine, I's gots work to do."

By this time, the strong smell of drying tobacco hanging right in Sandy's face made her sneeze. Oh, my God! Oh, my God! she thought. What if he hits me? They think I'm a ghost! Bubba turned to the sound of the sneeze and picked up a shovel. "Dat don' soun' like no ghos' t'me, Faye—dat soun' like a gal, run'way slabe, mebbe." With that he started poking the tobacco with the shovel. Fay knew what she had seen, and she still tried to convince him.

"Bubba, I see' dat ghost' wit' ma own eyes come outta pure air!" she moaned. "Be careful!"

Shovel in hand, Bubba didn't even hear Faye. With one jerk of the shovel, he flung the tobacco to the ground and exposed Sandy. "Come owd heah 'foe Ah call da oberseer on ya." Sandy felt as if her heart would jump through her thin shirt, but she stepped forward until she was almost in the middle of the barn. She didn't know what to expect.

But nothing happened. Faye was still behind Bubba, and Bubba was still staring at Sandy, but that's when things changed. Now Bubba looked scared to death! He was trying to decide whether he should run or stay there and defend Faye. One thing he was sure of and that was that this ghost was a woman, and this coupled with the fact that she was black gave him some degree of courage. He stood where he was and stared her up and down, first at her Nikes, then at her jeans. Now Sandy wished she had not changed into pants after supper. She was sure they had never seen a black woman wearing pants. Bubba looked at her pony tail and then back down to her digital sports watch which now chose, of all times, to beep. Both Faye and Bubba bolted for the door, but Sandy couldn't let them go. They would probably make it worse by bringing more people.

"Stop, please!" They stopped right in their tracks, but Bubba's legs turned to rubber and wouldn't hold him up. He slid to the dirt floor. Faye turned back to Sandy, helping Bubba regain his senses. Sandy wasn't afraid anymore. She just felt the urge to explain to them how she got there and why. She needed to make these two people trust her if she intended to do any good here. Getting them to trust her would clear the path for others that must be in the fields and about. So she gave it her best shot.

"Listen. I'm not here to hurt you, Bubba. I've come to make things a lot better for you and for your people. I'm not a ghost or anything; you can even touch me. See?" Now she dared to take a step forward, and she pinched her own arm. Bubba and Faye cautiously reached out and touched her. Now Bubba sensed less danger from Sandy, but he was still wary because of the way she was dressed.

"Iffen yo ain' no slabe ghos', den what be ya? An' way yo come from? Ah ain' nebba seed no ghos', but Ah ain' nebber seed no human dress' like dat befo' needa." Sandy felt her spirits soar. He was talking to her!

"My name is Sandy. I've travelled back . . . to help you. I live in . . . in another place, in another time . . . over a hundred years . . . in the future! In my time, slavery has been abolished. That means there aren't any more slaves. Do you follow me?"

Bubba was perplexed. But at last Faye spoke.

"If they ain' no slabes in yo time, den who take care ob de white folks and de white folk's chillins an' dat kinda thin'? An' who take care a da niggas?" Bubba, whose eyes kept going back to the watch on Sandy's wrist asked again as though all the other questions meant nothing.

"What 'bout dem clothes? Ya got on breeches jus' like a man an what's dat on yo arm?" Sandy sat down on the hard-packed dirt floor of the barn; she gestured at the floor in front of her, and they sat down too. Bubba never took his eyes off Sandy and that watch.

"How much time do we have before you have to go back to the fields?" she asked.

"Well," Bubba answered, "We was jus' gettin' ready t' eat when Faye saw ya, so we still gots a lil' time. Besides, we gots a new oberseer and he a fat, lazy man," Bubba offered, nervously. "He'll holler when it time to work." Faye just sat there.

"This piece on my arm is called a watch. It shows what time of day it is. Look!" she said, holding out her arm for them to see. Bubba jumped right on it.

"Uh huh," he said, bobbing his head. "Ah seed de fine white peoples wear dey time piece on a gole chain in dey ves pokit, but ah ain' nebber seed one up cloz', but ah know dey got nummers in em, but not like dis un." He reached and touched the watch and told Faye to touch it. "How come it doan' tick?" he asked.

Sandy started to say, "because it's digital," but how would she describe "digital" to them? Instead, she ignored the question and went to something more important instead. "Bubba, Faye, listen up. I want you all to go tell the other slaves about me being here. Tell them that the white folks can hear me, but they can't see me or hurt me, so I'm going to walk back to the slaves' quarters with you all when you finish in the fields today and meet the other slaves, OK?" The two agreed, stood up, and walked out of the barn, glancing back at Sandy as they went.

Now that Sandy was alone, she decided to explore a little bit. She peeked out of a side door. She had to be careful. She didn't want another slave to see her until they all were warned. Looking out at the vast sea of green tobacco, she crept cautiously outside. From not a far distance she heard the overseer call the slaves back from their break. Stepping carefully, Sandy found a hard-packed red clay path that snaked between the tall plants and decided to follow it. As she walked, she took in the unfamiliar sights and sounds.

The unsolicited aromas coming from the earth were exhilarating. Soon, she could hear the slaves singing. This reminded Sandy of a dream she used to have. After walking about a quarter of a mile, she saw a cluster of white-washed frame huts, about 20 in all. Just beyond them to the east was a quick-moving brook that emptied into a small pond. To the right of the pond was a small gathering of pine and cedar wood trees. The smell of fresh cedar was luscious to her. All of her senses filled with the sensations from a new world. She felt taut, like a compressed steel spring ready to uncoil. Whatever she did from now on, she meant to do it well. She knew she could make a real difference in these people's lives. Coming to a dip in the path, Sandy caught sight of what she thought was the most beautiful mansion she had ever seen. Breathless with wonder, she stood nearly gasping. This must be the plantation house! And the huts were surely the slave quarters!

Sandy wrinkled her nose as she walked closer to the white huts. The smell of sweat and urine hit her like a wave. But her attention was on the big house. Now she would test the ivory and see if she would really be undetected by the free men. Sandy intended to go inside the mansion. Just as she cleared the small, white-washed huts, she almost walked square into a little white girl about six years old who was playing under a live oak tree. She wore a blue pinafore and had the palest blonde hair Sandy had ever seen. Then Sandy saw that under her, horsey style, was an even smaller black boy.

While Sandy stood watching, she heard the little girl yell, "Gee yup, mule!" The boy strained to keep his arms straight and his back arched. He pursed his lips to gain strength. Then he looked up . . . right into Sandy's face!

"Whatcha stoppin' for, mule," the little girl demanded. But he didn't speak or move. "Aw right, mule, I'm gonna whip yew!" She held a small riding crop in her hand and struck the little boy, but to no avail.

"Look, missy, look," the boy whispered hoarsely, motioning with his head to where Sandy stood. The girl looked up but saw nothing.

Stomping her foot in anger she asked, "What's wrong, Jimmy Lee? I don't see a thing!"

Sandy took a step forward, bent over, put a finger to his lips, and whispered in his ear, "Be quiet, little boy. She can't see me. Look!" She moved right in front of the little girl's face and waved her hands. With that the boy jumped to his feet, spilling the little blonde rider on the ground, and in a flash he ran into the nearest white hut, screaming and flaying his arms.

Seated on the ground, legs splayed, the white haired girl yelled at him to come back. "I'm gonna tell mammy you've been mean," she yelled. Sandy realized now that she couldn't go to the big house right then; she would have to wait until the house slaves had been told about her. So she walked back to the barn to wait. What she didn't know was that almost all of the slaves on the plantation knew of her already.

The slaves had learned of her through a network they called 'the grapevine.' No one but the slaves themselves knew exactly how it worked. After what seemed an eternity, she heard the nasal voice of the overseer call the work day to an end. Minutes later, Faye slipped into the barn.

"We's 'bout to go on in from de field," she whispered. "De udda slabes done been tolt already." She looked intently at Sandy. "Is yo sho' da white folks can' see ya?"

To assure Faye that they couldn't, she told her what had happened with the little girl. Then she and Faye made their way out of the barn.

"Afta we go in and fix de las' meal an eat, we always gatha roun' late and sing, an so den yo meet ebby one."

Sandy nodded her head as they slipped into an already moving line of slaves. As she passed the overseer sitting on his steed, she again had the chance to test her ivory. Sure enough, he looked right through her. The other slaves tried very hard not to stare and make the white man suspicious, but most of them gaped. Giggling, Sandy gaped right back at them, hoping her mock terror would put their fears to rest.

Why, they look so healthy, she thought! They are ragged and burned black from the sun, but they look so fit! Never had Sandy seen better looking bodies than these. They were bone tired and the smell of human musk was strong, but it was not offensive. It was like the smell of healthy horses, strong but pure. As Sandy fell in line behind Faye, she knew for sure that she would start with their personal hygiene. Almost every woman she saw had on head rags. Sandy wondered why. An obviously pregnant woman in front of Faye moved with amazing grace and speed. The woman looked back at Sandy and grinned.

Sandy marvelled at how calmly these people seemed to take her having appeared to them out of nowhere. She knew she looked like a creature from another world to them. She later learned that many of these slaves had been purchased in Charleston and had Haitian or Jamaican backgrounds where voodoo was commonplace. These people didn't find her being among them entirely strange or impossible, and some of them from time to time would offer tales of magic or unexplainable events in their own lives.

Before she knew it, they were in the slave yards and the people disappeared into different doorways. Sandy was gaping again when Faye's strong fingers grabbed her wrist. "I stays in dis howz, ober here," she said, pointing and pulling Sandy along. Faye's cabin was larger than the others, and there were several young women standing on the porch. Entering the house, Sandy was surprised at its neatness. There were at least twenty corn shuck mattresses lined up against the wall. The rough pine board floor was worn but spotless. In the back was a potbellied cooking stove. The shelves on the wall held cooking and eating utensils and what looked like dark, clean rags. The windows had no glass, but the shutters were neat and in good repair.

"This is fantastic," Sandy thought aloud.

Faye responded. "Dis where mos' ob de youn' women lib. S'times a slabe is bought from de slabe market house in Fayetteville, o' she been sold away from her mammy and pappy, o' maybe her folks lib here on dis plantation don' wan' her stay wid dem no mo, she come here. If da massa picks out two slabes t' jump da broom, he always get de gal from here. He always put a dark skin one wid a light one ta get de brown ones mos' slabe massas like. Worthinwood slabes is talked 'bout by ebby body." Sandy watched the girl puff up with pride. Faye smiled. "Now ya'll come close. Dis here is de gal dat Bubba slipped out de fiel' to tell ya'll 'bout. She called Sandy."

Sandy looked at them and, lacking something better to say, mumbled, "Ah, good news travels fast, huh?"

A very dark, smoothed faced girl with beautiful dancing eyes said, "You show talks funny."

Faye ignored that, but the other girls agreed. "Ya'lls gon hear how she gon help us out? Now, Ah wanna gib her ebby one name." Putting her hand on a girl's shoulder, Faye went on. "Dis one name Cleta." Sandy nodded at the pretty sloe-eyed girl and smiled. The girl put her hand up and wiggled her fingers shyly. "She my sista," Faye said. "De rest ob dem can tell ya dey own name stead of starin' at ya like a fool!" With that the other girls fell on her, touching her watch, clothes, and hair. They all tried telling her their names at once. Some of the girls were as young as twelve, and some were as old as nineteen. Many were pregnant.

The pregnant slave that was in front of them in line from the field was called Fanny. She was a beautiful girl with laughing eyes, dark skin, and big luscious curls of hair. She was one of a few girls without a head rag. She was the sister of the other dancing-eyed dark girl, but Fanny was stunning. Her features were as delicate as a porcelain doll's. She had a small, shapely plum mouth. Her nose was narrow, short, and turned up slightly. But her teeth were what struck Sandy: they were the whitest, the tiniest teeth she had ever seen. The black irises of her large, slanting eyes seemed surrounded by snow; her long, thick eyelashes and dark eyebrows gleamed like raven's wings. Still staring at her, Sandy asked why she was in the fields in her condition. The girl threw back her finely shaped head and laughed. "Ah won' out der cuttin' 'backy! T'day Faye and me jes walk' de rows and pass out watta. Ah wanted to go cause Ah need ta hurry and drop dis young 'un. Ah's been hired to da big house to nurse Missy Kate's baby boy and he been born seben days ago. If Ah don' hurry up, sum body else gon get dat job."

'Sides," Faye interrupted, "Dis her third baby. De massa sells her babies fo lotta money cuz dey come heah lookin' like her."

Sandy felt sick when she heard this, but she had read about this somewhere, so she wasn't surprised. She knew that the white baby would be nursed by his black nanny while in most cases her own baby got leftovers if there wasn't another slave mother nursing. In the case of working pregnant women, it was up to the overseer to decide which women should or should not continue working the fields. If he made a bad decision and a baby was lost, he could lose his job, yet the overseer didn't want the slaves to deceive him. So an older slave, usually a woman, had to keep a vigil and report to the masters about who could or who couldn't handle a full day in the fields. No one person could be absolute in determining who should or shouldn't work. As a general rule, masters found hardness to be their best policy. But sometimes there was the risk of turning a treatable problem into a fatality for both mother and unborn child. A small-time farmer with only a few slaves worked everyone because he had to sustain labor at a minimum cost. At crucial times during the care of his tobacco, breaks in discipline could mean disaster to the year's crop.

Deep in thought, Sandy noticed that the girls were running their hands through her hair again and trying to take her watch off. Sandy wanted to make sure she wasn't dreaming. She asked the girls what year it was, and she was told that it was 1821. She asked about the town and state, just to reconfirm her whereabouts. Everything was as it appeared to be.

Most of the girls had lost their fear, but Fanny and Faye were the bold ones, touching her the most and asking lots of questions. Sandy took her watch off and let Fanny hold it. Just like a baby she put it to her lips and tasted it; then she put it to her ear. She was absolutely astounded. One of the girls wanted Sandy's shoes, so she took them off and watched her as she put them on the wrong feet. A little, chubby, beaver-looking girl with slow, deliberate movements kept exclaiming about how good Sandy smelled. When Sandy told them that her curls came out of a bottle, Fanny's sister LeeLee looked at Sandy as if she had two heads.

"It's called a perm," Sandy explained. When she told them that she could give each of them a perm, everyone's mouth popped open.

A tall willowy girl called Skeeter turned to the window because she heard noises. There on the porch and in the yard floated a sea of black men's faces. There were old ones, young ones, tall ones, and short ones in almost every shade of black one could imagine, and in front stood Bubba. Stepping outside and onto the porch, Sandy and the girls stood facing the crowd. The men stood silently until Sandy spoke.

"Well . . . uh . . . Bubba probably told you who I am and how I got here. It's all true. Call it voodoo if you want; I believe God has allowed me to come here to help you folks. I live in the year 1993. I've come to help you in anyway I can. I never would have believed anything like this was possible, but if I can believe in the Bermuda Triangle, I shouldn't have knocked this."

After her little speech, there was complete silence until she saw someone walk up to her left. It was a young man she came to know as Stoney. He was about six feet tall and had the body of a weight trainer and a very dark complexion. He asked her several intelligent questions and she answered them. Sandy felt strangely moved by this young black slave, and, not realizing it, she was gazing into his eyes, seemingly transfixed. Not until Faye intentionally coughed and interrupted her conversation with Stoney did Sandy notice that Stoney was gazing into her eyes, too. Their behavior did break the tension, though, and everyone relaxed and began to talk.

She smiled as everyone sought somewhere to sit. Some sat on the steps, some squatted where they stood, and others leaned or sat on the porch. Sandy felt as though she were among friends and family. Everyone clamored for her attention while she struggled not to stare at Stoney. She was sure that he purposely ignored her, too. It wasn't until someone handed her back her watch that she became aware of the time. Standing abruptly, she signaled for Bubba to follow her to the side of the hut. "Bubba," she whispered when they got out of the others' sight, "it's time for me to go home. Tell everyone that I'll be back tomorrow about the same time and place." Bubba looked down at the ground and shuffled his feet.

"Huh. Ah can' get yo no hoss, miss Sandy; Ah get in trouble iffen a hoss come up missin'." Sandy assured him that all she needed to leave was already in her possession. Not wanting to frighten him, she asked that he close his eyes while she palmed her ivory and began to chant. As her head started to spin and the heat in her hand grew, she gave a little shutter and disappeared. She didn't see the peeking Bubba faint when she vanished. When Sandy came to her senses again, she was back in her bed. Uncurling herself, she glanced at her digital alarm clock on her bedside table; it was midnight.

"I've been gone for hours," she said aloud. The excitement of her first journey into the past should have been enough to keep her awake, but in two minutes she was snoring.

CHAPTER THREE

When Olivia finished getting Richard off to work, she sat down on the porch swing with a second cup of coffee and watched the morning traffic go by. School would be starting soon, and there would be no more warm summer mornings to rock leisurely on the porch. She loved this time of day. Sometimes she believed that God had made this time of day just for her. A small, gray haze covered the morning, however. Sandy's problems with slavery were on her mind as they had been, off and on, for most of the summer. Maybe Olivia'd been too liberal in letting the kids watch too much TV. No, she couldn't blame TV for Sandy's behavior. Her daughter was just a moody person. Maybe she'd just sit back and let her daughter solve her own problems for a change. She would be there for Sandy in case she reached out for help; after all, she was 16 now. Yes, Olivia thought; let her grow up. She can handle it.

Sipping her still hot coffee, Olivia looked out at the pecan trees that stood in her yard. As a child she hated the leaves that covered the yard in the fall. She and her friend, Clara, whom her brother John W. would eventually marry, would have to rake those leaves from the back, the front, and the sides of the yard. When she was young, the yard seemed so large. There were so many pecans that fell to the ground then that the girls couldn't help but walk on them.

Back then, there used to be a stop light at the intersection of Pine Street and Fourth Street until the traffic was re-routed because of the new by-pass. Jesup now had a population of twenty thousand, but when Olivia was growing up, it was half that. There was only one school for blacks then—Wayne County Training School— and it went from first grade to the twelfth. After integration in the 60's, the school turned into the present elementary school. Mr. Robert Robertson was principal until the change. Even now, he and his wife and son Robby still lived within shouting distance of the school.

Olivia recalled how there had been several dirt paths, or lanes, in Jesup when she was growing up. One lane in particular ran from Olivia's house directly to Cooter's, one of the town's two teen recreation centers. After church on Sunday, all of the kids went to one of these two centers, but if you were too sick to go to church, you were too sick to go party. At one center there was music, dancing, and swimming. At Cooter's there was just dancing and music, tunes like "Under the Boardwalk," "Ain't Too Proud to Beg," and "Stop in the Name of Love." Olivia thought those were the days, and nothing on this earth would ever be as exciting again.

A noise in the kitchen interrupted her musing. Either Sandy or Larry had awakened and had come downstairs. Olivia stood up to go inside just as Larry came to the screen door.

"Why aren't there any peaches in the fruit bowl, Ma?"

His mother rolled her eyes skyward. "Good Morning to you, too, Mr. Larry." The sarcasm in her voice made him imitate his mother's eye roll. "Larry, is there an unwritten law that says you can't put anything but peaches on your cereal? You can have something else, like pancakes or waffles."

Larry opened the screen door for his mother and stood to the side to let her enter. He wasn't going to answer that. As stubborn as he was, he just grunted and stuffed his fruitless cereal into his mouth. After eating, he put his bowl into the sink and headed out of the kitchen door to the shed to get his lawn mower.

Cutting grass was serious business for the boy. He had made enough money this summer to buy most of his school clothes, especially the ones his parents thought were ridiculous looking. Olivia and Richard were so proud of him. They even let him get away with a few trivial things. They had agreed that as long as he showed no adverse reactions to having his own money, they would leave him alone. Right now, Olivia felt like thumping him on the head as she would a ripe melon, but she couldn't help but smile as she went to the utility closet to get the vacuum and cleaning cart to start her chores.

It wasn't until 10:00 a.m. that Sandy woke up. She lay looking up at the ceiling for a while wondering if everything had been a dream. Going back in time was impossible, wasn't it? There is no physical way to go back into a time that's dead already. Once a second passed, it was gone! That's all there was to it! While she was thinking this, her hand—as if it had a will of its own—reached for the chain and ivory around her neck. Yes, it was there! Touching it, Sandy pushed her bed clothes back and jumped to her feet.

"Oh, my Lord," she exclaimed. Looking down she not only had on the same clothes she had worn yesterday, but, bending over, she inspected a speck of green entwined in her shoe laces. The doubting girl couldn't describe her feelings when she discovered the tiny but unmistakable piece of tobacco leaf strung up in her shoe laces! She sat back down on the bed to collect her thoughts. She wished that she could at least tell her daddy . . . .

Richard Tucker was sitting in his patrol car on the corner of Walnut and Main when the Pickett's old, beat-up '79 Toyota pickup came speeding through the yellow light. Richard put his siren on and pulled out onto the two-lane road. Checking his own speed, he estimated the pickup to be going about 85 mph. He called in to the station and asked for back-up after giving his location and the direction of the chase.

They passed Tom Jones Funeral Home (the only black mortuary in Jesup) and sped toward the city limit. The speeding cars were approaching the railroad tracks, and Richard could hear the noon train in the distance, so he began putting on his brakes. The officer watched as the pickup raced across the tracks, barely missing being hit by the train by maybe twenty feet.

I don't believe this, Richard thought. People don't put their lives on the line like this unless they've got a good reason. By the time the train had passed, the pickup truck was long gone. He knew looking for the pickup now was useless, so he reported in and returned to his patrol area.

It was quite a while later before anything else happened. Richard was getting bored again when he saw a silver Nissan Maxima slow down on Oak Avenue to turn right onto Third Street. The car lost control for no apparent reason and struck a parked Toyota van. Richard reported what he had seen on his radio before he approached the car. Tapping on the driver's window, he could see that the people in the car were dazed, but they appeared unhurt.

The young man behind the wheel had his blonde head bowed over the steering wheel, but, in response to the officer's knock, he looked up and rolled down his window and unlocked his door. The smell of alcohol assaulted the officer's nose instantly. Looking at the driver carefully, he asked for his license. Richard saw that the boy was blind drunk and so was the young man on the passenger's side. By the time his backup arrived, he had found what looked like two gallons of milk jugs in the trunk of the car, but they were full of pure home-made corn liquor. These kids couldn't be much older than Sandy, he thought.

Sandy's head cleared once she had her shower and had cleaned up her room. She hesitated before she sucked the withered piece of tobacco leaf into the vacuum that her mother had left in the upstairs hallway. Going down the stairs, she made sure her ivory and chain were inside her shirt. She took skim milk for her cereal from the refrigerator and sat down at the table to eat. Eating slowly, she remembered the days as a little girl when breakfast consisted of creamy buttered grits with cheese, country slab bacon with crispy skin, homemade biscuits with strawberry jam, and scrambled eggs. She was rather pleased that now Olivia only cooked like that on special occasions, when relatives stayed over or on some Sundays and holidays. Sandy glanced at the marmalade wall clock in the kitchen and saw that it was well passed noon. Olivia and Larry were out already.

This was the first summer since seventh grade that she didn't have at least a part-time job doing something. All summer she had kind of floated around the mall and hung out with her friends. Now something incredible was happening, and it was only three weeks until school started. Washing her bowl and flatware, she dried them and put them away. Later, Sandy decided to walk down to the section of town called the Hill and watch the pickers that worked in her Uncle Junior's vineyard. But, first, she had to check her makeup.

She was really into her makeup now, thanks to a new friend she met last school term, but Verma went back to Chicago with her father during the summer. Verma's parents were divorced, and during the school year she lived in Jesup with her mother. No one approved of their friendship, and her family and friends were constantly on her case. Sandy thought that her friends Julie and Robin acted like green-eyed monsters because she was growing up and they weren't. She wasn't interested in their baby stuff anymore. When her friend comes back from Chicago, Sandy would cut

Julie and Robin off if they didn't grow up. These three girls had been best friends since first grade, but was it her fault that her old friends weren't as mature as she and Verma?

Right now she was bursting at the seams because of the ivory! She wanted so badly to share this with someone, but she knew she mustn't say a word. When she was young, her grandmother had told her that she was a special child, special because people could tell what she was thinking, how she was feeling, just by looking at her. "You will always be able to let people know you mean them only good," her grandmother would say to her. If she were clairvoyant, as her grandmother said, maybe she wouldn't have to tell anyone exactly what happened to her. Somehow, they would sense from her all that they needed to know—yet not know how or why. She would have to be strong enough to believe in her Grandmother's words—strong enough to execute this privilege by herself.

Sandy was passing the Shaw house on her way to the Hill when five-year-old Anita Shaw ran up to her. "Hey, Sanny," she blurted. "I can do Wanda. Look!" Sandy laughed as tiny Anita crossed her eyes, turned up her top lip, and said,

"F'real Doe." Sandy applauded her young entertainer, but Anita wasn't through yet. "I can do Sha Na-Na, too. See?" The small girl arched her back to make her butt stick out and rolled her eyes and said, "Come home, Martin! Oh, my goodness!"

'Jello,' as Anita was called, was Sandy's favorite person, and she was a pleasure to sit for. She was pretty, and she was as smart as a whip. There were only two children in the Shaw family. Anita had an eighteen-year-old brother named Carnell; he was as sexy as Anita was pretty. Their parents had been married six years before they were blessed with Carnell. Years later, after trying for another baby time after time, they decided Carnell would be their only biological child. Imagine the total joy and the thanks they gave God when he blessed them a second time with this wee girl!

Having been an only child for thirteen years, Carnell surprised everyone by showing a passionate big brotherly love for his little sister. The baby needed only to whimper and he was at her beck and call. Defying the popular logic which concluded that the little girl would be spoiled by so much attention, Anita grew into the most giving and trusting person Sandy knew. In fact, Sandy didn't think Anita could be spoiled.

The child seemed unaware of the long curly lashes that cast shadows on her cheeks while she slept. She had incredibly large, dark eyes like her brother, eyes so dark they looked black. They both had dimples in their chins, but their resemblances ended with their physical appearance. Their personalities were distinct, one might even say opposite in some ways. The elder child had always been sober and serious, but nevertheless lovable. Anita, on the other hand, was always bubbling over. She never met a stranger and always had a smile for everyone. Laughing, Sandy picked the little girl up and gave her a quick hug and kissed her soft neck—she always smelled like baby powder.

By the time Sandy reached her uncle's house, it was well past the lunch hour break. Because of the heat, the pickers had gone home to stay. Passing the vineyard, she saw tools and machinery and high stacks of baskets . As a child, she used to love coming to Uncle Junior's place. She got to eat all of the scuppernong grapes she wanted, and, if the year had been warm and dry, the grapes grew in such abundance that they threatened to break the vines. Even when the vines were skimpy, she was allowed to pluck as many as she wanted so that she could set up her own little fruit stand. Only a small percentage of her uncle's grapes were used to make wine. His grapes were for eating and making grape juice. Just thinking of the vinegar that was sometimes made from grapes made her pinch her nose. She saw the beechwood sitting-barrels beside the baskets. They usually made vinegar in a rare year when they made wine. But sometimes mildew destroyed so much of the fruit that her uncle and his wife Sharon could only harvest enough for vinegar, if God were merciful; if not, a parasite called the vinegar eel would prevent even that bitter harvest. This would be a pleasant visit because the weather was perfectly hot. But, even so, she wouldn't be harvesting any of the fruit to sell because she felt that she had outgrown that type of thing. What would Verma think of 'Sandy's Grape Stand'? It embarrassed Sandy to think about it.

In another part of Jesup, still thinking of how young his two culprits were, Richard took the two drunk teenagers to the station and finished his report on them around 3:00 p.m. He was back on his beat on the corner of Elm and

Fourth Streets when he was radioed that an autopsy he had been waiting to hear about had just been faxed to the station. Arriving at the station, he found that the young man finally had a name—and a police record. The autopsy showed that the red-headed youth, Clifford 'Climmy' Pope, died from lead poisoning from a bad batch of homemade corn liquor. He had been found face down in an old tobacco barn by two teenagers that probably used the barn for something other than curing tobacco. The dead man's clothes were imbrued with alcohol. He had been dead about twelve hours before he was discovered, and flies had already deposited eggs and larva in his eyes and mouth. Crimes like this very seldom happened in Jesup, and this one had the small staff at the Wayne County jail confused.

Pope was from Hinesville and not Jesup. His father came to Jesup to claim him. What was not clear was why a twenty-two-year-old of legal drinking age would come to Jesup, where it's semi-dry, to buy liquor—unless someone in Jesup were making moonshine and selling it dirt cheap. In Wayne County, you could buy beer and certain wines with very low alcohol content, but not liquor. Richard voiced his concern that someone in Jesup was making corn squeezing.

"It doesn't take a friggin' genius to figure that out, Tucker!" bellowed the desk sergeant. David Montgomery had been desk sergeant since Richard could remember. His little rat-like eyes were beady and out of place in his otherwise generous face. The other police officers called him 'Piggy.' But Richard took him seriously and understood that he ran off at the mouth because he was envious of the other police officers because, for some reason, Piggy was given a desk job from the start of his career. Anyway, Richard had a gut feeling about this case. Looking down at Montgomery but not really seeing him, Richard knew he was on to something.

Sandy's visit with her uncle and his family went well. Her cousins Kianna and Jovan were more than happy to tag along as she walked all over the vineyard talking with her uncle. It was 5:00 p.m. when she got home. At dinner, all of them discussed the days events.

Larry was ecstatic he'd finally made enough money to buy the three-wheeler he and his dad had talked his mother into letting him buy. Olivia talked about the new mall over in

Hinesville. She thought the prices there were outrageous. Sandy cleared the table when the meal was over and started doing the dishes. When she had them done, she told her parents, who had retired with iced tea out on the front porch, that she was going for a walk. After a large meal like this, how in hell could they just sit around like that, Sandy wondered, as she walked across the yard and onto the sidewalk. Olivia had served fried rice, cabbage, grilled pork chops, fried green tomatoes, and cheese-cake for dessert. Whew! She felt stuffed, and she was the only one that didn't get dessert. Of course, what Sandy was also trying to do was to pass the time. She couldn't seem to get to her room quick enough and caution had to be taken. She couldn't risk getting caught—she had plans to carry out.

The evening was still young as she passed the Hines' house. A car pulled up to the stop light with the stereo booming: "I'm every woman . . . . Its all in me . . . ." Sandy could see one of the twins from the Thomas house riding shotgun with two white men on either side. The car pulled off and parked in the back of The Grill, the only black bar in Jesup. Sandy re-traced her steps and started back toward home; maybe she wouldn't take that walk after all.

Just as she passed in front of the Miller house, eight-year-old Tammy Miller yelled at her from across the street.

"Sandy, my momma had a new baby last night."

Sandy looked up at the child and smiled. "What did she have, Tammy?"

Learning that the baby was a girl, she told the little girl to tell her parents Congratulations for her. Then she made a mental note to visit them once Mrs. Miller and the baby were home from the hospital. The last time she'd seen the inside of the Miller house was last year when she went over to take them some of Mrs. Julia's rhubarbs, pie plants Sandy used to call them when she was a child.

As she entered her yard and neared the front porch of the house where her parents sat on the swing, the phone rang and her mother went to answer it. Sandy approached her father. "Dad, how's it going at work? I'm still sorry I missed having breakfast with you."

He was very sensitive to Sandy's situation regarding slavery. Anytime she was bothered by something, big or small, he was concerned, and now was no exception. He knew that there was something troubling her, but the last thing he wanted to do was to ask her about it. If he gave her space and let her know that he would be there if and when she needed him, Richard thought, she would eventually seek his advice and help.

"It's OK, hon; we'll have lunch one day—you say when. We're trying to piece a puzzle together a the job, and I think I may have my work cut out for me."

Richard sometimes spoke in metaphors when he talked about his job. That was his way of not really bringing his work home. Sandy smiled at him. He could always make her smile, no matter what. "You know you want to tell me the whole story, daddy. Did you all ever find out who was robbing the museum?"

Puffing on his old pipe, Richard looked at his daughter over the top of his glasses. "You, little girl," he said, putting emphasis on the 'you,' "have not been reading the newspaper. But to answer your question: we don't have a clue. It's going to be tricky tracking down a kook that makes his living stealing copper tubing . . . ."

Before he could complete his sentence, a thunder of music boomed from an open upstairs window. Larry must have lost his earphones again and was blasting his Rap tapes. Just last week he was forbidden to listen to anything made by 2 Live Crew. His tapes were taken from him. But Sandy was willing to bet that Larry had purchased more. Right now he was playing Dr. Dre. Sandy liked Dr. Dre, but her favorite artists were Whitney Houston, CeCe, Peniston, TLC, SWV and Shai. Sandy would listen to hard Rap discs if she were with Verma, but she knew never to bring them home. The music and lyrics seemed to put her father's nerves on end.

Putting his fingers in his ears he shouted over the music for Sandy to tell her brother to cut the box off. "And tell him to bring his 'droopy ass' down here . . . . Now!"

Richard was constantly buying tapes and videos—the wrong ones—for his son. He could appreciate his sons love for music, but why couldn't he listen to the tapes he bought him? In the late 50's and 60's when Richard was growing up, his parents complained about the loud, nerve-racking James Brown and the tight, tight skirts most girls had adopted. In the 70's, the mini skirts and go-go boots almost caused a civil war between the middle-aged adults and the baby boomers. If Richard's parents could see what the kids of today wore and if they could hear the music they listened to, it would be a war.

It took Richard Tucker to tell you about the lost days of wholesome living. He read anything he could get his hands on about the fading baby boomers. Fading? Ha! If only the youth of today were remotely as moral as he and his fellow teenagers were 2 1/2 decades ago. He was the last to say that his generation was physically chaste, but they didn't make a mockery out of being young. Richard had spent seven days at Woodstock and he did his share of non-hallucinogenic drugs, but he left with his values and priorities intact, and he went into the army to serve for four years. Olivia never asked about his trip to Woodstock, and he never brought it up. Anyway, it was before her time. This year he and Larry had their father-to-son talk about sex, and, afterwards, he had the feeling that Larry already knew everything they had talked about. He felt that he was being just a wee bit patronized.

When he heard the music shut off and his son coming down the stairs, his anger tapered. He didn't expect the boy to be philharmonic; but couldn't he just play his music a little less noisy and a lot cleaner?

The night was slow and breezy, and, if not for hungry mosquitoes, it would have been perfect. People passed by on the sidewalk and said 'Good Evening' and nodded their heads. There were not too many things in Jesup worse than passing someone's house and not speaking. And if you passed another person walking, you said 'Hey' no matter what. It had been like that since Sandy could remember.

At 9:00 p.m. Mrs. Conyon Walker stepped out on her porch and, as she did every evening, she called for her daughter Kim to come in for the evening. Mrs. Walker lived on the other side of the Tuckers, but Sandy could never remember her ever stepping a foot in the Tucker house, or vice-versa.

A car full of teenagers rode by in Lenora Ellis' 'heavy Chevy,' and you could hear Ice Cube pumping. As the family gathered up their empty tea glasses and dessert dishes, Sandy's cousin on her Mom's side OraBell and he husband Charles Horton strode by. The two had only been married since April 1st and were already expecting their first baby. OraBell—whom everyone called 'Honey'—was a strikingly beautiful young woman. She declared before her nuptials that she wanted twelve children. Charles, whom everyone called 'Mr. Charlie,' worshipped his wife. "Good Evening," they spoke, and smiled as they passed. Everyone in Jesup loved Ora. She was Sandy's favorite female cousin.

At 10:00 p.m. everyone but Sandy went inside; she told her parents she'd be in after a minute. She stayed on the porch and took a deep breath. The crickets and frogs made a symphony. Somewhere in the dusk a dog barked. Today had been a long day for Sandy. Before they went in, she overheard her mother thanking God for his mercy. Sandy wrapped her arms around herself and marveled at how tranquil she felt.

Now Sandy was ready. She would make her second trip tonight. She had made it through the longest day of her life. It was 11:30 p.m. when Sandy finished her good nights and went up to her room. She didn't bother to get permission to lock her door. But Sandy had always thought that was a dumb idea anyway.

She brushed her teeth and, after showering and changing clothes, she closed and locked the door. Walking slowly to the bed, she pulled her chain out of her shirt and palmed the smooth ivory. It felt warm in her hand. She had a mission to accomplish. “And I will see it done,” she vowed to her image in the mirror facing the bed. Sandy began her chant. The room began to spin and Sandy’s disappearing body left a trail of thin blue neon light in her wake. At midnight on the dot, Sandy was gone!

She became conscious in the same place and at the same time of day as she had the first time. She sat up and stuffed the ivory into her shirt. She shook her head to clear it, then looked around her. Bubba and Faye were waiting. Sandy saw a bit of apprehension in their eyes and they seemed in a hurry. Bubba was the first to speak.

“Sho is glad yew was no dream, Sandy.” She felt his nervousness as he spoke. “Me an’ Faye tol’ de res’ ob de slabes we was gon’ bring ya wid us when we’s done in de ‘bacca fiel’s.”

Sandy stood up to brush her clothes off and ran her hands through her hair. She looked over at them and saw that her clothes had them in awe again. Today, Sandy wore a large shirt over a short blue jean skirt and sandals. She tried to blend in a little more, but this was as close as she could get—she chuckled to herself—unless she went to the bridal shop and came up with something like Scarlett wore in *Gone With the Wind*!

Faye had finally gathered her wits about her and told Sandy that the way she dressed really was so strange that it would always shock her. After having been reassured that Sandy was really there and would be there when their work in the fields was done, they rushed back to the fields.

Sandy decided to resume her search of the big house and the surrounding grounds. As she retraced her steps on the narrow dirt trail, the white overseer on his slate gray steed cut across the trail, whip in hand. It was obvious that he was returning from his lunch break and expected to see some of the blacks gold-bricking so that he would have a good reason for whipping someone's bare black back. She would have yelled that he was coming, but she was sure they heard him.

She wondered how she would be accepted by the house slaves. She knew they had been informed about her presence and her appearance. From what she learned from her first trip here, the slaves did not expect to have a complete understanding of everything that happened around them. In fact, how could they? And they did not blame themselves for what they couldn't understand. They were comfortable with the unexplainable.

Most of what the slaves couldn't figure out they attributed to voodoo. A lot of the slaves here had West Indian backgrounds; they had been told fantastic tales from generation to generation. Sandy would just be one of the characters in a tale they would pass on to their children . . . .

Before Sandy knew it, she was standing at the kitchen door of the big house. Tapping lightly on the door and pushing it open, she saw the widest, roundest, blackest woman she'd ever seen in her life. Mammy Cinda was her name and minding everyone else's business was her game! If Mammy Cinda had not heard it, it probably wasn't true. Sandy's first glimpse of Mammy was of her back end. If you've ever seen *Gorillas in the Mist*, you've seen the biggest male gorilla's rear end. Well, that's what Sandy seemed to see as Mammy was bent over the potato bin. She looked like a gorilla with a sheet over its rear hump.

When Mammy Cinda turned to face whoever it was tapping on 'her' kitchen door, Sandy saw what first appeared to be the animated eyes of a cartoon character! Her face was the color of a prune, but of a prune with no wrinkles. Mammy's skin was as tight as a fully blown balloons; the whites of her eyes and of her even teeth were almost as pure as Fanny's back at the slave quarters.

Just as Sandy thought, Mammy had already heard of her and her mission. A tabby cat on the window ledge hissed at Sandy and ran away. Mammy drew Sandy deeper into the kitchen. Sandy was still amazed at how completely these people accepted something as strange as her appearing from another century. While the slave went on and on about the strange clothes Sandy wore and about voodoo, Sandy took in the old-fashioned furnishings.

Except for the stoves and lack of modern appliances, the kitchen looked like some of the very expensive kitchens she had seen in Better Homes and Gardens. A fireplace with a large hearth took up one corner of the room. In the fireplace and on the hearth stood black cast iron pots of every size. There was also a large pot belly stove of cast iron in the opposite corner with three steaming pots on it. In yet another corner was a large basin under a hand pump. The floor was made of brick and had been scrubbed so often that it was smooth and shiny. There were counter tops made of oak, as were the pantries. In a little alcove off from the kitchen hung onions, parsley, garlic, mint, and a number of other herbs and spices. In a pantry next to the alcove, the canned fruits and vegetables sat on shelves from ceiling to floor, and the flour, grits, rice, coffee, tea, sugar, corn meal, and other perishable staples were in barrels in another closet. She learned that right outside the kitchen door in the backyard sat a smokehouse with ham, bacon, herring, ribs, beef, turkey, and other meats. The spring house next to it was for storing milk, butter, cheese, ice, and icy-cold and clear sweet water—the best Sandy ever tasted.

Mammy Cinda was telling Sandy about another 'ghost' that came to this very plantation six years ago. "It was sad," Mammy said. "De wo-jo woman was de onny one what coul' see or hear dat ghos'. But yew is here an' we all is seein' ya."

Before another word could be spoken, in walked the lady of the planation. Sandy froze and Mammy Cinda's face went blank and ashen. The lady was there to make sure Mammy remembered they were having three guests for supper.

Missy Teresa was the backbone of the mansion, and, in some cases, she had control over the entire plantation with the exception of the fields. But lately, on several occasions, she had even gained control over them. Teresa had found reasons to fire three different overseers and was clever enough to make her husband think he had done it! 'Lady Teresa,' as she had insisted her equals call her, had her husband, Coard, hoodwinked most of the time.

The couple had two daughters, Misty and DeeDee. DeeDee was seventeen and Misty six. Some in the household wondered, though, how any children were conceived from their marriage. The couple slept in separate rooms, and it was a rare night if at all that he visited her room. Coard, standing six feet tall with dark copper hair, a square jaw with a cleft chin, and green eyes, had grown up on this plantation. He was the only child of Coard Worthinwood III. And it was Coard IV's duty to bring a mistress to the Worthinwood planation and have sons.

Coard grew up believing that a high bred white girl wasn't made to enjoy sex but to endure it for the sake of procreation. On her wedding night, Teresa had to fake virginity and pretend to hate the act she had learned to enjoy as a teenager on her father's plantation.

As a well-bred white aristocrat, Coard never even mentioned sex around his wife. He had secretly compared the bodies of his wife and other white women he'd sexed to those of the rounded, lusty bodies of the slave girls he consumed regularly. His wife's body was very thin and flat. The slaves were round and sweet. The buttocks of the slaves he visited were so firm and full that thinking about them brought on a trip to the slave quarters. To be sure, Lady Teresa knew about these midnight liaisons. "Coard couldn't hide a needle in a haystack," she was often quoted as saying.

But, right now, Lady Teresa was standing not an arm's length away—Sandy was face to face with the mistress of Worthinwood Plantation! Mammy Cinda stood staring from Sandy to Lady Teresa with her mouth agape. Both Mammy and Sandy were temporarily stunned. Could the mistress see Sandy? Sandy had proven that the other whites couldn't, but what if, somehow, she could? How would it go for the other slaves and Mammy? But before either Sandy or Mammy could stick a foot in their mouths, Teresa spoke.

"Well, Mammy, you seem to have everything under control. When I walked up I could have sworn you were talking to somebody." She looked around the room and even peeped into the alcove. "In fact, I heard another voice. Mammy, you shore you're not hidin' a man in this kitchen?"

Mammy, so relieved at not getting caught with such a strange looking and sounding creature as this ghost in her kitchen, threw up her hands, rolled her eyes skyward and whinnied gratefully, "Lord, Missy Teresa, I ain't had me no man in so long I done loss coun'." Mammy picked up a piece of whet-stone and started sharpening the already well-honed cutlery with vigor. But much to Mammy's dismay, Sandy in her funny clothes, now assured that she was indeed invisible to Missy Teresa, was walking around and around Teresa waving her hands in her face.

"Mammy, are you feelin' poorly? You look positively ill!"

Teresa walked up to the servant and lay a very white hand on her brow. Sandy could smell a scent on the lady something close to the honeysuckle cologne her mother used to wear. She was so close to Teresa that she could see the white rice powder clinging to the pores of her face.

Sandy saw that Teresa could've been beautiful, but she was so white, so pale her face had probably never felt the sun for more than a minute or two. She had beautiful hazel eyes and, although her mouth was none too generous, her oval face with its widow's peak was striking. Her uncinate nose could have spoiled her profile, but Teresa's hair more than made up for any shortcoming she had. Waist-length, the color of wild honey, and thick and glossy, her hair fell like a curtain when it wasn't caught up in a bun around her small head. The one clearly visible flaw was that the Lady of Worthinwood lacked the small hands and feet that were so coveted by the women of her era.

Taking a list from her pocket, Teresa started checking off the items of the menu, one at a time. "Ham? Mustard Greens? Corn bread with cracklings? Cream potatoes? Field peas? Duck in orange sauce with wild rice?"

"Yessum," Mammy answered each time.

"Biscuits?"

"Yessum."

"Candied yams?"

"Yessum."

"Now, Mammy, what about desserts?"

With pride, the big cook listed sweet potato pie and milk chocolate buttercake. Satisfied that her orders were being carried out, Teresa spun around to go back down the narrow walkway that connected the kitchen to the house, but she stopped short.

"Mammy, I keep smelling the prettiest aroma. What is it?" The butter knife Mammy had picked up to ice the cake with clattered to the floor. Sandy put her hands to her mouth and tried to stifle a giggle. Teresa glared at her servant. "Mammy Cinda, are you laughing at me?"

The big woman shook her head so hard that Sandy thought her snow white turban would fall off. "No ma'am, Missy Teresa, I was jus' clearin' my throat." She clutched her throat and coughed loudly. "I is gettin' a mite sickly, but it ain't nothin' dis ol' hide cain't fight. Yessum, I can fight it. You jus' go res' yo sef. Let ol' Mammy Cinda take care-o-things." She shuffled over and pushed Teresa gently toward the walkway.

Turning toward Sandy, she put her hands on her hips and tried to point her sternest look at Sandy but failed miserably and had to cover her own mouth to muffle the deepest belly laughs Sandy ever heard. Mammy's whole body shook like jello and tears coursed down her cheeks.

By the time Sandy returned to the tobacco barn, the slaves had finished their work in the fields and had lined up for the walk back to the quarters. Standing to the side of the path as the procession passed, she watched intensely, looking each person in the eyes. Their utter acceptance of what, to them, was the supernatural still amazed her. Sandy felt like crying as the ragged, dirty, and completely exhausted line passed, but these poor souls still had more work ahead of them. When Faye walked passed, Sandy fell in step with her.

"Well, Faye, what do you do next?"

The little slave was so tired that she seemed almost incapable of the sigh that Sandy barely heard. With a visible struggle, Faye told her friend that she had cut tobacco today. Now, they would do things that needed to be done for their own survival. Some would chop wood to cook tonight's supper. Some would go down to the stream to bathe or to draw water. Others had clothes to wash or to take off the lines. Faye had to gather some produce from the little garden behind her hut—nearly every group had its own little patch in the back of the huts. She had her own clothes to wash and she wanted to bathe. "I be so hot today. Dat oberseer onny gib us a break to drink watta; we had to eat standin' up."

Soon, they were entering the women's hut, and, as they entered the room, all the girls stopped what they were doing and gathered around Sandy and Faye. The sweat and heat of over twenty young girls was overbearing even though the room was well-ventilated. It struck Sandy that these people probably had never used deodorant or shampoo and conditioner before in their lives.

"Faye, what kind of soap do you use?"

The tired woman looked at Sandy as if she couldn't believe she had asked the question. "We use lye and ash soap when we can get enuff talla' t'make it. Why?"

"Do you use that to wash your hair, too?"

"Who got time to wash dey hair?!"

Cleta asked, "Why is you askin' us deez ass backward thangs?"

Now Sandy was very excited. "Yes!" she yelled and grabbed Faye by the arms and danced around and around with the poor tired slave. Everyone in the room and even some that had been outside nearby ran into the hut and got caught up in the moment. Sandy got everyone to settle down and to gather round, and she briefly explained to them some of what her grandmother had told her about them. "One day," she began, "I will tell you all about the 20th century."

But right now Sandy was holding the ivory in her palm. She gave the amulet a squeeze, and, as if in response, it grew warm in her hand. She actually felt it throbbing, echoing her excitement. "Right now I'm going to furnish you with soap, deodorant, shampoo and conditioner, toothpaste, toothbrushes, and hair picks and brushes!"

The little beaver-looking girl Sandy had learned was named Dorsey edged close to Sandy and asked if they would smell nice like her. Sandy nodded. "I'm going to show everyone how to use everything once its here; this is my first time, girls, so bear with me."

Closing her eyes, she asked the girls and some of the men whose curiosity had drawn them in to join hands and to form a circle.

"Now, please, everyone, be quiet—Don't say a word." Sandy started chanting under her breath. "Close your eyes and don't open them until I say so." No one heard the words she said. In a tremulous voice, barely audible even to herself, she delivered her request. She felt the ivory give a solid shudder and then quit. Drenched in perspiration, did she dare to open her eyes? She did so, very slowly.

Sandy let out a squeal of delight at what she saw. "It worked!"

There, at each of their feet, was a medium-sized plastic bag filled with Creme of Nature shampoo or Posners, Crest or Aim toothpaste, a Reach toothbrush, Lever or Irish Spring soap, Mennen Herbal Scent Deodorant or Ban Roll-on, a powder box of Shower-To-Shower, a towel and wash cloth, and some Water Babies 35 SP Sun Block! Sandy watched with tears in her eyes as these people marvelled over what she had always taken for granted. Like little children on Christmas morning, they smelled the items and asked how to open this or that; they compared what was in each of their bags and laughed. One of the girls named Cookie came up to Sandy and tried to kiss her hand.

"You is a good magic woman. Now us'll smell better'n doze white fo'ks. Dey ain' even got nothin' liken unto dis stuff. Why, Missy Teresa ain' nebber seen nothin' like what we's done got from you!"

"That's right, Cookie," Sandy told her. "Nobody will have this stuff, not for another hundred years!"

Sandy spent the rest of the evening with the slaves, showing them how to use all of the gifts she'd wished into their lives. It was just like Christmas morning and she was the happiest gift giver ever!

She would return home after this trip knowing that her Grandmother Mary would be very pleased . . . and proud.

CHAPTER FOUR

Richard had not been at work long when a call came in that Woodworth's Drug and 5&10 Cent Store had been robbed. The pharmacist and a clerk came in an hour before opening time as usual and found certain toiletries missing. As Richard was in route to the store to investigate and to take a report, he remembered when some of the stores in Jesup weren't too happy with their black customers. Woodworth's was one of them.

In those days, if more than one black came into the store at the same time, the manager would call a stock clerk from the warehouse for back up. This went on until a few years ago, in spite of the King Marches. Woodworth's still didn't like to serve blacks at the snack bar, but they had no choice.

Q Moony's, an expensive clothing store that had been in town since the Tuckers were babies, was another example of discrimination Richard recalled. During the '50's, '60's and '70's, most local blacks could not afford the prices offered at Q Moony's. But the few families that could were not treated with kindness. Blacks were not allowed to try on clothes nor were they encouraged to browse. Richard remembered his second anniversary. He went to Q Moony's because he had saved enough to buy Olivia this beautiful blue hat he knew she wanted. The day after his anniversary, he went back to return the hat, Olivia's mother had given her the same one. Entering the store, he gave the hat to the clerk and explained. The clerk took the hat into a room behind the counter, and for five minutes another clerk followed Richard as he browsed in the store—step for step.

Finally, a young man came out and asked how he could be of assistance. Richard explained again.

"Well," the young man said. "We can't take the hat back, but we can sell you something else at half price." Richard and his family had not set foot in Q Moony's since.

When Richard and Patrick O'Mallary, his partner, arrived at the store, they found the manager and his first shift clerk taking inventory of the missing merchandise. Richard began looking for the point of entry while his partner took statements from the irate manager, Ron Tart. Finding absolutely no forced entry, he went to report his findings to the pharmacist and to ask him a few questions.

Wayne Larky, the pharmacist, explained that not one thing was disturbed or missing from the pharmacy. The cash registers, receipts, and safes were untouched. The thief wasn't interested in anything of real value. Richard wondered: could it be that this robbery and the museum robbery were pulled by the same person or persons? Even though the museum showed signs of forced entry, nothing of real value was taken from either place. Copper pipes and metal kegs from the first crime; soap, shampoo, deodorant, and other toiletries from the second.

After talking to the pharmacist, Richard walked over to the front of the store where Ron Tart and Gabby Schmidt, a female clerk, were still giving an account of the missing inventory to O'Mallary.

"I still believe it was one of those colored boys and he got scared off before he could get to the drugs and cash," Tart was saying. He was silenced by a jab to the ribs by his clerk when she saw Richard approaching, but he overheard anyway.

A bit stiffly, Richard said, "Well, Mr. Tart, we will do our best to solve this, but if you find anything new that may help us clear the case quicker, please feel free to inform us."

As the men drove off in the patrol car, Richard was reflective.

Three summers ago a large group of white kids started gathering in an empty parking lot downtown on Friday and Saturday nights. On Sunday mornings, you could find gads of empty beer cans, broken soda bottles, used condoms, empty marijuana baggies, and discarded wrappings from food. Sometimes, you could find panties or a bra, but the town of Jesup didn't mind. So what if you could hear The Grateful Dead three blocks away? The kids were just being kids, the officials were quoted as saying. After all, wasn't the mayor's eighteen-year-old son one of the gang?

There was a video arcade on the white side of the tracks and a tennis court complete with refreshment stand. On the other side of town (the black side) the kids had the recreation center. Like their white counterparts, the black youngsters found an abandoned parking lot downtown across from Hardees, and a crew of them began meeting there with loud music—leaving beer cans, broken soda bottles, wrappings from food, marijuana baggies, and used condoms. But the town of Jesup (and its nearly all white police force) minded terribly.

The black kids only met six weekends before the police went in and made them clean up and get out permanently. They obeyed, but not quietly, of course. They labelled the white chief of police a 'shit-eatin' son of a bitch'. The black youngsters were told by their elders to leave well enough alone; there was still the rec center, wasn't there?

Well, Richard recalled, it seemed that it was OK when the kids were only using the center for dancing and swimming, because it closed at 11:00 p.m. But when they started using the park behind the center on Friday and Saturday nights, the police would come over and demand that they turn the music down to a whisper, and the kids would—until the police left. Naughty by Nature would be pumping "Hip Hop Hooray" through the airwaves and kids would be hyped up and having fun. After having been duped by a group of black teens over and over, the officers thought that it was time for the chief of police to make a personal appearance.

One night, two other white officers and a rookie accompanied Chief Weller as he ostentatiously demonstrated a technique adequate to the purpose. They brought in dogs that were efficient in sniffing out the youngsters with marijuana. Five drug arrests were made. After a few cars loaded with kids left, news got back to the Park that the police were pulling drivers over and charging anyone smelling of alcohol with DWI. Afraid of being charged and going to jail, some of the young drivers walked over to the rec center to use the outside pay phones. If they could get someone to pick them up, great, if not, they left their vehicles and walked. But even after the arrests some of the diehards would still hang around the park on weekends and, much to his chagrin, Weller could find no reasons to arrest them. Most of them fled through the woods when they saw police cars, and they stopped bringing joints to the park, so it was a waste of city funds to bring the dogs out.

Not to be outwitted, Weller had ordered a curfew. Ages 21 and younger were restricted to homes and private yards after 11:30 p.m. on Friday and Saturday nights. It seemed that there was nothing that the black teens could do legally. On the other hand, the white youths met in their car lots in town, leaving their usual debris behind. The police would make a public show of putting the teens out, but it didn't take a high intelligence quotient to see that a public show was all it was.

Tempers were running hot in the Hood. At the rec center one night, a young man (Kurt Gilbert, but known only in the community as "Goat") exploded in a paroxysm of anger. He and a number of the diehards that still frequented the park announced that they were tired of having to be home by 11:30 after working hard all week. The crowd agreed in unison. Richard happened to have some spare time that evening and had come to the center to shoot some pool. Goat had everyone's attention.

Now, Richard knew that all of the kids had questions, but this group wanted answers . . . now! Each and every one of them had passed downtown and seen the white kids having a good time in 'their' parking lot at one time or another. And to add fuel to the fire, this young man was a proficient speaker. This kid could manipulate an angry crowd like his father, Curtis Gilbert, decades before him. The elder Gilbert led non-violent protests when Martin Luther King was marching for freedom.

But Goat's intentions weren't non-violent. This was not a high school debating team. The heat was getting hotter, and Goat (The Warrior) wanted to stain the arena with blood. Goat wasn't a naturally violent person, and he didn't come from a dysfunctional family, at least not from the public's view.

When Goat was five, the family moved to the Bronx, NY where the boy lived until he was thirteen. When they returned, he was very opinionated and his small town peer groups supposed he knew everything. If Goat didn't know, nobody knew, at least not another child. Goat was given his nickname at a very young age he would eat anything. But he was a thin baby, and he would be a thin adult. His mother always said he was so thin because he never stopped moving. He had an abundance of nervous energy, but his mind was capacious, and once he heard something, it stayed in his head.

Richard had listened as Goat asked how many kids in the room remembered the incident at Hardees? As echo's of 'yeahs' went around the room, Richard decided to defuse this time bomb before it exploded. Richard knew that reaching an armistice was foremost at the moment. He finished putting his cue stick back into its case and walked over to the crowd and stood beside the twenty-year-old Goat. One thing Richard knew about this group was that if he could appeal to Goat's empathy, the crowd would be amenable. But the last thing these youngsters wanted to hear was a bunch of police psychobabble. A ponderous lecture and the kids could've kissed their future's goodbye.

After speaking to Goat in private—appealing to the young man's good sense and concern for his friends—Richard convinced Goat of the foolishness of a violent approach to solving the problem. The crowd reluctantly, but wisely, dispersed. Richard walked home.

In addition to saving lives that night, Officer Richard Tucker had turned an approaching disaster for Goat and the others into a lesson in patient resolve: things could be changed, but violence wasn't the answer.

That incident happened three summers ago, and, today, the thought of it made Richard feel depressed and helpless as he and Pat headed down Main Street.

Things would start simmering again if the blame for those robberies were put on a black kid, and he was almost sure it wasn't a crime that the kids he knew would do. Richard was deep in thought and would have missed his turn at a four-way stop if O'Mallary hadn't whistled and waved a hand before his face.

"Tucker, I know you overheard what Tart said, but I hope you know I don't share his opinion."

"Fuck what you think, man, or even what I think!" All of a sudden, he felt he would suffocate if he tried to swallow the shallow sympathy coming from his partner. At that moment they were passing the white kid's parking lot, and two city workers who were picking up trash with their sticks waved. "It's scum like Tart that slink around ejaculating their racist shit-coated poison into the minds of supposedly decent white people. But it's the decent white men that spew their twice-eaten shit into the black community. It's the decent white men that talk about helping to bring about 'equality' to what he calls a struggling minority!" By now, Richard was banging on the steering wheel. "And the same decent white men stomp on the fingers of that struggling minority when they reach up to grab some of that equality."

The crackling of their radio made O'Mallary jump, but he was glad to have the interruption.

Richard just stared at the road ahead as they sped to the next crime scene. He wondered if his children and their children would forever live in a divided world.. . .

Sandy slept very late, but by one o'clock she was at the park with Julie and Robin. She'd had an early lunch with Larry before he left to hang out, and she had washed her mom's car for ten dollars. Now she was standing in the park with her two oldest friends, dancing and flirting.

A week ago, Julie had borrowed Sandy's CD player and Sandy had told her to bring it to the park today because she'd purchased a new CD by TLC and wanted to play it. "Hat 2 Da Back" was blasting now, but she really liked "Shock dat Monkey."

She and the girls were having fun. There were not many people in the park, just a nice comfortable amount. The girls were doing the Electric Slide. Sandy had learned to do the dance when she was with Verma, and she knew all of the latest little twists and turns.

"How come you have to make the dance look so sexy?" asked Robin. "Look at these boys ogling your butt." She spat out the word butt.

Today Sandy had worn her Guess Jeans with rips and holes everywhere, even on the rear end, but she had skin-colored unitards under them, and her black hi top Fila's. She knew she looked good and this is how Verma would dress.

Perfecting a pretty pout, she said, "I can't help it if I be slammin' and the fellows like what they see." She gave a little turn and shook her hips. Robin had stopped dancing and was sitting on a bench in front of them. The little crowd that had gathered were all dancing and having fun. But having the most fun was Sandy.

One of the kids that came over was a tall, skinny, curly-headed boy named Alvin. All of the girls liked him. He never moved very fast and Verma would say, "His clothes have it goin' on!" Alvin would be a senior this school term and captain of the basketball team. Sandy knew he had noticed her because he and his friends had stopped shooting basketball to come over. They were doing the Electric Slide with them, but Alvin was out of step. She had to bite a hole in her lip to keep from laughing.

"Al," one of his friends laughed, "you don't know these steps!"

"Damn, man, this dance is getting old."

A guy named Tommy persisted. "How come you can't do the steps, man?"

"I'll get it, I'll get it!" Alvin said, laughing at himself. Tommy laughed too. "Nigger, the music's stopped. Sit your constipated ass down."

It was 4:00 p.m. when Sandy, Robin, and Julie left the park. No one spoke until a car-load of boys passed, making cat calls and yell-ing, "Baby's got back!"

And Robin yelled back, "And so does your mama."

Sandy glared at her. "Now what if they'd heard you, asswipe?"

Before the two girls could square off, Julie stepped in, all 5' 11" of her! She had enough. She loved both friends, but Robin and Sandy had been bickering all summer.

It started in school with the arrival of the new student from Chicago, Verma Wells. Sandy was the first to make friends with her because that's just Sandy's personality. She was always witty and relaxed, and she never let anything or anyone shock her. If you told her a UFO visited your bedroom, Sandy's jaw would go slack, her eyes would open wide, her mouth would pop open, and she would ask you what planet it was from! Despite her apparent gullibility, she never made anything below a B in grades . . . until Verma showed up. She still made good grades, but she didn't mind the occasional C.

Sandy had a profusion of talents, but one thing she wasn't and that was overly critical in her evaluation of others. To Sandy, everyone was 'a nice person' until they proved over and over again, unfortunately that they weren't.

Verma acted and dressed a lot older than her fifteen years, and her grades left a lot of room for improvement. Robin had tried talking to Sandy but was told to butt out. So Julie and Robin left Sandy to Verma for the whole ninth grade term. Imagine Sandy's surprise when Verma left Jesup for the summer and her two best friends welcomed her back! Robin was pretty sure that in Sandy's eyes she and Julie were just filling in for Verma until her return from the big city, and she had no qualms about telling Sandy that. Sandy walked the rest of the way home by herself after the two girls turned to go on the hill where they lived. Until the last minute, she had planned to go visit her Uncle Junior's house. She could see him everyday and still not see him enough. Everyone in town that knew George Frasier Junior, black or white—loved him. Sandy was seven years old when her uncle came home for his mother's funeral. He planned to stay only until the reading of the will and even his baby sister Olivia couldn't sway him. After joining the Marines, Junior had moved to California when Sandy was only two. His stint in the Marines lasted only four years, but he met and married a little nurse named Sharen and decided to make Sacramento his home. However, he hadn't a clue that his mother would leave him more than ten acres of land and the Frasier vineyards.

His father and older brothers made a living from those vineyards, and by the time he and his sister were old enough to help, the family was stable enough to hire a full staff of workers and increase the production. George Senior died that same year from neglected diabetes mellitus before he had a chance to sit back and enjoy the leisure that hard work had afforded him.

Junior accepted his inheritance gratefully, and, after selling his little bungalow on the west coast, he and his wife Sharon made the vineyard their lives. Even hard work wasn't aging her uncle; his hazel eyes were clear and warm, and his soft curly hair made his 6' 7" and 259 lbs frame less intimidating to his little niece. I'll just see him tomorrow, she thought.

Olivia was livid when Sandy walked through the door. "Where have you been? I've called all over the place for you. Did you forget that you're supposed to sit for the Shaws tonight?"

Sandy's eyes and mouth popped open simultaneously.

"Oh my gosh, Mom . . . . I absolutely forgot! How could it slip my mind?"

Before Olivia could say another word, up the stairs Sandy dashed to grab a book, her phone book, and a toy microscope she had picked up at a flea market for Anita. She ran about half way up and stopped in her tracks. Squeezing her eyes shut, she turned around slowly.

Sitting on the floor in front of the TV in her PJ's with her sleeping bag and Raggedy Ann doll was little miss Anita grinning from ear to ear.

"Sandy, you didn't see me because I was invisible," she said as she walked over and stood by the bottom step as Sandy walked back down. Sandy picked her up and hugged her. "You were supposed to be over to my house at six, and its seven already." The little vixen was up to something, Sandy thought. She put her down and Jello walked over to Olivia. "It's kinda OK, though, 'cause I got to come over here instead. But if Sandy gives me two percent of her babysitting money, I'll forget it ever happened, and so will Mizz Olivia. Right, Mizz Olivia? We'll call it 'even stephen'."

Sandy and her mother laughed. For an hour the three of them talked.

Anita had this little game she played. When she was happy she was 'cherry jello' and put red bows in her doll's hair. If she were lonesome, she was 'lemon jello' and used yellow bows in the doll's hair: she was 'lime jello' with green bows when she was busy; 'blueberry' with blue bows when she was sad. Anita was hardly ever sad and recently she started using white bows for pretending she was invisible, saying she was 'water jello.' Tonight, the dolls black yarn hair sported many red and white bows. After putting Anita's doll to bed and rubbing mosquito repellant on Anita and herself, Sandy took her charge out to sit on the porch. It was only 8:30 p.m. and still very hot. They were playing jack stones when Nadine Morgan passed the house.

Nadine was not a pretty woman, and it would be an exaggeration to even call her cute, but, as if to make up for her homeliness, Nadine was flamboyant—to say the least. Tonight she was wearing pink. Everything she had on was pink, even her wig. Despite its color, her clothing was plain, but Nadine's walk was anything but plain. Her moving hips reminded Sandy of a swinging pendulum.

As she walked by, she said her usual 'Evenin'.'

Anita looked up from the game and said aloud to Nadine, "You go girl!" Nadine hesitated and looked at the child with raised brows. Anita being the ham she was asked Nadine, "'S'up, Nadine?"

Nadine couldn't help it; she and Sandy laughed, and Anita kept playing jacks.

She wasn't trying to make a joke. Anita was just being Anita.

Later, Sandy faked anger at being beaten five times by the little girl, which made Anita laugh. "You gotta learn to take your hard knocks with a grain of salt, Sandy. Your time to win will come soon enough. I can't just keep winning. I'm not THAT good."

Sandy really struggled hard to keep from laughing and just settled for hugging and squeezing the little girl. Everybody loved the innocence of Anita. If Sandy had a younger sister, she would've had to be just like Anita.

A car pulled into the Miller yard and blew the horn. It was one of the twins and the same white guy that was driving the other night was driving a different car tonight. The door to the house opened and 5 or 6 of the Miller kids poured out.

"Uh, Oh, here comes Be Be's kids," piped Anita. Sandy tapped the child's hand.

"Jello, be nice. I thought you liked Tina and Kayla." Anita looked surprised and hurt.

"I love them," she said, tilting her head to one side. "They're in my Sunday school class. Be Be's kids are loved too. I only meant that in the nicest way, San."

By this time they were sitting on the porch swing. Anita had popped her two middle fingers in her mouth and laid her freshly shampooed head on her sitter's lap. As soon as she was asleep, Sandy picked her soft little body up and laid her on her sleeping bag in the living room. Sandy kissed her sweet, baby powdered neck and put her Raggedy Ann in her arms.

It was 10:00. Anita's parents had gone to a gospel concert then out to dinner. They would pick Anita up at 11:00. Sandy went to her room to get her journal. Curling up in her dad's recliner and munching an apple was a comfortable way to spend the time until 11:00. She planned to leave early tonight because she had a lot to do.

Suddenly, Sandy remembered that no one had mentioned her chain and ivory. It was as if no one saw it. Today at the park, it was displayed in full view, and no one seemed to have seen it. Even Jello hadn't seen it. "Well I'll be a . . . . "

Before she could utter another word, a car pulled into the driveway. Seeing it was the Shaws, Sandy unlocked the screen door and started gathering Anita's belongings—a toy doctor's bag, a barrette box, her robe, and a deck of Old Maid cards. After paying Sandy, the Shaws took their precious bundle home. Sandy was glad they came back before 11:00. Now she could get an early start and get back in the morning early before anyone came knocking on her door. If she kept 'sleeping in,' somebody would eventually get suspicious and come to investigate.

Finding her mother in the den sewing, Sandy kissed her and told her she was tired and was going to bed and asked permission to lock her door. Permission granted, she locked the downstairs doors and windows and went up to her room. Her father had been shooting pool with her Uncle Junior and Uncle Edward at the Rec Center, and Larry was playing video games. It was 10:25.

The house was quiet when she locked her door and transported herself into the past.

Sandy expected to come to in the barn as always, but she didn't. Before she opened her eyes, she noticed the smell of tobacco wasn't there and she wasn't on a dirt floor. Opening her eyes, she saw that she was in a beautiful room, and instead of dirt, she was lying on a highly polished hardwood floor, and the smell of green tobacco was replaced by the scent of cedar.

Sitting up, she tucked her ivory into the scanty top of her unitards. Getting to her feet, she thought she was in someone's bedroom, but there was no bed. Walking over to the window, she found that she was upstairs and the room she thought she was in was actually a hallway.

The hall's generous-sized furnishings gave it a room-like appearance. The window at the south end of the hall had a secluded little window seat loaded with pillows of all colors and the prettiest afghan she'd ever seen. The hardwood floors (which she later discovered were all cedar) were covered with the most elegant area rugs.

Sandy then drifted from one room to another. The elongated windows were not only beautifully dressed but served another purpose as well; they let cool air slip into the rooms near the floor, forcing the warmer air to float to the ceiling. The windows also captured lofty views of the magnificent old trees outside.

Every room she went into had a cedar trunk and a canopy bed with mosquito netting that opened and closed with the tug of braided rope hanging at the four corners of every bed. Kerosene lamps sat on bedside tables and pewter candle holders sat on window sills and fireplaces. Every room had its own pattern of wallpaper. The rooms were large and immaculate; the thick blankets and homemade quilts hung neatly on brass quilt racks at the post of the beds.

Instead of closets, chifforobes sat in corners, and instead of dressers, chiffonniers with mirrors sat next to the old-fashioned toilets which consisted of a shelf with a basin and a pitcher.

Under the shelves in a little enclosure sat the ceramic slop jars which were emptied and cleaned every morning and the little vase-like contraption beside the toilet was filled with a soft ecru-colored paper. It was pretty to look at, but where were the showers?

She had looked at seven bedrooms already, and each had its own coat rack and bathroom, but not one had a shower because there was no indoor plumbing. Even so, every room was beautiful. The last room had a beautiful iron bed with a brass bed warmer and candle snuffer stored away tastefully atop a brass and cedar trunk. The other side of this room was the landing of a beautiful, highly glossed staircase.

Standing on the landing and looking down took Sandy's breath away. Clean lines molded the rooms surrounding it. Reaching the bottom step, Sandy found the beauty to be overwhelming. She walked around the big open room and touched the vases and statues. One of the big rooms to the right of Sandy was a magnificent dining room. Hanging from the ceiling was the most elegant chandelier Sandy thought was ever made. In the place of electric bulbs there were many tiny, slow-burning candles. The chandelier was centered over a long oak table with twenty places—nine chairs on the right and nine chairs on the left and captain chairs at either end. The place settings were ready, always set up for the next meal.

To the right of the dining room was the library with wall-to-wall bookshelves. The big leather-back books with raw silk bindings filled every shelf. Their three-dimensional, fourteen carat gold print was of large Latin box print. Even the family portraits (paintings in oils on canvas) in their heavy gilded frames were neat and in order. In the center of the room was a large oak desk with a handsome leather chair in burgundy. All of the windows had exquisite drapery treatment of heavy velvet and tiebacks to match the gold knobs on the shining oak secretary. Sandy was about to go into a room that looked very much like a parlor when two women emerged from it. One woman looked to be the mother of the other. They were both very well groomed and rouged, and their clothes were immaculate. The elder was a petite slip of a woman with brown hair and beautiful blue eyes; her mouth was generous with evenly shaped but small teeth. Though she looked meek, she had a look about her that betrayed the frailness the Southern women struggled very hard to possess. Kate was her name, as Sandy would learn later, and the young woman walking in her wake was her niece DeeDee, "Deidra." DeeDee was sixteen, and the only thing she inherited from her mother, Lady T., was her iron will. Even their paleness was different. Lady Teresa had a paleness that was uninterrupted by spot or blemish. Her daughter, on the other hand, was pale with green eyes that sometimes turned hazel; her long thick hair was carrot orange, and she didn't have an inch of skin—aside from the palms of her hands and the soles of her feet—that wasn't covered with freckles. DeeDee was homely, and everyone knew this but DeeDee. Her father agonized over this.

Coard Worthinwood of Worthinwood Plantation could make a whole plantation of people cower just by raising his voice. He could own anything money could buy, but he couldn't change his child's looks. Her uncinate nose was a permanent part of her chubby face and her weak chin was there to stay.

The youngest child of Teresa and Coard was also (much to their disappointment) a girl. Baby Misty, as she was known by everyone, wasn't a boy, but she could climb and jump as well as any of the little slave boys she played with everyday. She could spit farther and run just as fast. Misty's happiness was with the slave children. She didn't know prejudice yet and would rather eat at the cabins of her friends than to come in and eat with her family. Her parents drew the line at sleeping over, but, aside from this, they left her alone.

Misty was nursed by Faye until she was thirteen months old and had developed a fondness for the slave, though she couldn't remember why. The little slave that she loved most was Faye's son Jimmy Lee. Jimmy Lee was much smaller than Misty, but much stronger. His mother swore that he was smaller because Baby Misty took so much of her milk that many a time Jimmy cried from hunger. He more than made up for it now because he ate nonstop. This boy never turned down food, and there wasn't a child on the plantation white or black in his range that was smarter than Jimmy Lee.

Sandy watched as the two women stopped at the foot of the stairs and exchanged words. They walked right past her! Sandy laughed aloud and the older woman, who had gathered her skirts in her left hand to go up the stairs, stopped and looked back at DeeDee.

"Do you find what I've told you funny, Dee?"

Sandy watched crimson creep into Katy's face. Sandy slapped her hands over her mouth; she had forgotten that she could be heard! Dee looked behind her and up the stairs before she answered her blushing aunt.

"Why, no. It wasn't me, Auntie," she said in her thick Southern accent. "I don't think anything you've said was either cute or funny."

Sandy turned to go into the parlor and found herself face to face with what she could see were house servants. They were both no older than sixteen or seventeen and wore starched white aprons over floor-length plain black dresses. They both wore white turbans over their hair, and they were both beautiful girls. One of the girls held her dustpan like a weapon. The other looked poised to run. Looking back at the stairs, Sandy put her fingers to her lips to shush them. In a low voice, she explained that, though the whites couldn't see her or touch her, they could hear her and smell her, and her visits had to be inconspicuous for a while.

The two maids had heard about Sandy, but they never thought they would see her. Unlike their superior white counterparts who were pious in their tailor-made Christianity and had faith only in what their minds and their power could control, slaves believed in all forms of the mystical.

The slave maids—Charlotte and Gail—were fascinated with Sandy's attire and her hair and jewels, but Sandy was overwhelmed! This was her Charlotte! She didn't know HOW she knew, but, even before the girls revealed their identities, Sandy knew that this was her great, great grandmother! Sandy also knew she shouldn't tell her now.

The three girls walked to the veranda, where they could really talk.

When Sandy asked Charlotte about her parents, the young woman dropped her head and hesitated. Her father, she explained, was beaten to death four years ago. Sandy asked her why, and she dropped her head even farther. Feeling that it was a very ugly situation, Sandy tried to change the subject, but Gail insisted that Charlotte talk.

"Dis here is a ghost; she can't hurt you," Gail said.

Sandy learned that the master of this plantation was preceded by his sire, Coard Worthinwood IV. It seemed that Geata, Charlotte's mother, was born on this plantation, and, as was the case with many other slaves, her father was Master Coard III. Charlotte's dad, Jace, was purchased when Geata was fifteen. He quickly fell in love with the beautiful slave and asked for her hand. Master Coard Senior granted permission and the two jumped the broom. They quickly produced two boys and one girl.

The problem occurred after the older master died and Coard Junior had taken over completely. When Charlotte turned thirteen, she was every woman's nightmare and every man's dream. At 5'6" she had the tiniest waist around. Her breasts were ample and high, and, although tiny, she had rounded hips and buttocks. White women everywhere were having the stays in their waist clinchers as tight as possible, and they still couldn't come close to the slaves's eighteen-inch waist. When there were house guests at Worthinwood, the women would turn absolutely green with jealousy. They were clinched so tightly into their stays that they could hardly breathe, and here was this slave with hardly anything under her dress with a waist so small that she herself could put her fingers around it. Her feet and hands were tiny also.

Jace was very protective of his girl child. He ran off any young boy that dared sneak around her. He also watched her every move. None of the bucks on any of the surrounding plantations dared cross Jace when it came to his daughter. But pain and heartache came when any slave father couldn't protect his daughter from the unwanted advances and eventual rape of the slave masters and the other white male guests that the masters could grant permission to. But, for a while, Jace thought his daughter was safe. Young Master Coard had come to Jace himself and asked if he were keeping the 'wolves' from Charlotte. Jace assured him that he was, and Young Master declared that no man, white or black, would have his pleasure with the beautiful young slave. He and Jace would see to it, he said. Jace was honored, to say the least; he assumed that his Master realized the Worthinwood blood that ran through Charlotte's veins. After all, she was his niece.

But Geata knew better all along. Wasn't she used goods when Jace took her in their marriage bed? Jace knew firsthand that black women were never a protected class. They were working, productive labor. Putting all pretense aside and all Southern belles in true lights, the female slaves were much more sensitive than their higher-class white sisters, but fragility has its own place in any class.

Black women were taught to act as tough as their men. Their backs were bared and they were beaten just as savagely, especially if they should be so brave as to spurn their white masters' advances. Jace always bore pain by pretending all was fine. He would never bring nighttime problems into the light of day. He couldn't and wouldn't allow his mind to even think that anything so hideous could happen to his daughter. She was his life. She made going from one day to the next worth the struggle. It was ironic that Jace even thought that Young Master meant what he had said to him.

Charlotte's virginity, however, was of paramount importance to no one but her family.

Charlotte remembered, when she was about five, how the old Master came down to the quarters and into their cabin. Charlotte and her two brothers—Wade, who was six, and Bernie, who was eight—were asleep on straw-filled pallets in a corner of the one-room shack. Her parents were asleep on the only bed in the cabin. The Master just pushed open the front door and barged in. Jace sat up, but no one moved when they saw it was Old Master Coard. Old Master Coard greeted her father like it was 6:00 p.m. instead of 2:00 a.m. He told Jace to put on his pants, and he picked up a pair that was hanging on a chair and tossed them at him. Charlotte never forgot the sight of his engorged white manhood as he pulled his tan suede riding trousers down.

Sensing that the children were awake, he pulled the tattered curtain around the bed. Her father walked away from the porch when the first of the disgusting sounds coming from his master started. Charlotte's brothers Wade and Bernie lay very still, but she could tell by their breathing that they too were awake. This was their mother's father raping her!

Before Charlotte knew it, it was over, and her father was sitting on the edge of his homemade bed with his head in his hands, sobbing. Her mother just sat there, dry-eyed, trying to comfort her husband. Jace, being a very subservient slave, went about his duties, and with an obsequious duck and bob of the head, he would grin like a Cheshire cat every time he had reason to be near any white master or the white overseers, even though it was eating away at him like a cancer.

But three months after Charlotte's thirteenth birthday, everything came to a head.

The field hands were late coming in. They were plowing the fields to get them ready for sowing. It was hard work. The long days were arduous and taxing. Most work in the fields did not require a high level of skill, but it did demand care and thoroughness. Careless plowing could ruin animals or equipment; improperly turned soil would have to be plowed again, wasting time. Some days Jace would be on hands and knees picking out large stones. When that was done, two to three days later his hands and knees were so raw they were swollen almost double their size and bleeding profusely. After Geata washed him up and put him in his nightshirt, she fed him his supper of fried salt pork, cabbage (from their own little patch) and rice. He had to soak his hands in a basin of salt and water to toughen them up because, bright and early the next morning, he would be back at it. This was only the first day, and he was asleep before his head hit the pillow.

Jace was awakened by someone crying. Shaking the fog from his head, he realized that the sobbing came from his daughter, and his wife was trying to comfort her. It took a few minutes before he saw Young Master Coard standing at the doorway. He could see that the master had come for Charlotte, and Jace wanted to know what she had done wrong. Getting nothing but silent tears from Geata and near hysterical sobs from Charlotte, he tried desperately to calm her. But not getting anything from his family, he implored his master to tell him.

"Go back to sleep, Jace," his master's voice drawled. "There ain't a whole lot you can do here."

As it became obvious to Jace what was happening, he began to plead and appeal to the part of this man he thought was human. He thought Coard saw his daughter in a family light, as remote as it would be. But Coard stopped him.

"Now, listen to me, boy. This gal here is a damn slave just like all the other slaves on Worthinwood Plantation, and every darkie here belongs to me to do with as I please." Jace was on his knees now, blubbering and begging. His sons just sat huddled together. They knew what was going to happen to Charlotte, and they knew that their father was about to cross a line that no slave dared cross.

Coard walked over and grabbed the horrified girl by a wrist and left the cabin with a crawling, begging, and totally out of control Jace following him. As master and slave disappeared into a barn that housed tools, Jace had followed as closely as he dared, falling to his knees and getting back up to follow some more. Geata was hanging on to her husband trying to get him to stop and come back inside. Charlotte had been told time and time again by her mother that this could happen, but she never told Jace that she'd been warning the girl for a year now.

Depositing Charlotte in the barn, Coard came back out and told one of the big fellows to chain and fetter Jace and to be down at the big house instead of going to the fields the next morning and to bring Jace with him. Coard didn't touch Charlotte that night, but he instructed her to go to the female dorm to stay that night and forever. The next day, Jace was strung up and whipped to within an inch of his life. His cries made the flesh of anyone within hearing range crawl. There wasn't an inch of skin left uncut on his back, buttocks, or thighs. He died eight days later from a massive infection and fever.

Charlotte sniffed and wiped at her face as she finished her story. Sandy saw that Gail was crying also. Sandy found that, soon after Jace died, Charlotte's mother and brothers were sold away to a rice plantation.

CHAPTER FIVE

Richard's day had started at 5:00 a.m. He always got up to take a brisk walk around the neighborhood before showering and having a nice breakfast. This morning he knocked on Sandy's door to see if she wanted to walk and have some breakfast with him. He knew that Sandy had gone to bed with permission to lock her bedroom door, but she was also instructed—as always—to unlock it before going to sleep.

When he didn't get an answer, he knocked harder, bringing Olivia down the hall. He explained that he couldn't wake Sandy. After her attempt proved futile, they both agreed that Olivia should open the door with a little screwdriver she referred to as 'the emergency-only key.'

The shock of finding Sandy no where in the room left Olivia weak in the knees; she had to sit on the neatly made bed while Richard checked in the closet and underneath the bed. It didn't matter that it was a little weird looking under a bed for a fifteen year old; all he knew was that his baby girl was gone. Of the two windows in the room, one held a small air conditioner, and the other was open. Standing in front of the opened window, he looked down at the trellis outside. The lattice work made a perfect ladder leading from the window to the ground below.

He called to Olivia: "Vernell"—He only used her first name when he was troubled or angry—"I think Sandy slipped out during the night and just hasn't slipped back in yet." Olivia looked up at her husband as if to get permission to walk over to the window. Looking down, she asked him nervously how he could be so sure Sandy wasn't taken by force. "Honey," he clipped his words, voice tight, "this trellis would break if anyone over 120 pounds climbed on it. Sandy's 110 pounds, so she simply climbed down. Figure it out for yourself."

They decided to close and lock the bedroom door and to leave things like they were. If Sandy wasn't back by 9 a.m., they would report it. . . .

Sandy let Charlotte and Gail look at her 'funny' clothes and 'good, good' hair. She told them she would be back, but she didn't tell Charlotte of their kinship. The girls walked her around the mansion and Gail rushed back in. She was Missy Katie's maid while she was at Worthinwood, and she knew she would be missed.

Sandy ambled across the grounds slowly, looking at everything she passed. This is great, she thought.

The field hands were piling out of the fields. She would just jog on over to the female dorm and wait. After she'd gone inside and spoken to all of them, they followed her to the front porch to wait for the tired and weary workers.

In the women's quarters you could smell food cooking. Earlier in the day she had heard what sounded like a bunch of chickens clucking and was told the slaves that didn't work the fields were killing chickens for their suppers tonight.

"What's cooking in your kitchen, Tulla?" Sandy asked the big, red-skinned woman standing in the doorway wiping her hands on a flour sack apron.

Tulla grinned, showing her large tobacco-stained teeth and cackled, "Glory, chile. I cooked some chicken and dumplin's an' we always hab rice."

Sandy could tell that something was going on. She said aloud, "Oh! I almost forgot . . . the toiletries!" Oh, wow, it smells pleasant today, she thought. Everybody jumped around and tried to get closer to Sandy so she could smell them. Even Hettie smiled shyly at Sandy. With all of the girls blowing their breath in her face and holding their arms up for each other to smell, she had to admit it really was nice. The girls explained to Sandy that they waited until they were sure everyone from the big house was settled, and they gathered the toilet articles in the lunch bags they all owned and went down to the stream to bathe, brush their teeth, lotion up, and powder themselves. The deodorant was fabulous, they said, and they were fascinated that this deodorant stuff took away the bad odor and wetness all day. But Sandy had to reiterate that they had to use it every night *after* they bathed.

By now, the field hands were back, and as soon as Faye saw Sandy, she grabbed her arm and pulled her off to the side. "Sandy, that 'deodorit' ya gave us? Well, everyone whats don't hab it wonts it. I been hot all day long, but I had dat powda on—it soak up dat sweat an' musk."

Sandy was so happy for them. "Well, before I leave, I'll leave everyone some," she told Faye. "But I want you to find me a clearing in the woods not too far away, and I need you to do it now! So hurry."

Faye called another girl and beckoned her with her finger for her to come with her. Sandy turned her attention back to the occupants of the room and saw that this hut was filled so tightly it was hard to move! The porch was packed and even more hung in the windows. The yard was filled with still more trying to get as close as possible to the hut. The slaves that had gotten the packages were showing them off, and the ones that didn't were begging for a sample or, having got a whiff, were trying to get close enough to Sandy to beg doggedly for a packet of their own. Sandy tried to reassure everyone that they would get one.

As soon as Sandy saw Faye trying to push her way toward her, she asked in the loudest voice she'd dared to use since her first visit, "Please everyone, shh! shh!" It got a little bit quieter, but not much. "Please!" Sandy beseeched them. Then she had a brainstorm.

Grinning like the fox she could be, she held up both arms.

"Is everyone hungry?" Silence. "Aha! Does anyone want to try the kind of food I eat?" A chorus of "huhs?" and "um hums" quickly rose up from the thick crowd. Sandy had their attention now, but talked quickly. "I'm going to order subs and pizzas," she said. "I know you don't have the slightest idea what 'pizza' and 'subs' are, but, everybody that wants to eat, put both hands together like you are holding something flat." She demonstrated for the benefit of those that could see her, and it spread around fast. "Now close your eyes and keep them closed. No peeking!" Sandy started chanting after cupping her ivory in her fist and closing her eyes. She could feel the excitement about her. She hadn't completed the first chant before she heard the first shouts.

Sandy opened her eyes as the hot food started popping in. Women and men alike were staring with open mouths and bulging eyes, and the smell of hot pizza and hot meatball and cheese subs filled the air. People started opening pizza boxes and tearing the thin papers off of the subs. She stood on a chair and demonstrated how to pull the tabs off of their Pepsi cans. There were pepperoni pizzas and hamburger pizzas; sausage, pepper, onion, and cheese pizzas; and hamburger, green pepper, and mushroom pizzas. There was tomato sauce all over little fingers and noses. Cheesy chins wiggled with laughter, and greedy little glugs could be heard as those first tastes of bubbly soda slid down throats, tickled noses, and made people belch. The meatballs and nice, thick, crusty Italian bread made eating almost unbearably good. Ooh, la, la, that cheese!

Sandy had ordered chocolate milk for the kiddies and told parents to give them this and not the more tingling sodas. Little kids drank up heartily. Their eyes sparkled with joy. Their mamas didn't bother to wipe them clean before they drifted off into a happy sleep. Sandy had seen most of these little ones at one time or another. There was one little four-year-old orphan that looked very much like Jello's twin. But, unlike Jello, she and the others were ragged and didn't have any soft pajamas to snuggle into. Their little bare feet were filthy and caked with dirt or had open, infected wounds from stepping on rusty nails, glass, or sharp stones.

Sandy saw that everyone had finished eating and didn't know what to do with all the wrappers and cans. Some wanted to keep the cans and boxes. Faye was collecting the paper that the subs came in. This puzzled Sandy because she was only collecting the paper. She asked her why. She explained to Sandy that this thin paper would feel a lot better than the dirty moss and leaves they had to use after a trip to the outdoor toilets. Most slave families collected corn cobs to use as toilet paper.

"Sandy," Faye said with one hand on her hips and the other full of the thin paper, "I ain't trying to figure what you and yo' family swab yo' tails wid, but me and my peoples is tired o' havin' sore tails!" Sandy and most the people around them laughed.

"Wait," Sandy laughed. "Put all that junk down. There is a paper we use in my time called 'toilet paper'." Since everyone was finished and not a crumb of food lay anywhere, she asked everyone to close their eyes again. Everyone gladly obeyed. Sandy cupped her ivory and began her second chant of the day.

First she made the trash disappear. Then she popped in nice, soft pajamas for the children, six packages of toilet paper per family, and simple shower shoes for everyone—men, women, and kids alike—toilet articles for those that hadn't gotten any the first time, and baby wipes. Sandy heard the little gasps and the cellophane paper rattle before she opened her eyes. Looking she noted all the red and moist eyes of the mothers in the room. Some of the fathers and single men still seemed to be in a daze. Sandy's own eyes grew red and moist. Standing on a chair, she looked slowly at different faces in the dense crowd and tears kept filling her eyes and running down her face.

The love she had for her people filled her with awe; only she and they could fully understand it. The love she felt for God and his son Jesus, she believed, was uppermost and could not be touched, yet the love she felt for her 'family'—and she believed all blacks were her family—was extraordinary.

Since she was still standing in the chair, she told them how to use the toilet paper, and told the people that knew how to use the toiletries to show the people that didn't know.

"Mothers, take your children home and bathe them before they go to bed. The clothes you just got are for sleeping only."

Sandy told them to thank the Lord, not her. The pizza she ate was making her lazy; she had skipped a meal before coming this time. She wouldn't do that again.

Suddenly, the room was deathly still and some were looking toward the door with terror on their faces. Following their lead, she too looked stunned for a moment. Standing in the doorway blocking out the light was Master Coard himself!

"What in the hell is going on in here?"

Slaves scampered, babies cried, men that were sitting leisurely jumped up and stared down at the floor as they started to shuffle. Coard came into the room, but the slaves would not meet his eye; that is, until he walked up to Mammy Tulla. Staring right in her eyes, he asked, "What is that smell? Tulla, what's cooking?" He sniffed hungrily at the air. "I don't think I've ever smelled anything so wonderful," he sniffed again, "in my entire life! Tulla, I bet you've cooked up on of them creole dishes your ole mammy use to cook!" But remembering why he was there, he pulled himself up short and it was business as usual. "What is almost every slave I own doing all clustered in and around one hut? Well?" There was a long pause. "I don't hear any explaining!"

Master Coard could be a dangerous man to cross, but as long as everything was going his way, he could at least be amenable with his slaves. Still, they all were afraid. No one had been mutilated on the Worthinwood Plantation in two years, but not one slave wanted to explain anything to their master on this matter. No one but Stoney. He stood before his master and told him that the Voodoo Woman out in the everglades gave them some new herbs and spices to cook with, and Ole Tulla volunteered to cook everyone's meal in the women's hut. But another thing Coard wanted to know concerned the plastic bags that everyone seemed to be holding! Even Stoney was hard pressed for an answer. Everyone was scared to death and it showed in each of their faces.

Stoney again spoke up: "It's magic, Master Coard. We's callin' it Voodoo."

The big white man's face flushed magenta. Sandy jumped down from her perch on the chair. Aw, monkey shit, she thought. No way is Coard going to believe that! Something in Coard's face made Sandy's blood run cold. She knew that the absolute force in the master's hand was barbaric.

Coard could take any slave in this room and have him staked out on the ground or held down by one of his own peers, stripped to the bare flesh, and beaten with a variety of instruments, from a whip to a blunt weapon. Lord, Sandy thought, I can't let any one of those people be punished for grabbing a little pleasure out of life.

Thinking fast, she grabbed one of the little babies from its mother, and, holding the child at arm's length, she walked over to the slave master and waved the baby up and down before his face. Sandy accentuated her voice to sound like a hill born white woman and said, "Coard dear, leave these people to th'air lil' get together and go back to the big house or I'll cut your tongue out as you sleep tonight! Go! Go!"

Coard's flushed face blanched from red to white, and his eyes bulged in their sockets. He couldn't see Sandy! All he saw was this sleeping little baby floating in the air speaking to him without moving its lips! The master whimpered something unintelligible and stumbled from the room backwards. Everyone in the room was frozen with their mouths open; even Sandy just stood there, still holding the baby frozen at arm's length. Coard was headed toward the big house walking like a drunk man.

"If he keeps walking backwards, he's gonna break his ass!" Sandy remarked as she took the still sleeping baby back to its mother. "What you just saw, my family, is a true coward." As soon as she said this, she regretted it. She looked at the sea of faces around her.

In some she saw amusement, in some indifference, but the majority showed fear. Stark, raw fear. Sandy felt like a bucket of ice water had been dashed over her head. Slaves trying their master's patience was a general part of life—negligence, awkwardness, ineptitude, forgetfulness, haughtiness—all of these were everyday words in the white vocabulary. Blacks were said to taunt their master until he exploded with rage, crippling and maiming any slave he wanted. For a white slave owner, justice was served only when a slave was punished for making his owner or any other white man feel fear.

Sandy knew that, for a slave, even learning to read could result in his or her death. If a slave owner had trouble learning to read as a child, and as an adult had troubling comprehending, it could mean perilous times to what a master thought was his 'dumb struggling nigger' if that slave was caught reading. It stirred fear in the white man if a little slave three or four years old practiced the art the master couldn't accomplish when he was ten or eleven. If a master were to catch his black sycophant reading and, when questioned, he hesitantly but completely explained what he had read . . . Death! When whites learned that blacks could learn as fast and as thoroughly as a white person, what a nightmare! When owners learned that their slaves weren't naturally and incessantly illiterate, something had to be done; the members of the white race could not admit to themselves that this race of people could be their equals if given half a chance. So, many a slave owner hid his illiteracy and, after maiming and in some cases killing the reading slave, the white man declared all writing, reading, and arithmetic illicit acts.

Sandy decide to trust spontaneity. "I see that what I've done has frightened many of you." Some heads bobbed up and down; some covered their mouths with their hands to hide nervous giggling, and still others continued to stare at nothing with their mouths open. "Well, Sandy hedged, "do you all want me to send these things back?"

That did it. Nearly everyone responded the same way: "No! Is you crazy!"

Everyone was talking at the same time and holding their plastic bags close to them. Faye got to her feet, and after the noise stopped she addressed Sandy and the crowd.

"We all know dat Massa Code is fair mos'a da time. But we wuk hard on dis plantation. Massa ain't go'n do nuttin' diffunt din he done no other year. Mos' ob us been bawn right here. Once a year afta da first fros' we gits cornmeal, salted pork meat, and some mo lasses. Evy hut gits dis. Now evy person gets some clothes to keep us wome in de winters. Shoes ain't for chillins; dey is fo us olda folks—pants and shirts for men, and for dey women's is dresses. Da linsey-woolsey long shirts is fo' chillins. An' all o' us gits blankets. I ain't gonna gib dis blessin' up dat Sandy hab given us."

Sandy hugged her friend and with tears in her eyes she told them she had to go home. "I love all of you, my sisters and brothers, and if the Lord is willing, I'll be here tomorrow. I won't try to tell you how to handle your master. I'm sure you've mastered that."

Sandy didn't try to hide. She cupped her ivory, closed her eyes, and—right before their eyes—faded to nothing.. . .

Richard had just returned from his walk and was headed upstairs for his shower when he heard noise coming from Sandy's room. He snuck back to the kitchen and told Olivia. Having tip-toed up to Sandy's door and listened for a minute, they listened again. Olivia heard enough. She knocked on the door and Sandy answered. Richard asked her to open the door.

"Dad, I'm not dressed yet," Sandy said, trying to sound sleepy but succeeding only in sounding nervous and hurried.

"San, open this damn door before I kick it in!"

"O.K. Just a moment, daddy. I'm coming. Let me get my robe." Her voice had become tremulous; Richard heard her nervousness.

Sandy cracked the door open and stood behind it with only her head showing. Her eyes looked like large marbles in her face; her coloring was ashen, and the hand holding her robe closed at the neck shook badly. Olivia knew that if she didn't say something, Richard would start feeling sorry for this child and believe anything she said.

"Take your robe off, Sandy."

Sandy opened her mouth to speak but Olivia tore her hand away from the neck of the robe and snatched the tied sash off. There Sandy stood with the same clothes she had on yesterday; she only had time to kick off her sandals.

With her head down, she knew it wouldn't be wise to lie to Olivia right now; she had been caught red-handed. Although she wouldn't lie, she also could not tell the whole truth. Olivia sensed this, and her eyes filled to overflowing. She had never been given a reason to be this harsh with one of her kids, and Richard had always worn kid gloves when it came to his daughter. There was not a girl child in the world more loved by her father than Sandy. But he had always drawn the line when it came to any apparent disrespect for his wife. Olivia was the only one that he loved more than he loved Sandy.

"Well, Sandy?" He spoke like a man going to his doom. "Where were you? And why?"

Before he even spoke the words, he knew she wouldn't tell him either. Olivia threw the sash back to Sandy and told her to shower and dress and then come downstairs to the kitchen. "If your dad is going to make it to work, he needs to get his shower too."

Olivia was sitting at the kitchen table drinking hot tea. When Sandy sat down, Olivia filled another cup with hot water and put a pack of tea inside it. She pushed the cup and saucer gently toward Sandy. Sandy accepted the tea and poured cream into it. She looked up at her mother and saw hurt and fear in her face. She knew she would say something, but whatever she said would have to be the truth or she might as well not say anything. The love she had for her mom was deep and the look on Olivia's face right now made tears sting in Sandy's eyes.

"Mama, I think you know that I'm not going to lie to you." Olivia nodded her head, sadly. "But I can't tell you where I've been either." Olivia opened her mouth to speak but Sandy stopped her and went on. "It's not that I WON'T tell you; it's like I CAN'T tell you. I love you and daddy, and I promise to tell you two as soon as I can."

Olivia felt sure that she knew her daughter better than anyone else, and right now Sandy was being as honest as she could. Her daughter had gone through some major changes in the last year. Sandy was always a very emotional child, and she loved life.

When Sandy was twelve, her family went to visit her Aunt Dootsie in Jacksonville Florida. Dootsie was Sandy's favorite aunt, and she had promised the child that they would go up to the attic and go through trunks and boxes and play dress up in some of her grandma Nana's clothes that she'd worn before she married grandaddy Tucker. Well, the first trunk they opened amid the dust and cobwebs was the home for a nest of newborn field mice. The mother mouse scrambled to get out and lost her life to the formidable Dootsie who broke the neck of the poor unfortunate mouse with a swipe of an old, faded, blue umbrella. Young Sandy was shocked.

"That mouse is the mother of these babies." Tears dropped from the young girl's eyes, making clean streaks on the cover of an old and dusty ceramic dinner tray laying on the trunk. "Who's going to take care of these babies, Aunty Dootsie?"

Dootsie peered into the box and cringed. She knew what her niece was getting at.

"I guess we could take over." Sandy's tears stopped almost instantly. Suddenly bright-eyed, Sandy set about to find a shoe box to make a new nest.

"Aunt Dootsie, we'll get them big enough to give'em to a pet store."

"Good, Sandy." Then she muttered to herself, "I thought you'd want to return 'em to my dagburn attic!"

Olivia reminisced that, up until the time that Sandy met Verma, she was always pulling for the underdog.

In the summer she would fill the laundry room with hurt and homeless animals. Her care and loving didn't just stop at forlorn animals. It was doubled for her loved ones and friends and even strangers. Everyone loved Sandy. If a new child came to her school, she would look them up and make sure everyone was nice to them. If the little Tucker girl liked someone, the other kids would like them too.

But, about a year ago, Olivia and Richard first took note of the change in her. The first odd thing she did was to give away her hamsters. One day, Olivia asked Sandy to go with her on her weekly trip to the dog pound. Olivia was a volunteer at the shelter to help find homes for as many dogs and cats as possible. This was one trip she knew her child loved. But Verma was visiting that day, and Sandy seemed embarrassed when her mother asked her to go with her.

"Mom, who wants to visit a stinking old dog pound? That's nasty!" Olivia knew that those words were more Verma's than Sandy's . . . .

Now, with tears in her eyes and looking at tears in the eyes of her daughter—tears that fell into the cup of tea she had given her—Olivia knew that the changes in Sandy may have reached a critical point.

For her part, Sandy thought she saw a look of hopelessness in her mother's eyes, a look she had never seen before. It frightened her.

"Sandy, I have to ask you this now, and, on my word, I'll never ask it again. I know the ethics and morals your dad and I instilled in you and Larry are rested deep, but we as humans are subject to make mistakes." Olivia braced herself. "Are you involved with a boy?"

"No."

"So this has nothing to do with sex?"

"Mom, do you mean am I having sex?" Olivia blushed. "No. If I were about to do that I would've come to you first, mom." Olivia sagged visibly with relief. But she had to ask her daughter more.

"Is what you are doing dangerous at all?"

"No."

"When will it stop?"

Sandy stood and walked over to her mother's chair. She motioned for Olivia to stand and then put her arms around her. "Mom, I'm not putting myself in any danger. To answer your last question, it'll all be over in less than two weeks. Please, you'll just have to trust me . . . .

Relieved but frightened, Olivia squeezed her daughter in her arms. . . .

When Richard arrived at work Wednesday morning, the precinct was humming with the news.

Pac and Save, Pizza Hutch, and Woodworth's had been burglarized during the night. Again, there were no signs of forced entry, and none of the stores reported anything of real value missing. Pac and Save and Woodworth's had been robbed of toilet articles and children's pajamas.

"Pizza Hutch?" Richard thought out loud, turning to the desk sergeant.

Montgomery nodded, "Yup. The crazy thing is that the thieves only stole pre-made pizzas and subs. And everyone knows that Pizza Hutch keeps the previous day's receipts in a flimsy safe." Richard nodded as if in agreement as 'Piggy' continued. "We've got men at each location. You know, Tucker," he offered, as a matter-of-fact, "I think its just a bunch of kids that don't know how much trouble their causing. After all, what professional thief would take pizzas, subs, and the like when they could've taken a safe with the whole day's receipts?"

Richard felt cold and hot all over when Montgomery said *kids*. Ten minutes later, he was on his way to the patrol car, and he ran into David Chestnut coming in. He and his twin brother were two of the four cops that went out to the crime sites.

"Come up with anything, D. C.?"

David slowed his brisk pace to a stop and turned back to face Richard. The twin brothers were not identical. In fact, they were opposites: D. C. was a tall, athletic type, and C. C. (David's brother, Charles) was short, overweight, and going bald at twenty three. David took off his cap and ran his hand through his thick shock of amber hair.

"There's some crazy shit going on with this case, Tucker. You know the thirty large pizzas and other food that were stolen from the Pizza Hutch?" Richard nodded. "Well, we found the boxes, the pepsi cans, and the sub wrappers littered all over that parking lot near downtown. You know, the one where the white kids spend their weekends? Didn't someone tell us that there was a black girl hanging with that gang?" Richard nodded and gave D. C. a nervous 'What gives?' look. "Chief wants us on this one right away."

Both D. C. and Richard knew that the longer a case like this took to solve, the less likely it was ever to be solved. "You know, Tucker, we had that theft at the museum, the DWI and moonshine, the confirmed homicide and lead poisoning and now these thefts . . . ."

Before he could continue, Richard waved him off as if he were listening but in a hurry. He hastily retreated to his patrol car, a bit shaken. He was thinking about Sandy.

In his car, he rested his forehead on the steering wheel and prayed: "Oh, God, let all of these crimes be coincidences. Please don't let my Sandy be involved . . . ."

He and Olivia had agonized over the changes in Sandy during the last school term. She had gone from shy and sweet to bold and sassy overnight. It seemed her attire used to be fit for a girl her age, but now it consisted of jeans so tight they looked painted on, and, as if that weren't enough, they had to have rips and tears all over them. Her blouses were put away because she only wanted to wear shirts or tee shirts. Some of them had large neck openings and she would wear sports bras under them and just let the shirt fall off her shoulders. He knew that Sandy felt like she had outgrown her old friends. He knew she had become friends with a new student.

Verma came to Jesup after her parents had divorced. Richard had gone to school with Verma's mother, Barbara, who had left Jesup after graduation and eventually married a man from Chicago. Their offspring, Verma, was a beautiful child, beautiful but troubled.

By the time Verma reached puberty, she had learned to use her looks to open many doors, some of which should have never been touched. Her introduction to sex was her Pandora's Box. Barbara's courageous attempts to vivify her daughter's morals were pitifully ineffective, to say the least. To say that the girl's set of ethics were no longer than a peppercorn would sum it up nicely.

But the most disquieting thing about Verma was her outward show of 'personality'. She dressed in gaudy colors and scraping-the-bone-tight pants and skirts. Her hair was wild and her make-up wilder.

Talking to her parents and teachers with anything but a conciliatory manner was extremely difficult for Verma, but she managed.

Richard saw through her if Olivia couldn't, but they couldn't find a good enough reason to prohibit Sandy from befriending Verma. No, Verma didn't fool Richard, but he was convinced that Olivia had been taken in. So Richard left off expressing his opinion on the subject, but he never doubted himself as a judge of her character. He knew that Verma was gone for the summer.

But the crowd of boys that had started following Sandy and Verma was still around . . . .

CHAPTER SIX

It was five minutes after 6:00 p.m., and Anita and her parents were sitting on their porch. The Shaws were all dressed up and ready to go out to dinner and afterwards to a gospel concert. Anita had been fed, and all Sandy had to do was to give Anita her bath and put her to bed at 10:00 p.m.

The child kept running out to the sidewalk to see if she could see her sitter coming. The Shaws felt grateful that Sandy was willing to sit for Jello even though Sandy told others she wouldn't be doing any kind of work this summer. The Shaws believed in schedules, and they had pleaded with Sandy to sit for Jello this summer. They knew Sandy was good for their gem and wouldn't trust anyone else.

"She's coming! She's coming!" Jello said and ran down the sidewalk to meet her best friend. She squealed as Sandy picked her up and swung her around. "Sandy," she said, "You are five . . . no . . . six minutes late! You've got to start being more responsible, okay?"

She had Sandy's face between her palms and put her face so close to her sitter's that their noses touched.

"It never fails," Sandy said laughing. "Jello, you never fail to crack me up."

After the Shaws left, Sandy saw that Jello's doll had yellow bows for lonesome and red for happy. Later, Jello went into the house to get her purple boom box and her Kriss Kross tapes. When she came back, she had also brought her microscope that Sandy had given her. She put everything down on the porch and asked Sandy what tape she should play first.

"Since you love Kriss Kross so much, play them." Sandy had never looked through the stack of tapes but had assumed they were all just Kriss Kross. Jello shook her head.

"I've got Michael Jackson and Janet Jackson in here, too. I've got Janet Jackson's video, too. I took it from Carnell. He's spent a lot of money on a great big collection. First of all, I like Janet Jackson. LaToya can't sing, and Carnell says she has more plastic in her than a

Tonka toy. Besides, she's not pretty, just painted. You know, San? You can take an old ugly board and paint it, and you would make it look pretty. You see?" Sandy held back laughing. "I like Michael," Jello said, "but 'Toya don't have any decent fans. Did she have to show us her hiney for people to like her? Everyone already knew she couldn't sing, so why would anyone buy her records?"

Sandy was hysterical with laughter by this time. Obviously, what she was hearing was Carnell's opinions flowing out of this five-year-old's mouth. Jello went on.

"I have all of Janet's records, even the old ones." Jello never laughed when she spoke like this. That's what made it so funny. The Shaws had her IQ tested last year, and it was 130! After Sandy was laughed out, she agreed with Jello a little.

"I guess LaToya has gone as far as she could go, so what's next?" That was Jello's cue.

"She can dye her hair blonde and get blue contact lenses!" But true to her nature, Jello had a row going. "Michael can dance better than anyone else in the world! And he's still the best entertainer, even if he did use more than four percent of that you-know-what on his skin. His sister probably takes a bath in it just to be fair." Jello batted her eyelashes and did her best LaToya impression. "Michael only does those crazy things to keep his many millions of fans from being bored to death while he's in between shows. But LaToya paints herself and gets silicone because she wants to be pretty like her sister Janet. I can't blame her, can you, Sandy?"

After Sandy humored Jello, they had a snack of graham crackers and milk. While they were sitting at the dinette table, Sandy mentioned the bows in her doll's hair.

"When I got here, you had red and yellow bows in her hair. How can you be lonesome and happy at the same time?" Jello looked at Sandy with a gleam in those incredibly large eyes and left the room. When she returned, she was holding up her Raggedy Ann with only red bows.

"See, I took them out right after you came. Today, Carnell went to Savannah to get himself ready for State in the fall, and Mommy and Daddy were busy." Jello was wide open now. "I didn't have anybody to help me get germs for my microscope, and they said I couldn't do it alone. I have to have a grown-up. You're grown up, San! Can we look for some germs now? Please, San? Please?"

Sandy couldn't say no, especially not after Jello had told her that when she couldn't get anyone to play with her, she had put lonesome and invisible bows in dolly's hair and disappeared into the tree house in her backyard earlier. Once outside, the two of them went just a little farther than the lip of the woods in the Shaw's backyard. They found all kinds of 'bacteria'.

Jello was about to pick some berries off a bush when Sandy yelled "No!" She startled the little girl so badly that Anita's bottom lip trembled. Sandy hugged her. "I'm sorry, babe. I didn't mean to scare you. That is poison oak, honey." She let Jello look at the plant and then showed her poison ivy. "Never touch this, Anita. Some people have such allergic reactions they die from it." Sandy could still feel Jello's little heart beating fast as she held her close.

When something scared or hurt Jello, she put her two middle fingers in her mouth as she was doing now and sucked them hard. She slept with her pacifier too, but she didn't pull on it as she did on her two fingers when she was scared or hurt. She mumbled through her fingers now.

"San, why don't people just go through the forest and kill them?" Sandy had no good answers.

"Well, it would be very expensive, Jello." She was carrying this precious child and her bag of germs and her microscope and was heading back to the house when Anita took her fingers out of her mouth. She wiggled to get down.

"Hot water kills anything."

The Shaws got home at midnight, and Sandy's father came down to walk her home.

"Daddy, I hope you believed me today. I'm glad I postponed my sitting job with Jello until 6:00 tonight so I would be home when you got there this afternoon. I know you knew I couldn't possibly be involved in those robberies. By the way, you never told me what was stolen."

Before Richard could finish listing things, his daughter realized that the things she gave the slaves were from the burglarized stores in Jesup. While she struggled to refocus, she remembered wishing that the things her people needed would come from the stores of the white business owners that had a reputation for discriminating against black people. Now she knew her wishes had come true. Her father was convinced of her innocence, but he also knew that, somehow, her knowledge of the burglaries exceeded his own. How she knew, he wasn't sure, but she did know something he didn't.

"San, sugar, please let me in on this. What's going on?"

But Sandy said nothing.

It was after 1:00 a.m. when Sandy sent herself back to the plantation and Mammy Cinda's kitchen.

"Well, Lo' hab mercy, here goes my lit ghos' chile." Sandy stood and brushed herself off. She had come awfully close to Mammy's black wrought iron stove! "I's hopen ya could'a cum earlier. De voodoo lady n'ha daughta come ober heah dis moanin'. They say they cum to bring me some herbs and spices, but I don't believe none of that. See, they done herd talk 'bout ya, and they figger if Mammy ain't seed it, den it ain't de troot."

Mammy walked over to where Sandy stood and peered right into her eyes. "Iffen yo wants to go ober der I kin take ya, alls you got ta do is wait 'till I's done gettin de las meal togatha. I knows ya a powful ghos' but don' no ghos' try to do me no harm. Y' kin sit yo're self down for a spell an' wait on Ole Mammy Cinda to get dinna dun. I don' hab to serb it. De butla and Lucretia do dat."

Sandy very much wanted to meet the voodoo woman and her daughter.

Sandy had been formulating a plan to help her people, and this voodoo woman, who was part of—and not part of—the slaves' lives, would be important to Sandy's plan. Sandy had sent Faye out to find a spot in the everglades north of Worthinwood Plantation that would not likely be disturbed by anyone in the surrounding plantations—especially by the white slave owners. Faye had come back to tell her that she had found a spot, but it was very close to Madam Valery's land. Sandy had taken the news well, despite Faye's warning that Sandy was sure to have a run in with the voodoo woman. Somehow, Sandy knew she'd convince Madame Valery of the urgency of her plan and what an indispensable role Madame Valery herself would play in it. Sandy would wait for Mammy to finish and then confront the voodoo woman herself.

So Sandy talked and Mammy cooked. Sandy asked if Mammy had seen the things she had given the people. Mammy looked askance at Sandy, pretending not to hear her question.

"I gots to make up a pan o' biscuits now. They's hard to whup up an' we cain't go ober there till I's done."

Sandy knew what Mammy wanted, but she wouldn't ask for it. She took out the ivory and wished for a pan of thirty-five big, fluffy and buttery biscuits, but she didn't stop there. After the cook hugged and kissed her, she asked Sandy to wish up some food that she had never seen before.

"I wants to see some stuff you peoples eats," Mammy said.

An impish grin spread across Sandy's face.

"Are you going to serve whatever I chant for Mammy?" Smiling from ear to ear, Mammy stood showing those long dimples in her cheeks and nodding 'yes'. Sandy was going to enjoy this, and so would Mammy. "Okay, now, here we go. Mammy, count to ten and then open your eyes." Sandy was just about done when she heard the maid gasp.

On her ready-to-serve table was a flaming Cherries Jubilee, complete with its own little bottle of rum to make it flame. On a push cart sat a large crystal punch bowl filled with sparkling, fizzing peach-colored lemonade with little frozen lemonade ice cubes. There was a duck stuffed with wild rice and complete with papillotes. Mammy beamed as if she had prepared all of these dishes herself.

"Sandy, these white peopa's gon tink I made all o' dis." Sandy too was proud of this display, but there were two more things she wanted to get. From her first meeting with Mammy, Sandy felt like challenging Mammy and seeing what she could do to shock her. So, closing her eyes and chanting, she popped in a large tray with a peach-colored Jello molded to look like a large peach sitting on a bed of lettuce, and standing up proud and stately were four whole pineapples so fresh and ripe that they still had water clinging to the leaves.

Mammy tried to pick it up, but Sandy stopped her before she spoiled the mold. As the Jello shook and glimmered, Mammy squealed that she could see herself in it. She declared it was like looking into a moving, pink looking glass.

When all was prepared, Sandy pressed Mammy to hurry to take her to see Madame Valery. Confident that she could leave and be back before she was missed, Mammy led Sandy away from Worthinwood Plantation. They had been walking for a while and were almost at their destination, and the old cook was still talking about that Jello.

While walking to Valery's cabin, Mammy informed Sandy that Master Coard was really upset with the voodoo he had seen out at the slave quarters. After Sandy had gone home, Coard sent for Madam Valery and her daughter Renee to get some explanation, but the two of them were out somewhere looking for the roots, herbs, and spices that they kept hanging from their ceiling. Next, he sent his valet, Almon, to walk out to the quarters with Mammy Cinda, and they were instructed to report everything they heard or saw.

Mammy reported to Sandy how when she and Almon arrived they noticed right away that the rooms didn't smell of body odor. Mammy had left the women's dorm and had gone to one of the private family huts in the back and then to another, and both huts smelled wonderful. Mammy had started back to the women's hut to get Almon when she noticed a little girl about four years old wearing a pair of shorty pajamas. They were pink with little ruffles on the back of the panties, and on her feet she wore little pink shower shoes. To Mammy, they looked like rich white folks' clothes. She stopped and picked the child up and sniffed at her. Mammy was tickled red. Her people were really moving ahead on the Worthinwood Plantation! "We can smell good, too," she had said aloud to herself. "And I ain't tellin' Massa Coard nuttin'! Not one lil' thang." Under her breath she muttered, "and needa is Almon." Putting the little girl down, Mammy Cinda had said, "Dees white peoples tink dey da ony people dat wants to be people."

Mammy told Sandy that, on their way back to the big house, Almon wasn't sure what he was supposed to report. He said, "Sho' tings smells better, and dee slabes look cleaner, but Cinda, I ain't seen no voodoo. What I'm go say?"

By this time, Sandy and Mammy Cinda were approaching Madame Valery's little cabin. It looked like the other little slave huts, though slightly larger, and it had been recently whitewashed. The front door was open, and all the shutters were opened, but it was dark inside, and the room was musty.

As she and Mammy entered the home, Sandy saw all kinds of drying or dried plants hanging from the ceiling, and on shelves below the ceiling were stored what looked like drying animal parts in jars and rolled in papers. There was incense burning thickly in some type of hardwood bowls. In the shadows sat two figures—they seemed to have been expecting visitors.

Madam Valery and her daughter Renee looked enough alike to be twins. The only difference was that the older woman was a very deep coffee brown (Madam Valery called it *cafe noir*) and her daughter was that same shade, but with milk (Madam Valery called that *cafe au lait*). The two women were tall and stately, not beautiful—the words *comely or picturesque* came to mind. Both had very smooth skin and very long, black wavy hair. Aside from that, every other feature was average. Madam Valery stood up when she saw Mammy and Sandy come up the wooden steps.

"Cinda, Cinda, maybe I should make you a *Lias sez passer* to come on my property, yes?" Mammy chuckled and hugged her old friend.

"Lo', Valery don' go talkin' dat Frenchy stuff to Mammy Cinda, now you noze betta. Dis here strange looking gal is the one that sent that wench out heah to find some clearing." Madam and her daughter looked at Mammy like she was crazy. Mammy went on. "Girl, I nos yo ain't skirdt o' no ghos'?" Sandy figured it out. "Mammy! Look! They can't see me! These are free people!" On their way to the cabin, Mammy had told Sandy of Madam Valery and Renee.

They once lived on a sugar cane plantation in New Orleans. Valery's mother had been a strikingly beautiful woman of pure Mandingo stock, and women everywhere of every race admired her beauty. After the master of the plantation died, Valery was set free, according to a will that was left behind. As it turned out, the plantation owner was Valery's father. He had, upon his death, set free Valery's mother, who he had taken as his wife. The only reason the plantation wasn't left to them was that slaves weren't allowed to own property.

Valery's mother had refused to leave her husband's home and settled in with some of his distant relatives that took over the plantation. But Valery and her two-year-old daughter—whose father had been sold away by the new owners—set out to find a place of their own. If they stayed on in New Orleans, they would wind up in some brothel or be forced to live a nomadic life. They heard about others in similar circumstances, so, with her mother's blessings and some of her belongings, they came by train to Savannah and found out that the Worthinwood Plantation was surrounded by lots of land and that Coard Worthinwood III was a fair man and would probably rent them a square acre or two for a while. That's how these black magic women from Louisiana came to Worthinwood.

Sandy looked around the quaint little room and appreciated the way Madam Valery had put her hut together: it was apparent the furniture consisted of pieces she had from her late master's mansion. The small but unblemished secretary was a true work of art and it was well tended. Aside from the black horse hair sofas and the jade green chaise lounge, everything else was homemade, even the area rug on the lacquered pinewood floor. The four windows in the hut were treated with jade green print curtains of heavy linen. The two women seemed pretentious with large dangling turquoise earrings.

After the elder Worthinwood died, Coard stopped charging Madam Valery to live on his property in exchange for the medical cures that the plantation needed so badly. Madame Valery also began supplying Mammy with herbs and spices for her cooking. Coard and the plantation owners surrounding Worthinwood also came to appreciate the little love potions the voodoo woman concocted and her ability to tell the sex of a baby before its birth. It was common folklore to hear of many magic feats Madam Valery had done. Every plantation usually had such a 'doctor' that knew a lot about childbirth, herbs, spices, and other useful knowledge that most slave families would suffer without. There was a profusion of things Madam Valery had done—people she'd saved and lovers she'd paired up.

Sandy, standing close to Mammy Cinda, whispered, "Mammy, if they aren't slaves, they won't be able to see me." Mammy looked perplexed. "But deez is black folks!" she whispered back.

"Whoa-kay," Sandy sighed louder than she meant to. "Watch this." Clearing her throat, she turned to Valery. "Madam Valery, you can't see me because you and your daughter are free people. My name is Sandy, and I live in the twentieth-century, but all my life I've dreamt of doing something for my people. That is, rather, my people that lived in this time, this time of slavery to be exact. Recently, I was given the opportunity to do just that. Please don't be afraid." As Sandy spoke, her voice grew more confident. "I came to make things easier for the slaves, no matter what color."

As Sandy spoke, she saw Mammy's back stiffen with indignation. She saw Renee cover her mouth, first with one hand, then the other. Madam Valery had fear written all over her face before she remembered that she was a voodoo queen. She wasn't supposed to be afraid of something like this, was she? Mammy started to sputter. She let Sandy *know* she was angry and insulted.

"Gal, don' yo' go talkin' crazy. Ain't no white slabes need no hep from no black ghos'." Sandy and Mammy seemed totally to forget Madam Valery and Renee. They bickered back and forth until Madam Valery held up her tiny little hand and commanded them to stop.

"I can see that our ghost is well known to our Lady Cinda, yes? But let's not have bouleversement." Madam Valery knew what to say to calm Mammy. When she called Mammy a lady, it had never failed to placate the jolly fat cook who could be prickly at times. Immediately, Mammy's bottom lip was sucked in, and she giggled. "Lo', Madam Valery, I sho' is glad to see ya'll." Mammy totally changed the subject and spoke as if she had just walked in the door. Sandy understood that her disagreement with Mammy would have to be postponed to another time and, from that point, she practically ignored Mammy and Madame Valery as they had a close conversation of their own. For now, the room had Sandy fascinated. "Wow, I can't believe this! Look at this stuff." She picked up a demitasse and saucer from a sofa table and took pleasure at floating it through the air, or at least it looked like that to everyone but Mammy. She was making Mammy jittery.

"Madam Valery, if I'da known yo wouldn't been able ta see dis gal, I wouldn't brung ha heah." Madam Valery shrugged. She was trying hard to appear as if such things as these happened in her life all the time. Renee was sitting so close to her mother that she was almost in her lap.

Sandy was intrigued by the herbs and spices hanging or in glass jars. Some of the roots and leaves were familiar to her from her reading about slaves and their herbal medicines. Her Grandma Mary would tell her stories about such things, too, as they swung on the front porch of the Tucker home. There were about ten jars of the dried or powdered All Heal that belonged to the many assorted family of plants *valerianaceous*. There were jars of bats' body parts, and when Sandy saw this, she laughed until she felt dizzy and fell down. Madam Valery and Renee almost jumped through the tin roof.

Mammy's eyes were tiny, mean slits in her face. She looked ready to put her ghost over her lap. Sandy had the floor to herself.

"I'm dreaming. I can't believe I'm in the home of the voodoo queen." Instantly, Madam Valery jumped up and asked Renee for her portemonnaie. Grabbing the black velvet purse, she opened it and flung the contents in the direction from which Sandy's voice came. Little crystals hit Sandy's face and arms, and Madam Valery screeched some chant that was supposed to make a spirit concrete. Renee grabbed her arms and stopped her.

"Mother, I don't think she is something we should fight." Turning towards Sandy who was holding a jar in her hand, Renee made an offer. "We have turned this into an unnecessary battle. Let us clear the air. If there is something you want from us, tell us what we can do for you. I know that you know my mother and I are weak entities, to put it mildly. At the risk of sounding presumptuous, we want to have what you have, to be as powerful as you."

Sandy put the jar down and picked up the little black bag that Madam Valery had thrown to the floor. Sniffing it, she noted, "Chrysarobin, made from goa powder, Renee, is only good for skin disorders." Renee said nothing, so Sandy prepared to speak on, but Madame Valery spoke first.

"Sandy, what is it that you wish of us?"

"I sent Faye out to find a secluded spot in these everglades so that I could store some things here for my people at Worthinwood. She thought that the spot she chose was too close to you. If white people come upon this spot, they may or may not be able to see and destroy its contents, things that I want to leave here for my people to use."

"What is it you want to bury in the glades, Sandy?"

Now that Madam Valery was talking it meant things were smoothing over, so Mammy's face relaxed, and she tried to pretend she was okay with all these goings on.

"Lo', y'all jist go on an' tauk, don' worry 'bout ole Mammy Cinda." Mammy was once again her old jolly self.

Sandy had felt triumphant. Sitting down, Sandy started explaining. She told Madam Valery the story from the beginning. When she was done, she explained that she needed a piece of land in a clearing, about one-half acre. She explained that one of her two weeks was almost spent, and she wouldn't be able to come back. But she wanted to leave a 'fountain of youth' containing many different things—tubs and tubs of shampoo with conditioner, body lotions, neutralizers, all with soft soap nozzles, birth control pills, five bath-tub size vats with curl activator, straight perms, S curls, curly curls, perm rods, sun block lotion, and deodorant.

She would also leave yards upon yards of different types of cloth, emery boards, clear polishes, diapers, and safety pins; perfumes (Poison, Jovan Musk, Chloe, Youthdew) and bath oils for the women and splash-on for the men (Drakkar), medicines, bottles for babies, powders, pacifiers, combs and brushes, hair dress (oils), toothpastes and a host of other things—panties, bras, clothes, and blankets.

Sandy told Madam Valery that freemen may come across the clearing and destroy it if they could see it, so she needed the voodoo woman's help. She wanted it close to Madam Val's so she could watch it and waylay anyone about to discover the cache. There will be enough stuff there to last three plantations for a lifetime if used correctly. Madam Valery walked over to where Sandy's voice was coming from.

"Sandy, if I give you a potion to make your cache invisible to freemen and prayer to keep anything from turning putrid, what will Renee and I get out of it?" Sandy had anticipated this. Ready with an answer, she told them she'd give them anything within her powers, and they would be free to use whatever was in the cache. "Sandy, Renee and I would love two thousand dollars in gold and five thousand dollars in silver, a brace of horses, and a carriage." Sandy agreed and told her that as soon as she had finished protecting the cache, the two of them would be compensated.

With little ado, Sandy and Mammy left Madam Valery and the everglades. Mammy had seen more voodoo in the last hour than she'd ever heard of in her lifetime. Sandy had gone on to the slave quarters, and Mammy had come to her kitchen to do last minute preparations.

Lady Teresa had just about finished her toiletry when she dispatched her personal maid to the laundry room to iron her blue afternoon gown. While she waited, she decided to go down to the kitchen to make sure the menu was going to be not just savory but also ready to be served on time and elegantly. Tonight, she would be formally introducing Christopher Frazier to sixteen-year-old DeeDee.

Christopher was, in Teresa's eyes, the best and most eligible catch around. The reason for this was that the man lived within thirty miles of Worthinwood and had known the Worthinwood family for many years. DeeDee had already had a debut when her mother paraded the homely child around as a desirable woman. At least, she had tried.

Walking into the kitchen, she spotted something pink amidst a bed of green. Inquisitive, she went over to get a closer look. As she peered down at the Jello, she bumped the table and the mold wiggled. Lady Teresa blinked several times and shook her head before looking again.

"Whew," she said aloud, "I must get some rest. I'm starting to see things." But before she could finish the sentence, she bumped the table again. This time Teresa didn't close her eyes. She stared down at the mold. As it shook and shimmered, she could see her reflection, and she was shaking along with this pink glob. She covered her mouth to hold back the scream that was building in her throat. Lady Teresa couldn't take her eyes from the Jello mold. She backed away slowly, her face as white as a sheet. Just as she felt close enough to the door to turn and run, she turned right into Mammy Cinda's arms. Lady Teresa slammed into Mammy so hard that she knocked the wind out of them both!

"Missy Teresa," Mammy said trying to catch her breath, "Lo! What's done put a scare in my missus?"

Teresa was babbling and sputtering and pointing at the serving table. The rice powder she had so painstakingly applied to her face was streaked.

Mammy held on to her until she was making sense. "Lordy! Lordy, Missy, what done put a fire in yo bonnet?" Mammy asked. She had already figured that Teresa had seen the Jello mold. "Now you lis'en to yo ole Mammy. Dat what yo is done seed is some Creole food that I done got from Madam Valery. It like ice cream. It's got that spice yo's want me to put in that fish stew." By now, Lady Teresa had calmed down and was wiping her face with the hanky she always had in her camisole.

"Mammy," she said sniffing and trying to regain her composure, "I don't know what that is, but if yew are going to serve it this evening, make sure it is dead." She gave her head a shake, put her nose back in the air and said she was ready to check the menu with Mammy. "But first, go find that lazy Charlotte and tell ha to make shore she is bathed and clean since she will be helpin' Willy serve."

Yes'm." Mammy grinned and shuffled off to find the maid.

Five minutes later, Mammy Cinda was back, having carried Lady Teresa's message. She hurried and got back to the kitchen. For Mammy, time was moving so slowly. Charlotte was going to shock everyone tonight, and she couldn't wait.

She nodded her head as her mistress read off the menu. The *piece de resistance* would be the gigot. The appetizer was bouillabaisse, next yellow rice, corn on the cob, cornbread, sweet peas, broasted chicken complete with papillate on its legs, cabbage, smoked ham, iced tea with lemon and mint twigs, lemon tarts, petit fours, chocolate cake, and . . . cherry Jello.

CHAPTER SEVEN

Mammy's Jello went over big, real big!

When they finally decided to eat it, no one wanted to cut its pretty pink surface, but Mammy and DeeDee demonstrated. Mammy served it, and DeeDee ate the first serving. The people at this fiesta giggled and danced . . . and ate Jello.

DeeDee looked cute in her pea green evening dress. The color in the dress made her eyes sparkle. The dress had a low bodice and showed lots of cleavage. Her milk white breasts (dusted with rice powder) showed off a beautiful jade and diamond necklace given to her only that morning by her father. Her red hair was pinned up in a pretty chignon with a laced ribbon that matched the creamy beige ruffles on the skirts of her sleeveless dress. Her maid had strained DeeDee's stays and put her largest hoops and bustles under the skirts. She felt absolutely gorgeous. The rice powder, the grand finale, hid the freckles on her face, chest, and arms. But looking across the room at her daughter, Teresa was once again aware that nothing she did would ever make DeeDee a raving beauty. Her heart went out to her homely daughter, and her only consolation was her daughter's more than generous dowry.

Teresa signaled for DeeDee to come to the side of the courtyard she was on. She could see her daughter doing all the standard things that young girls did to snag a beau, but poor DeeDee looked clownish. This could be hard for her, Teresa thought, as DeeDee made her way across the courtyard.

Mr. Frazier, the man DeeDee and Lady Teresa wanted so much to impress, never noticed.

Chris Frazier was so tall that he even towered over DeeDee, and she stood five foot, nine inches tall. His straw-colored hair was worn long as was the style in that era, and it curled naturally. He had dark brown eyes and was well-muscled, deeply tanned, and had slightly bowed legs.

At that moment, his attention was drawn toward the part of the courtyard where the food was displayed. Following his eyes, Teresa spotted Charlotte carrying a tray of hors d'oeuvres. Teresa's mouth fell open at what she saw.

Earlier that day, after Charlotte had done her work, Sandy and Cinda had gone to the slave quarters to get Charlotte ready to serve at the party that night.

They were excited! Gail would be working in the kitchen most of the evening, so she and the other kitchen workers had to wear large red aprons, and their hair had to be covered. Cinda knew that the worst thing a master or his family could find in their food was a coarse, curled up 'nigger hair'. That could bring severe punishment, even a visit to the whipping post!

At the slave quarters, Sandy had Charlotte strip down to her undergarments and draped her with a sheet. Then she chanted in large-toothed combs and other beauty products like perms, make-up, lotions, and manicure kits. When Charlotte's hair rag came off, Sandy almost cried when she saw the condition Charlotte's hair was in.

As she combed it, she learned that these slaves had never used shampoo or conditioner, and they only washed their hair maybe two times a year with the lye soap the slaves made from tallow—from animal fat and pot ash, the ashes from the cooking fire. The soap was so strong that it bleached white clothes just like modern day bleach. There was no such thing as shampoo for blacks. In fact, the hair on a black person was not even considered hair, but wool. Sandy and Charlotte were packed in the midst of curious slaves, men as well as women. When Sandy combed the conditioner through Charlotte's hair, everyone became silent and tried to get a better look. Sandy asked them to pay close attention to every step because they would be doing each other's hair.

The S curl was simple and the straight perm, too. Charlotte's hair only needed to be washed and conditioned for the soft, wavy texture to wake up. Her hair was naturally beautiful, and so was she with her even features and pearly white teeth. Although her skin was an olive color, her eyes and hair were jet black.

There were many women whose hair would need something stronger than just a conditioner, and the coarsest hair would need the more complicated formula. These women would have to go to Madam Valery for the perm that requires perm rods. Faye and Madam Valery were the only ones that Sandy taught how to apply these beauty techniques.

Charlotte's hair reached past her shoulders when Sandy finished pulling the conditioning cream through it. She gave her the shampoo and moisturizer and sent the beautiful slave down to the lake to wash the solution out and pin her hair up to dry. Then Dial soap and more towels were dispensed as well for a bath. A little later, the women watched round-eyed when Sandy gave Charlotte pretty pink panties and a camisole with lace.

"Charlotte has to hurry because in one hour she has to be back in the big house before she's missed," Sandy explained. "However, every man, woman, and child has six pairs of underwear coming. You ladies and girls don't know what to do with a bra, but you'll be getting three each, and when I come back, I'll show you how to use them, or Madam Valery can show you. Wherever you keep your belongings, that's where you'll find your new things."

In less than a ten seconds, the room cleared as the women ran to find their new goodies.

When Charlotte came back from the stream with Renee and others who went to help, she was breathtaking. She stood before the mirror that Sandy had wished in. All of the solution was washed from her hair, and Sandy unpinned her hair to rub the rest of the moisturizer through the long luscious curls lying on her back and shoulders. The women and girls who had come back when they saw Charlotte returning stared with open-eyed wonder. The hair that Sandy first encountered on Charlotte's head a large mass of tangled, dry and damaged trouble—now shimmered and seemed to take on a life of its own. When she told the girls to hurry, she noticed that nearly every girl in the room had taken off her own head rag and was ready for the next step.

"Remember, girls, that Charlotte has got to get back to the big house before she is missed."

In ten minutes, they had her in the beautiful early-American style prom gown that looked just like the dresses the belles wore now, only this one came from the Bridal Shop in Jesup, along with sixty others and little ballet slippers with each.

Now dressed and ready to go to the big house, Charlotte looked like a doll. Sandy sprayed her with Poison, put just a dab of peach blush on her lips and cheeks, darkened her lashes and brows, and sent her off. Sandy asked some of the girls to help her get the rest of the gowns and slippers to the cache.

Earlier that day, Madam Valery had given Sandy a spell to make the cache invisible to free-men, male and female. The spell was a dance called a *passeul*, which meant, in French, 'a solo step'. Sandy had to do this alone and whisper her wishes as she walked all over the area that would be housing the goods. One whole area was for canned goods and dry foods. Everything that was wished for came by the bathtub loads. She made sure all of the families and other grown-ups had little plastic containers with compartments, as well as little shopping carts, that they took to the glades to fill as needed. Following Valery's instructions, Sandy danced the *passeul* to make the cache invisible as well as to preserve its goods. Unknown to Valery, however, Sandy clutched her ivory, just to make sure: in case Madame Valery's magic didn't work, Sandy was sure of the ivory's power!

Looking at the faces that ranged from prune black to coffee and cream, Sandy could see the problem that plagued all of the slaves. No one had ever taught them how to take care of their own hair—though they were good caretakers of their white owners' hair or any white hair for that matter. Now Sandy had news for them. She had already shown them how to do an S curl and a straight perm. Now, she would tell them about caring for black hair—their own! Today had been a long day for everyone at Worthinwood.

Sandy understood that every time the big house had a party, the slaves were allowed to celebrate also, even when it had nothing to do with them. This day was no exception for the slaves that didn't have to serve. It was almost 5:00 p.m., and everyone at the quarters helped to fix each other's hair, bathed, or cooked. The little girls and boys were getting bathed by older brothers and sisters in foot tubs. Big girls were getting all dolled up for their own party. Some of the boys and men were getting their haircuts and baths.

Sandy, with the help of some of the younger men, improvised a shower down in the lip of the stream by putting up four walls and a door. Overhead was a bracket holding a sixty gallon drum with a stopper or plug in one end and at the other end a long hollow tube or pipe going from the drum into the stream. That was all that was required for operation since the principal body of the stream was lower than the cause, which was a small waterfall. The shower was constantly busy, so some of the men bathed in the falls or the stream, which offered no privacy. The women were instructed by Sandy to never use the open falls again.

Some of the men snuck off of Worthinwood and brought back corn squeezin's. Women were still cooking and bringing big gourds and pots and pans filled with steaming hot food to tables set up in the middle of the quarters, but much to Sandy's glee, they still took time to see if their boys washed behind their ears.

Sandy felt the vibration of life in the air. The whole plantation hummed a vibrant, wordless tune. She knew she had to go home soon, but she had to see what was in those smoking pots they were bringing to the tables.

There were slabs of smoked, tender pork rib tips falling off the bone with sauce (barbecue sauce, thanks to Sandy), smoked oysters, she-crab soup, potato salad, fresh chowder peas with slab- skin fried bacon, cracklin cornbread, collard greens, turnips, and cornmeal dumplings. Sandy became acutely aware that she hadn't been eating right lately. She licked her dry lips as her hunger sharpened.

A booming, laughing voice rang out in Sandy's ear. "Um hum. Loo's to me like yo is gon need some o' dis food to eat so's yo won't git sick, ain't ya?" Mammy Tulla was standing behind Sandy with one hand on her more than ample hip and another pinching off a piece of white Wonder bread that Sandy had wished in—ten loaves in all. Right now, Mammy Tulla was right. Sandy needed something to eat, and then she'd go home.

Sandy had left for home just as the party—the black *and* the white—was in full swing.

She may have postponed her return, however, if she had known of Charlotte's reception at the big house: Lady Teresa couldn't believe what she saw.

Charlotte didn't have on her white turban that many slave owners insisted that the slaves wear because their hair looked so bad. Charlotte's hair hung in long, glossy spiral curls to her shoulders. Her face was scrubbed, and there was the slightest hint of blush on her cheeks and lips. There was something different about her eyes too, Teresa thought. And that dress! Where did she get that dress? It was every bit as breathtaking as the dresses worn by the young debutantes. Forgetting she had summoned DeeDee over to her side of the hall, Lady T. made her way over to Charlotte just as Chris Frazier reached the slave girl.

He was staring at the Charlotte like a man in a trance. No Southern gentleman *openly* admired a female slave like Chris was doing, Teresa thought. She snatched the tray from Charlotte's hands and ordered the slave to go into the courtyard foyer and wait for her. When Charlotte turned to leave, Teresa got a whiff of the most exotic scent she'd ever smelled. Chris also smelled it when he sniffed! Someone touched Lady Teresa's shoulder, and she spun around angrily.

"Mother, you called me over to yew and then yew ran awf!" Teresa pulled her daughter out of hearing range and looked into the face of her firstborn. Her heart went out to her. But like always, she affected a shaky smile and tried not to look at DeeDee's poor weak chin. The rice powder applied generously had done an adequate job of hiding the freckles.

"DeeDee," Teresa said half-heartedly, "you are simply beautiful, but why don't you go and talk to Mr. Frazier. You'll never be a bride, sweetie, by standing across the room blinking your eyes at him. Let your girlfriends mingle without you for a spell." DeeDee looked perplexed.

"Mother, yew said last night that I should copy Rosemary's every move."

Teresa sighed. She had indeed told DeeDee that, but that was before she saw how ridiculous DeeDee looked with size ten and a half feet, her rather large nose, and her almost carrot red, invisible lashes. If it weren't so sad, it may have been comical. She looked over at Rose playing coy with a potential beau, William Dreyfuss III, from one of Savannah's oldest families. The girl's skin looked like the petals of a magnolia blossom. Rose was looking up at the young man from under incredibly lush lashes. She was very petite, with black hair and dark blue eyes. She was a born flirt, but she had what it took to be one.

"Well," Teresa sighed with resignation, "my DeeDee is still my giglet, my precious little gem." That Rosemary, Lady T. concluded, looked and acted like a lasciviously experienced woman, hot in her pursuit of a man—any man! Teresa watched the back of DeeDee's head as she made her way back over to where Chris stood.

He wasn't trying very hard not to look in the direction that Charlotte had been sent.

Teresa stood watching her daughter try to act coltish with the debonair Chris, who paid her no mind. Teresa knew she would have to talk to Coard about adding to the already large dowry for this hunk of man to take poor DeeDee off their hands. She had to admit he was a very handsome man, and since DeeDee would be competing for a commitment from him, Teresa would pull out all the stops and push all the right buttons.

She looked around the courtyard before making her way to the foyer where the scared slave stood waiting.

Now standing before Lady Teresa, the slave looked down at her hands, the fingers of which were entwined in front of her. Again, Teresa smelled that heavenly scent. Looking around to make sure no one was looking, she leaned forward as if to whisper in Charlotte's ear. She took a deep breath and became lightheaded with the scent. Charlotte's body chemistry and the musk made an irresistible aroma! Teresa was sure that no man would be able to resist it, no matter what color he happened to be.

"What is that you are wearing?" Teresa snapped at the cringing girl.

Charlotte had already been schooled by Sandy and Mammy Tulla, so she knew what to say and how to act, but now she was so scared she wished she were anywhere but here.

Teresa never liked Charlotte. Watching the little slave go from cute to beautiful, her dislike intensified. She would never admit her jealousy and fear to anyone. Instead, Teresa would do and say nasty things to Charlotte in Coard's presence. Once, Charlotte was serving coffee and tea to the Worthinwoods and two of her husband's friends. Chris Frazier was one of them. As the girl bent down to refill Teresa's cup, Teresa skinned up her nose and said loudly, "My word, Charlotte, dismiss yourself and go wash yourself, gal. Yew smell like a wet dawg. When yew held your awms up, why, I almost lost my breath. Send Gail back to serve." When the humiliated slave scurried off with tears in her eyes, Lady Teresa apologized to her company and sat back to smirk, but her husband was on to her game.

"Teresa, how many times have I told you that, on top of them having a strong body odor from working all day long, they also lack the essentials that we have to ward off bad body odors. They can bathe all day and night, and if they don't have lip salves, powders, toilet waters, and baking soda to brush their teeth with, it's hard. It's a shame they don't make that stuff for niggers."

The most recent—and most dehumanizing—thing the dainty looking Lady Teresa did to Charlotte happened seven or eight months ago. The Worthinwoods were having their annual Christmas party. Teresa always insisted that her household slaves dress in red and green at Christmas, so she had given each slave a length of cloth in green and red for the women to make dresses for themselves and to make trousers and shirts for the butlers and valets. On the day of the party as guests began to arrive, some of them gazed too long at Charlotte. She did look lovely, but she hadn't tried to make her dress nice enough to compete with any of her superiors. Anyone could see that she had none of the nice chemises or camisoles. She had nothing under the dress except for a 'nigger slip,' a rough flour sack garment that rubbed and hurt her nipples and kept them hard and irritated.

Charlotte had noticed Teresa looking at her, and she had noticed that almost all of the men did doubletakes when they looked at her, some of them for an embarrassingly long time. Charlotte was very petite, but her little, round posterior and her firm, generous breasts wiggled when she made even the slightest move. Aware that the women were watching their men watch her, Charlotte kept her eyes cast down, shuffled a little, and smiled (or, rather, pasted on a bland smile).

Without warning, Teresa walked over to where Charlotte stood refilling her tray with mint juleps. Her tray held eight crystal cups, four on the left side with steaming minty green liquid, clear and pungent. The other four cups held a creamy white liquid. This thick, spicy chilled concoction was eggnog. Charlotte turned around with the tray, and Lady Teresa was standing so close to her elbow that she bumped Charlotte and splashed the hot and cold liquids all over her.

None of the liquid splashed Teresa, but, for her own reasons, the feisty mistress of Worthinwood reached up and tore the turban off the helpless girl. Charlotte's left hand and arm were smarting so much she didn't notice that her turban wasn't covering her hair. The women in the party room tittered and started whispering: Charlotte's shoulder length hair, an incredible number of dry curls, was amassed and packed on her head and looked like it was only two or three inches long!

But the girl had learned to play her role in this drama. Picking up her headrag, she kept up her pace. She was a slave! Nothing could embarrass her. Nothing could ever again embarrass her!

But now, looking at Charlotte's resplendent beauty, Lady Teresa had seen it all!

Still heady with the perfume Charlotte wore, Teresa repeated herself: "I asked yew a question, daggone it. What is that yew are wearing?"

Charlotte mumbled something indistinctly, but Teresa heard the word *poison*.

"Poison?" Teresa muttered, clinching her fists and gritting her teeth. "Gal, yew either give me straight answers or I'll have yew whipped to within an inch of your wretched life! Now tell me what toilet water it is yew got on and where yew stole it from?"

Charlotte entwined her fingers behind her back and kept her head bowed as she tried to explain. "Missy Teresa, I got dis cloth from selling dem beans'n peas out dat patch 'hind de hut we stay at. An' ya 'members dat ole cow my brother got for tendin' Unca Tillbert's garden whiles he was ailin'? Well, we keeps dat cow fresh an' sells da milk an' cheese." She was nervous now, but still defiant. Today, Charlotte knew she was just as pretty as the woman that owned her—even prettier!

Teresa narrowed her eyelids and through clenched teeth she hissed, "Tell me, damnit. What are you wearin'?"

Teresa reached down and grabbed one of Charlotte's hands from behind her. She thought the girl was hiding something, and she was, only it wasn't what Lady Teresa thought. Holding the slave's hand, Teresa gasped at the freshly manicured hand. The nails were filed ovally and shining clear with a tint of pink. The skin was soft, clean, and lotioned with a fragrant cream. She had two rings (not gold, not silver) just iron and steel. The blacksmith on the plantation was taught to make them by Sandy who read the directions to him from a book she'd wished in.

The young slave blacksmith Enoch was unmarried, so he didn't have to charge much to make them—five eggs for one pinky, ten figs for one thin band. A two-month old piglet would buy a thin, dainty wrist band or ankle band.

"I's wearin' Poison, Miz Teresa." Before she could say more, Teresa's hand came up and hit the now numb slave so hard it snapped her head backwards.

Charlotte didn't cry. She didn't even put her hands up to her face to protect herself. The obviously vitiated mistress of Worthinwood slapped the helpless girl again with so much force it knocked Charlotte to her knees. . . .

Madam Valery and Renee had sat around inertly for most of that evening. Renee wasn't talking much, but she, like her mother, was deep in thought about Sandy and her visit to their home earlier. Despite all that had happened that day, Mammy Cinda—upset about the way her mistress had treated Charlotte—had stolen away for a little while near the end of the evening and told them what had happened. Not that it was any surprise to Madame Valery and Renee; they understood how the lady of Worthinwood had always hated the beautiful slave.

When Teresa first married Coard and came to Worthinwood, she, like most women, was awed by Charlotte's beauty, and she drew no comfort knowing that there was Worthinwood blood running through Charlotte's veins. But it was apparent that blood lines meant nothing when some of it ran through the veins of a black man or woman. It was common knowledge that, like most men, Coard wanted to possess the girl totally.

Before Mammy Cinda left Madame Valery's to return to Worthinwood, the twelve-year-old boy that Madam Valery and Renee fed and let sleep on a straw pallet in a corner of their kitchen floor came running back to the forest hut before any of the parked carriages left. Missy Teresa, he said, once again had attacked Charlotte. Charlotte was sent out to the toolshed to spend the night and wait until noon the next day for the overseer to administer the lashes after stringing her up stripped from the waist up. Charlotte, it seemed, had talked back to Lady Teresa in the presence of most of the guests and Lady Teresa had to smack her. Madam Valery saw this mess for what it was.

"Missy has always been extremely jealous of that girl and any other beautiful slave," she said. . . .

Thursday morning when Richard walked past his daughter's closed bedroom door, he hesitated for a few seconds but went on to breakfast without stopping. When he bowed his head to ask the Lord's blessing, he remembered the little commercial that asked, "Do you know where your kids are?"

"I don't even know *how* my child is," Richard said aloud.

He arrived at work ten minutes early and was slapped in the face with more robberies with the same MO.

This time, Q Moony's was hit, along with Dixie Bell's Formals, J. T. Pinny's, Pac & Sav, and Cora Bell's Bridal and Formals. Missing were more of the same things, but in a much larger quantity.

The warehouses for Pac & Sav, Woodworth's, and Cloth World were entered and stripped almost bare. The pharmaceutical portion of Woodworth's was relieved of all of its antibiotics, bandages, gauzes, sponges, iodine, peroxide, condoms, birth control gels, creams and sponges, vitamins for children and adults, Monistat 7, and scores of other much needed medicines.

All of the perfumes, colognes, powders, and soaps were missing. Baby items were taken. All of the cloth diapers, rubber panties, clothes, and pajamas were gone. Detergents and bleaches were gone, along with large washtubs. Cloth World was deprived of all cloth, needles, thread, and all types of laces. The strange thing about this robbery was that the only Simplicity patterns that were taken were for women's casual and dressy long dresses and little girls' long pinafores and trousers and shirts for little boys and men.

Whoever was taking these things never left a clue, and, of all the things taken, not one left the warehouse or store with the tags on. The tags were left like ticker tape all over the place. Not one suspect fingerprint turned up on anything, only the fingerprints of employees that should have been there and who were clearly uninvolved in the thefts.

If the news of the robberies wasn't bad enough, Piggy also reminded Richard that the family of Clifford Pope was still waiting for an arrest in his murder. Usually, with each day that passes, the slimmer the chances are that the perpetrator of such a serious crime (especially a murderer) will be caught. The Jesup police still had no strong leads, but Richard had a theory.

He believed the Pickett boys had a hand in all of this. He prayed that he was wrong because, if those black boys were responsible for this white boy's death, there would be hell to pay. The Popes were very vengeful people and not easy to reason with.

One of the Pickett boys, Charles, had been stopped two days ago for an expired inspection sticker, and the officer found some copper tubing in the trunk of the boy's car, tubing that matched that stolen from the museum. Charles Pickett, having first denied everything, finally admitted he took the tubing from the museum plumbing, but added, "Ya'll kin kiss my ass if ya think I'm gon' say me or my family busted in some damn stores."

The boy was stolid and insisted that the police either charge him with what he had confessed to doing or charge him with the other robberies, too. He was charged with the museum robbery alone, and, after implicating his brothers, a bond was set and the boys were back on the streets before sunset.

Nearly everyone else in the police force was convinced the Picketts were guilty of the store robberies also, but after having questioned the boy, Richard was convinced that Charles wasn't lying. The person that robbed the McPherson Museum was not the same person that was burglarizing the stores in downtown Jesup. Richard also surmised, erroneously, that whoever was committing the robberies was also the killer of the Pope boy.

Richard was convinced, however, that there was a Pickett still. This, he felt, was obvious because of the museum piping. It never took Richard long to solve most puzzles, and this was no exception, but he was preoccupied with his daughter. He was hoping that the robberies and the murder were somehow connected: this would be an easy way to close two cases that were getting messier and messier as time went by. The racial overtones in the Pope case bothered him, and Sandy's disappearances at night had him at his wit's end. What was her connection with this mess?

Richard finished his report and, relieved at being done with it, gave it to Montgomery. He forced a smile as he turned to leave.

The sharp-eyed sergeant always noticed everything. "Hey!" The big man yelled at Richard's retreating back. Richard turned and saw him uncross his fat legs and remove them from his desk as he pulled his wheeled chair up short. "Wanna let me in on the joke?" he asked.

Richard slowed his steps and then stopped. "Wha's the matter stubby?" He shot back. "You think I smelled your feet this early in the day?"

P. Montgomery pointed his fingers like a mock gun and fired at the officer. Sometimes light banter was what kept the tension away, and this was one of those times. Montgomery, as serious as he may have appeared sometimes, had to laugh a little.

Richard was almost out of the door when the desk sergeant called him back. "You hear anything 'bout those Pickett boys?" he asked.

Richard shook his head no. "Well, don't give up," Montgomery told him. "Word is that there's been a hot-looking black puss riding shotgun with one of the Pope boys." Richard looked dumbfounded at these words, so Montgomery repeated himself.

Richard grew angry. "Who told you this?" he asked.

"I asked everyone to report any new developments to me, ASAP." The sergeant continued: "As soon as I got here this morning, I got this call and that was what it was about. Now I've only told one other person and that was Chief Weeler!"

Richard felt his anger turn into embarrassment, but he felt damned if he would apologize, so he walked off, but not fast enough to miss the remark Montgomery made.

"That's what's wrong with you people."

Richard knew he was joking because he said it in a stage whisper, but Richard didn't laugh.

He didn't even look back. . . .

Olivia heard her daughter moving around at 10:30 a.m.

Sandy got back at 8:00 and had two and a half hours of sleep and was now taking a shower.

Olivia made strawberry waffles for her daughter and sat with her while she ate.

"Sandy, you know you're losing weight, and you have dark rings under your eyes." She didn't want to make her daughter feel pressured because she had promised she would try not to interfere.

Sandy had said she was okay and not in any danger, and this was not about a boy, so Olivia tried to take solace from this and not push.

"Sandy, since Daddy and I know that you leave at night, why not go out of the front door?" Sandy looked up. She regretted what she was doing to her mother.

"Mom, I have to be consistent with my time and location, and if I were to try and explain, it would only confuse you more."

Olivia took a deep breath and looked down at her hands.

"Your father thought we should demand that you not leave this house anymore after 9:00

p.m." She held up her hand when Sandy started to speak. "Wait a minute. Of course we aren't going to do that because we know it wouldn't work."

"Well, why did you mention it?" Sandy asked. She knew her mother well enough to know it wasn't her father wanting this because he would've just done it (or tried).

Seeing that her daughter wasn't fooled, she went and got the newspaper. Sandy finished her waffles and stood up. She wasn't going to read the paper.

She knew what she would see.

"I'm babysitting today at 1:00 p.m. for Jello's mom. Oh! I almost forgot—did Larry get off okay?"

Larry's school age group went to football camp for two weeks. They were due back two days before the first day of school. Olivia told her everything went fine.

While her mom continued with her household chores, Sandy went upstairs to call Julie. She wanted to know if Julie wanted to come down to Carnell's while she babysat. Julie jumped at the chance. Julie had a crush on Carnell Shaw, and Sandy knew it.

"Will Carnell be there?" Julie wanted to know. Sandy had expected her to ask this question.

"No, stupid, if he were home, he would be keeping Jello himself. You know how Carnell feels about that little girl."

Sandy was looking forward to sitting with Jello today. Julie was coming with her, and afterwards they'd go to the park. After she helped her mom do a load of laundry and hose down the driveway, Sandy's chores were done. While she waited for Julie, she walked across to the Miller house to see the new baby.

Anytime Mrs. Miller answered her door, about six of her children came with her. Today was no different. She had the new baby nestled on her shoulder. Sometimes, all of the children—from the ten-year-old to the toddler—tumbled for a spot at the door. Mrs. Miller smiled as she unlatched the screen door then bent down and picked up the crawling baby by the arms and moved her around out of the way.

"Kevin, didn't I ask you to change Tina?" She asked her son in her soft voice. The oldest boy suddenly came timidly forward and with downcast eyes and a shy smile took the baby.

Of course, the baby put up a fight, but he carried her away anyway.

The new baby was a girl named Tuwanna, and she weighed in at six pounds. Sandy held the sweet smelling little girl. She had so much glossy black hair that you couldn't see her scalp. Mrs. Miller laughed when Sandy said, "You know it's really funny, but black babies are born with a head full of beautiful hair, and white babies are mostly born bald, but by the time they are three years old, the white babies are flush with hair and some of the black babies are going bald."

Sandy gave the baby back.

She began to reminisce about Jello and when Jello was born. Sandy was twelve years old then, and Jello was one of the prettiest babies Jesup ever saw. Jello's mother, Carolyn, and Sandy's mom had been best friends all their lives. It was common knowledge that the Shaws wanted another baby, but no one but Olivia knew how badly.

Carolyn had wanted a little girl when she was pregnant with Carnell. But she was content and very happy with her son. Carnell was five when they decided to have another baby, and Carolyn was elated at the possibility of having a little girl, but year after year went by with no conception. By the time Carnell was ten, Carolyn and her husband didn't care what the sex of the baby would be—they just wanted another baby. Going back and forth to different doctors proved expensive; and the medical reports broke their hearts: Carolyn was sterile.

When Carnell was older, the Shaws decided to adopt. After only one year, they found that they could be in for a long wait if they wanted a perfect newborn black child. However, if they would consider an interracial child or a child with special needs, they would have a better chance of getting a newborn.

One balmy spring day, their attorney called and said he knew of a girl who would deliver on or about September twentieth in Lawton, Oklahoma. She was black, but she got pregnant by her white, married gym teacher. Her mom and dad gave her an ultimatum: Give up the baby or leave home for good. On September twenty-first, the girl gave birth to a six pound boy but wasn't sure what she wanted to do. The boy they named Billy Ray Williams went to a foster home in Topeka, Kansas, the mother's hometown. He was a beautiful boy, and they nicknamed him Dudey. Although the baby was born in Lawton, Oklahoma, the adoption would be filed in Kansas. The Shaws waited anxiously for the mother to decide if she would give him up.

Meanwhile, Carolyn became ill and seemed to be tired all of the time. At first the Shaws attributed her condition to the strain of waiting to hear about the child they wanted to adopt. By the time the mother had made up her mind to sign the papers, Carolyn was almost out of her mind. Even Carnell wanted to get this over with. Finally, they were due to pick Dudey up at a Reverend James Dudley's home on February twelfth. On February fourth, Carolyn learned that she was pregnant. The baby was due on September thirtieth.

Sandy remembers when Mrs. Shaw had her sonogram. It was April twenty-first, and the baby was a girl. To make sure that the baby was healthy, they had another test performed, taking amniotic fluid and checking chromosomes. They were nearly one hundred percent sure that the baby was a girl and in good health. However, Carolyn's little girl decided she didn't want to wait until September to be born. True to Jello's nature, she was in a hurry to get here.

She was born with her eyes open on August third, weighing three pounds and five ounces. The day Jello was supposed to be born, September thirty, caught her fighting for her life. She was determined to get well, and, problem after problem, she fought for her life. She rallied and went home on October thirtieth, weighing five pounds. That was over five years ago.

Sandy walked to the door to leave the Miller home and almost forgot to give the little baby her gift. Mrs. Miller always pierced her daughters' ears before they were six weeks old, so Sandy had brought little silver loops for the baby. She had just walked back and sat on the porch when Julie walked up.

"Hey, I should have known you would be on time to go to *Carnell's* house." Both girls giggled.

Julie snapped her fingers. "You got that right." And they both succumbed to laughter again.

When they got to the Shaw house, Jello was just finishing lunch and was getting her hands and face washed. When Mrs. Shaw was finished, Jello asked for the sponge to wipe her Barbie dolls clean, too. As Carolyn was picking up her purse and checking out last minute details, she told Sandy that either Carnell or Mr. Shaw would be home at 9:00 p.m.

"Well, well! Miz Julie! I thought you had left this earth for another planet." Carolyn smiled at Sandy's friend. The two girls giggled and looked at each other.

"I went to cheerleader camp earlier this summer, Mrs. Shaw," Julie replied. "But right now, I'm just basically hanging loose and enjoying my last two summers before college and responsibility catch me and make a woman out of me. Next year, I'll have to deal with issues that I don't have to face now."

Carolyn patted the girl's hand. "You sound like you've got it together. I'm sure you'll make a good whatever-you-decide-to-be." Jello had run off to get her rag doll, and Carolyn whispered to Sandy, who was standing by the door to lock it after she left. "Watch out, Sandy. Jello has been a real handful today."

After locking the door behind Carolyn, she picked up the remote control and turned to the Black Entertainment channel.

Julie picked up the phone and pulled her phonebook out of her waist purse.

"Every time I bring you over here," Sandy said, scowling at Julie, "you either hog the phone or go digging around Carnell's room."

"That's right," Jello said coming down the hall. "You like Carnell, don't you? I bet if he told you to fix a hole in a water balloon with a needle and thread, you would try to do it." Sandy pursed her lips to hold back her laughter. For her own reason, Jello hadn't cared very much for Julie since she filled in for Sandy one night. Tonight, Jello told Sandy why. She said that Julie had tried to put her to bed as soon as her parents left. "She didn't even tell me a story."

Julie was an only child and had no interest in children. This didn't go unnoticed by Jello.

"She didn't even pretend she liked being here, San. I hope she makes a nicer grown-up than she does a teenager."

While Jello spoke, Sandy noticed that Jello had all lime bows in her doll's hair. Now she was taking them out and putting in red ones. When she turned the doll around, Sandy saw that at the nape of the doll's neck under her black yarn hair were two blue bows.

When Sandy asked about them, Jello explained. "Well, my mommy has important things she has to do this time of year, San, 'cause when school starts, her itin'rary has to be firm."

Sandy smiled.

"It must be kind of difficult for you seeing your mother travel from school to school, and you can't go."

Carolyn's job as a counselor kept her moving from place to place. Carolyn had stayed home after Jello was born and didn't go back to work until after her daughter had gone through the proverbial 'terrible twos'. Carolyn had waited for Jello to turn into the terror that her firstborn, Carnell, had been at two, but it never happened.

By the time she was three, Jello was reading. Carolyn had been teaching her the alphabet and the sound each letter made, when one day she noticed her baby reading anything that had writing on it. Jello would say the sound that the first letter made and sound it all the way through. For example, for go, she would sound out the g and run it into the o and say 'go' with 'away': "Ah... wah... a... ee... ." So Carolyn took pleasure in teaching her daughter arithmetic as well as reading.

Sandy hugged the child who had curled up in her arms. "You still didn't explain about the bows, Jello." Jello looked up at Sandy puzzled, but her brow smoothed out.

"Oh! Well, I put busy bows in because I didn't want Mommy to know I was lonely 'cause she would've felt guilty."

Sandy shook her head in amazement. "I love you, Anita."

Jello smiled shyly. "I put the sad blue bows in the back under Dolly's fat plait where Mommy wouldn't see that I was sad."

"Well," Sandy said in a husky voice and a hint of tears on her lashes, "you're not lonesome now, Jello. Let's pick up your toys and put them in the toy box. We'll have a snack later on, and I'll read anything you want."

"No, thank you, please, Sandy," Jello replied. "I want to read to you and Julie and stay up all night 'til Mommy comes home."

Julie had just hung the phone up and had heard the end of the conversation. "What do you want to read, Jello?" She asked, just to have something to say.

The little girl moved from Sandy's lap and jumped down from the sofa, and she went and got one of the *Little House on the Prairie* books.

Julie looked amused when she saw what Jello picked out. "Honey, you have to get something you can read, okay?" With this, Jello got angry. Sandy saw that her bottom lip trembled, and she stomped her tiny little foot, so Sandy tried to waylay the problem before it got too hot.

"Julie Ann Beck!" Sandy said with mock anger, "Jello can read, and she can read almost anything we can." Julie was searching Sandy's face for a laugh, but she saw that the situation was serious.

The smile left Julie's face. "You mean she can really read?"

Jello looked at Julie. "Don't talk about me like I'm not here. I can answer that. Give me your little black phone book, and I'll read it for you." Julie tucked her book back into her purse and snapped it shut. She was definitely not giving Jello her book.

"You little brat!! You really *can* read!" Julie yelled.

Jello had to have the last word.

"Yeh," she said. "And I'm not hooked on phonics either."

Sandy and Julie looked at each other and burst out laughing as Jello looked on, amused.

CHAPTER EIGHT

Richard drove his patrol car over to Q Mooney's where his partner and two others were taking statements and asking questions; the fingerprinting unit had already come and gone. What Richard saw inside the store was bedlam.

There were tags, pins, and hangers everywhere. But there were no signs of breaking and entering. The cash register was untouched. The guys that fingerprinted literally came and went: There was nothing for them to do in any of the stores. The warehouses that supplied these stores were stripped.

Richard walked out to the sidewalk where O'Mallory stood smoking a cigarette. He offered Richard one, and he accepted. Richard had stopped smoking about five years ago on his daughter's birthday. O'Mallory knew this, but he also knew that his partner would still smoke when he was really bothered.

"Tucker, I've never seen you get so bombed out over a case before," he said, offering Richard the flame from his lighter. "Are you still pissed off about those remarks that son of a bitch from Woodworth's made yesterday?"

Richard took a deep pull from the cigarette and exhaled the smoke slowly. Another toke and he threw it to the ground and stepped on it. "Pat ol' boy," he said, "don't worry yourself with trivial bullshit like that, okay?" O'Mallory shrugged his shoulder and followed Richard to the patrol car after stepping on his own cigarette.

Over lunch at the Woodworth's Diner, Richard talked about the murder victim. The day's newspaper article read "Man's Death Ruled Homicide—The death of a Wayne County man Tuesday has been ruled a homicide by the County Medical Examiner's Officer." Trying to talk around a mouthful of French fries, O'Mallory stated that he was glad this wasn't racial.

"In a town as small as Jesup," he said, wiping his mouth with the back of his hand, "that could destroy it." Cramming the last of his fries in his mouth he continued. "You know, Tucker, its not our young people that keep this racial shit afloat. From our generation on back, there has been a conflict between our God-given ability to love and the hate that our fathers and mothers stuffed down our throats. Richard, my father's people are from Ireland and they have a little land and money. They are healthy, good looking, and God-fearing people. But, on the other hand, my mother's people are from the hills of Alabama. They are generation after generation of dirt farmers. They are tobacco chewing, possum eating, incestuous bigots. They hate blacks and they love hating blacks and Puerto Ricans and Jews because they themselves are treated like scum, or poor white trash, and are at the bottom of the social scales of our own race."

Slightly agitated by his own story, O'Mallory sounded angry.

He continued. "Most upper crust white people put poor white trash lower than any black they know. Those upper class whites would not let their babies suckle a poor white breast, or they would not eat at the table with poor whites or eat any food they cooked. But you know, Tucker," O'Mallory wiped his mouth again and leaned forward on the table, "I'll bet the people on my mother's side eat more chitterlings than most of the blacks you know."

Richard chuckled at that. "I don't know, man; almost all of the people I know are black, and I don't know many of us that would turn our backs on a good plate of cleaned and seasoned chitlins. I'm going to tell you why blacks started eating chitlins," he said, getting caught up in the conversation. "Back in the days when white folks—like yourself," Richard joked, "slaughtered their hogs, they would throw away the feet, head, tail, and innards. The slaves would ask for these parts or take them out of the garbage. They would clean them very well and learned to cook and eat it. Most blacks in Africa don't eat pork, even today, but in this 'new place' they ate what they were given because even the best slave owners weren't going to give those poor black peons any of their *good* pork."

Richard had really gotten into the conversation as they paid for their meals and left. They forgot their troubles for a while and really talked.

They were still talking 'pork' ten minutes later when they turned onto New Brunswick

Road and were almost sideswiped by a car going about 80 mph.

Richard put on his lights and siren as he began the chase. O'Mallory called in the tag number and the make and model of the car.

The two officers could see four heads in the speeding car. Richard was having a time keeping up. The Nissan was going about 90 mph now, and Richard was pushing his patrol car to keep them in sight.

The station radioed that the car belonged to Tina Strickland of Hinesville. Richard remembered that name.

"I took a kid in just this week for DWI in that same car."

The speeding duo was approaching the hospital and a school zone. Although school was out for summer, Richard and O'Mallory knew that kids still went there to the playground.

Suddenly, the driver of the Nissan started pumping the brakes and made a wild turn to the left. The car careened on two wheels and then spun around several times before it righted itself and proceeded down a secondary road. Richard and Pat were catching up but neither officer had much hope of safely stopping the torpedoing car. Nothing like this had ever happened in Jesup, as far as these two could remember.

Richard glanced quickly at his partner's blanched face and felt sick himself.

"Do ya think we can force them off the road?" O'Mallory asked.

His voice trembled and a muscle under his left eye started to tick until he nearly closed his eye.

Richard was sweating profusely; fear knotted his stomach.

The police officers saw the Nissan approaching a railroad track crossing and the midday train was running. There were no crossroad guardrails, and the late noon day glare hid the red warning light.

The driver of the little silver car never even hit the brakes.

The patrol car braked and was able to come slowly to a stop, but the tremendous screeching of the metal train brakes and the impact of the train hitting and dragging that Nissan was by far the worst thing the two men would ever hear in their lives. While other travelers and onlookers gasped at the gruesome sight that etched itself on their minds forever, Richard, who never moved his eyes from the wreckage, called for an ambulance, fire truck, and rescue squad. He also suggested they bring the 'jaws of life.' Parking the car, Richard jumped out and ran to catch up with Pat.

The 3000 horsepower locomotive had crushed the little silver Maxima like an aluminum cola can and pushed it over 100 feet along the track before folding one-third of it under the train near a ditch. The train had struck the car on the passenger side, and the driver was flung through the window shield. Richard flinched as he passed the wreckage, but he ran over to the body in the grass.

It was the body of a young white male that had been tossed at least 50 feet from the car. As Richard looked at the obviously dead victim from a distance, the crushed upper body was barely recognizable as human.

People were gathering and crowds were forming. Someone asked if anyone had blankets or sheets in their trunks. Anxious to help, several people ran to their cars.

Bending over the obscenely twisted body Richard saw the face of the same kid he had encountered in the car crash that week. The sight of this inhuman looking pile of flesh and bone was horrendous.

The young man was lying belly down but his head was twisted so that his face was looking up. Both arms were broken and bent at unbelievable angles, and the left hand ripped off completely. Pieces of ribs poked bloody holes through his back, and one of them appeared to have come through this spinal column. His intestines were hanging out of a hole in his lower back and scattered around the body like bloody pink snakes.

People were sobbing now and some prayed. Richard heard someone behind him vomit, but he never took his eyes from the body. Pat finally got to him with some sheets and blankets. The blood around the stub where the hand had been was clotting like cold gravy, and Richard knew that blow flies would soon swarm the boy's body, so, covering the boy with the blanket, he went to assist elsewhere.

If Richard thought he could've lost his lunch over the first body, he almost did as he approached the next victim.

The second body—the boy on the front passenger side—was folded into the metal and was twisted under the train.

As Richard squatted to get a closer look, he saw the face of the third body—one of the passengers from the back seat—which was also trapped under the train. The train's wheel had neatly split the body down the center, but the train came to a stop while it was running over the head.

Richard and Pat soon heard the sirens of the fire truck and ambulance while they warily scanned the wreckage for the fourth body.

The rescue squad arrived first and had nothing to do after assessing the situation, but they couldn't leave until the fourth body was found. Everyone was rushing around looking for the fourth boy. The other bodies had been declared dead at the scene by the town coroner, but he hadn't left the scene because the two officers were certain they saw four heads in the vehicle.

The part of the railroad track that the accident occurred on snaked between thick pine woods on either side until it ran across a narrow two lane road.

Pat O'Mallory had walked from where the impact took place down to where the train stopped.

He was so sure that he counted four heads in that car!

He walked up and down the tracks while others worked with saws to cut the car off of the body and the train. It was pointless to use the 'jaws of life'.

Some of the workers covered big puddles of blood and gore up with sand. Soon, news reporters swarmed the scene. Police and patrols blocked the streets off, trying to keep the crowds away, but people parked their cars blocks away and walked to the site.

Richard remembered that he never took his eyes from the disaster as it occurred, but he never saw the fourth body being tossed from the car! He also knew that no one got out of that wreckage and walked away!

O'Mallory, seeking a quiet place to think, had stopped searching and stood under a canopy of tall pines and old oak trees. He still just couldn't shake this feeling. He had never been so sure about anything so puzzling in his life! Where was that fourth body?

As he stood there absentmindedly looking down at a small patch of clover and blue periwinkle, he saw something dripping on a little patch of moss near the clover. Looking closer, he picked up a twig and poked at it. Before he even looked up, he knew.

Hanging from the lower branches of an ancient oak was the fourth body—a female!

It was impaled by a sharp and strong leafless branch that pointed downwards; the pointed end of the branch couldn't be seen because it was buried somewhere deep inside the girl's body.

She was the person that had been sitting in the back of the car behind the driver. When the train struck the passenger's side, the velocity of the impact sent her through the window on the driver's side. She had been catapulted so violently that she was bent backwards at the waist. Her face lay pathetically against her buttocks. The limb went into her body on the left side of her neck and came to rest in the right thigh, snapping her back. It wasn't just blood Pat saw dripping; it was her vomit.

O'Mallory called for Richard, then leaned against a nearby tree for support. His legs felt like rubber, but he couldn't keep his eyes from darting up to look in the tree.

Richard came at once. He thought his partner was sick because the smell of raw blood and flesh was strong in the air as the bodies were being cut out of the wreckage. O'Mallory only nodded his head when Richard asked if he were OK, but he pointed up at the tree.

Richard turned slowly and looked up.

A rush like a tidal wave roared through his head and left him dizzy. He could only see a little of her face, but the black girl the desk sergeant told him about was hanging from this tree, dead. He had some trouble breathing until he noticed that the color of the dead girl's hair was not jet black—like his daughter's. Richard sobbed with relief. . . .

Sandy and Julie played with Jello in the backyard. After playing kick ball for an hour or so, both girls were ready for Jello's bedtime.

After a snack of graham crackers and milk, Jello was given her bath. The girls made a messy game of powdering her, and, blissfully tired, Jello went to sleep before her bedtime story, "The Baker's Daughter," was over.

Earlier while they played outside, Jello mentioned to the girls that there were real toadstools beside a tall, broken, and ugly shack down in the woods with a pond beside it. Sandy and Julie looked at each other, and they both gasped at Jello.

That pond was on the Shaw property, but it was a five minute walk down into thick foliage, and then there was that old, dilapidated barn that was off in a small hollow.

Sandy knew the spot well. As small children, she and Julie and Robin used to play there until they were forbidden to do so by their parents. No one, not even the Shaws, had been down in those woods since Sandy was eight or nine years old. In fact, Mr. Shaw told Sandy's dad a few weeks ago that he wished he could sell that property and that he was only keeping it because his great grandparents were born, raised, died, and buried in what were these forests—and now only these woods—in Jesup.

The two older girls knew that a pond could be dangerous to a lonesome little girl.

Sandy squatted so that she and Jello were face to face. She loved this precious little bundle of energy. Jello looked into her friend's face with wide-eyed innocence and told Sandy that she climbed the fence because she wanted to get some specimens for her microscope and, before she knew it, she had gone too far. She put her little palms against Sandy's cheeks so tenderly.

"I won't go again, San," Jello promised. "Please don't be mad. I'm sorry."

Sandy put her arms around Jello's soft little body and squeezed her.

"OK, baby. Just let that be your last time, OK?" Sandy said, kissing her. "Never, *ever*, go where there are no grown-ups!"

Jello put her fingers into her mouth but quickly pulled them out again.

"Hey, I almost forgot, San. There *was* a grown-up out there. He was cooking, but he never spoke to me. He just stood there and looked at me."

Julie, who had been standing beside Sandy, squatted now and asked, "Honey, what did he look like?"

Jello looked at Sandy and then back at Julie. "He was tall and had straw hair."

Seeing that Jello looked frightened, Sandy stopped her. "Oh, baby, it's OK. We just don't want you ever to go out there again without a grown-up . . . . I mean one that you *know*. Alright, now? We came out here to play ball. So let's go to it!"

Later, while Jello slept, the girls sat in the den watching TV. At 8:00 p.m. Carnell came home, and the girls left, but not before telling him about Jello's little adventure.

As Julie and Sandy walked down the street, a carload of boys passed them on their way to the center. Since the girls would have to pass by Sandy's house to get to the park, they stopped there long enough to freshen their makeup and to put on some scented oils.

All day during the summer, the rec center DJ played rap, reggae, and just plain good music. It was almost 8:30 p.m. when Sandy and Julie got there.

Also present was a local band that pumped the sounds and played all of Jodecis' latest songs. Then there was a girls' group that was slammin'. They sang like S.W.V. The boys' group was just starting on the first song, and, right away, Sandy was pulled off the park bench to dance.

Nadine was there in her green 'Daisy Duke' shorts with platform shoes and green Jerri Curl wig.

Sandy danced until her feet hurt. As she made her way to the concession stand for a Diet Coke, she ran smack into Alvin Parker, Jr. He was a hunk and (as Robin would say) 'ga-ga' over Sandy. And even Sandy, who had never had time for Al before, was glad to see him tonight. Usually, he was a royal pain. He even used to show up in church when he knew Sandy would be there.

Verma just loved him, but he only had eyes for Sandy. Verma had never allowed herself to believe that this hunk of man was merely nice to her because she was Sandy's friend. After all, she, not Sandy, was the fly girl from the city.

Right now, Sandy just smiled at him. Out of kindness or pity, Sandy decided to save a dance for him. After Alvin told her that he would break his nose if he couldn't get her to dance with him, she told him she'd meet him back at the bandstand. Sandy remembered a conversation she and Alvin shared last year.

She had just finished reading Alex Haley's *Queen*, and she and her friends had stayed after school to watch a football scrimmage. Sandy, Alvin, James Shipman, Robin, Julie, and a few other cheerleaders had stayed over also.

Robin remarked that, out of the fifteen cheerleaders, only three were black. Alvin said it was four black girls because the one girl that Robin thought was Italian was indeed a black girl with a fair complexion.

"Did you ever notice," Alvin had reflected aloud, "that most white girls are shaped different than you loud-mouthed sisters? Your backs stop at a point and twin globes flower out—round, swollen, supple, and tender." Alvin looked serious, but to lighten the mood he popped Robin with a towel he had around his neck. Robin put her hand out but failed to block the stinging blow.

"Who asked you for an opinion, asshole?" Robin joked. She and Alvin had dated off and on, but Robin was more like a sister to most of the guys she went out with.

"Actually," Alvin continued, "it's not just an opinion, Robin. Back in the days of slavery, the white men could hump any black female he wanted; he didn't want the pale, flat bodies of the white woman. When the slave master did touch his woman, he was finished in two, maybe three, minutes! She laid under him and just took it. When he had sex with his slave, she didn't just lay there—unless she wanted her ass whipped! She had to work those 'glute' muscles and thighs. All he had to do was lie in her and drool. This happened all the time because black females were born with round, tight butts. Call it evolution if you must, but a white woman is in no way equal to a black woman physically. You know, I had an old white man tell me that, 'if you haven't been in a black pussy, you haven't been in a pussy yet!'"

Sandy remembered flinching at that vulgar word, but that was one of the things she liked about that boy. She thought he was blunt, down-to-earth, and mature.

Sandy bought her soda and went back to the park benches. The boys' group sounded just like Jodeci. Alvin was dancing with Laura Horton, and Sandy was a little envious.

Laura was the youngest of a family of twelve children, ten of whom were girls. The only other girl in town as spoiled and pretentious as Laura was Mekka Tucker, Sandy's uncle Bruce's only child.

Mekka drove a 1992 yellow Geo Tracker and Laura had a 1991 Ford Escort. These two girls didn't get along—at all! they were always trying to outdo each other. Sandy wasn't crazy about either girl, but typical of Sandy, she kept it to herself. She smiled and spoke to them when she had to, but she was a pro at looking through people she didn't particularly like. She just pretended they didn't exist. If she were put on the spot, she would act nonchalant until the pest moved on.

Suddenly, someone pumped up the music, and everyone was headed for the dance floor to do the electric slide. Someone grabbed her hand and pulled her up to the platform. Afterwards, she was drenched in sweat and had danced to three songs. The last one was Whitney Houston's "I Will Always Love You."

"No way. I'm not dancing another dance!" Sandy sighed.

She was standing in the rec's ladies room when she heard the news: Annette Smith—

one of the twin sisters of Mrs. Miller, the Tuckers' neighbor—had been killed in a car accident around noon. All around Sandy, kids stood in shock; some looked scared and others didn't know what to feel.

Over at the bandstand, she heard Goat say that he had been wondering why the cops hadn't bugged them tonight; the accident must be the reason. The dance was cut short and the park cleared. Sandy and her friends quietly walked home.

Richard and Olivia were sitting at the kitchen table when Sandy walked in. If anyone knew the story, her dad would. She kissed them both and sat in a chair next to her mom and across from her dad.

"Dad, what happened?" She could plainly see that he was shaken, his hands folding nervously in front of him. She didn't have to ask him if he were at the scene; it was obvious that he had been. He gave her a few details and kept shaking his head. It was her mother who spoke first to the real matter at hand.

"Sweetheart, your dad was given reason this week to believe that you were the girl seen in the car with two of the boys that were killed today." Richard looked ashamed.

"Sandy," he said, "when I looked up into that tree, for five horrible seconds I thought I was looking at you."

Sandy's heart went out to her dad, but she just sat and looked at him. She started to speak, but her mother stopped her with a hand gesture. "Let your daddy speak, Sandy."

He took a deep breath and went on. "You know, Sandy, when it became obvious that the body in that tree wasn't you, my knees buckled. I was so relieved that I didn't feel any other emotion for a long time. When the shock wore completely off, I felt empathy for the Millers, but I only wanted to rush home and demand that you tell me what you are doing when you leave and stay away for hours. But I know you, San, and I would be wasting energy unless I was willing to put you in restraints. So, I'll ask you again: are you in trouble?"

Sandy shook her head and softly whispered, "No, daddy."

"Is what you are doing dangerous?"

"No."

"Will you tell us about it *soon*?"

Sandy heard the tears in her daddy's voice. Before he could say another word, Sandy flew around the table and into her dad's arms. They both cried. Olivia knew they needed to be alone for a moment, so she walked out onto the front porch.

She and Richard had already gone to the Millers to offer their condolences, but now she went over again.

Mr. and Mrs. Miller were fairly calm. It seemed that the Miller's knew that Annette was hanging around with those Pope boys but they didn't know why. It turned out that the 20 gallons of white liquor that was found was being carried to Brunswick, Georgia for sale. Annette had been having a lot of money on her of late, Jeanette too, for that matter. Now, Jeanette was in her room asleep. Old Doctor Jones had given her a sedative. Mr. Miller's mother had taken the four youngest children home with her, except for the baby.

Mrs. Miller had been crying. Her eyes and nose were red and she was subdued but needed to talk.

"Livia, when I found out that Annette was hanging around with that Pope boy from Hinesville, I begged her to stop. Then when that red-haired one was found dead, I begged her to get away before it blew up in her face. She laughed and showed me all the money she had. She told me I should be trying to talk Jeanette into hanging around with the Popes, too."

Olivia knew that the red-haired boy found dead, poisoned with liquor, had been Clifford Pope. The bodies recovered in the accident today had been identified as Leon Edward Pope, Ernest Hillson, Curtise Hillson, and, of course, Annette.

Olivia gave Mrs. Miller a firm, warm hug and told her to call her if the need arose; she would be right across the street.

Olivia walked across Pine Street at a snail's pace and then sat on her porch. She was so deep in thought that she barely heard and acknowledged the "Good Evening" that Mr. Cogdell offered as he passed by.

Sandy and her father were still talking; they were curled up on the sofa like a couple of best friends, so Olivia didn't want to interfere.

From all she had taken in of this illegal whiskey case, it was all finally starting to make sense: the Pickett boys—Billy, Charles, and Pee Wee—were the ones caught stealing copper tubing for pipes and coils to put on a still. The copper tubes, she knew, were used as a cooling device after the ingredients had been heated for condensing the vapor. The tube supplied cold water to the condenser. It was sometimes called a "worm," and if the wrong worm were used, lead could bleed into the outlet and poison the whole batch, making it deadly. The theft of the tubing itself proved that they had a still somewhere.

The Popes of Hinesville always had stills. If one was found and destroyed, they had five or six spread out elsewhere. Olivia and Richard surmised that the Popes had somehow found out that the Picketts had put up a still in Jesup, somewhere, and had taken away a lot of the Pope's customers.

Clifford Pope was probably poisoning the Pickett still and was caught red-handed. He could've been force-fed the lead-laden whisky he intended to put in the Pickett still. That would explain the bruises found on his body and the whisky-drenched clothes. But no arrest could be made without proof.

After Climmy's funeral, the Pope family reorganized itself and redoubled its effort to eliminate the competition.

Somehow Mrs. Miller's sister Annette—an old friend of the Pickett boys—had gotten into the middle of it all, as a spy or counter spy,

Olivia couldn't be sure. But, as Mrs. Miller had attested, Annette was being paid well for her involvement, whatever it was.

Now, an accident had taken the life of another Pope boy, and Daddy Pope, with only one son left, would be dead set on revenge.

Everywhere in black Jesup, the people were somber. Suppers were eaten in silence, showers were taken without songs, and babies were bathed without bubbles or toys. Temporarily, the streets were empty. The darkness on this August night seemed to cover the town with a question. But the crickets still sang, the frogs still croaked, and the mosquitos buzzed, still.

Whenever something like this happened to someone as young as Annette, the question that the darkness asked was, "Who's next?"

Tonight, Olivia served dinner late, even for a hot August night. Olivia walked into her kitchen to serve the leftovers she had warming in the oven. She had already made a salad and it was sitting in the salad crisper in the fridge. Ironically, dinner was more relaxed in the Tucker house tonight than it had been in a long time. Everybody missed 'ol' big head' Larry, but he'd be back soon enough.

Olivia had been left with a list of things he didn't mind her picking out for school. Olivia had asked Sandy to pick out some 'Shaquille O'Neal's', but Sandy had assured her mother that even Olivia couldn't mess that up, and Olivia didn't: the shoes she picked up were black, white, and blue, with black soles and pumps. When Richard saw them, he had given Olivia a wink and a thumbs-up sign.

Now, Olivia called from the kitchen, "I've got some chocolate cake! Anybody game?"

Richard swore he couldn't eat another bite, but when Olivia said she'd just put it in the freezer for Larry, Richard jumped up and grabbed a slice.

After lolling in the living room for a while, Sandy stood up and stretched. This was the time of night that she looked forward to, but she saw a brief shadow cross her daddy's face, and her mom wouldn't look up.

She went to kiss her mom and then her dad and then, with nothing to say, she climbed the twelve steps to her bedroom and closed and locked the door.

Because of the racial tension in the air—another Pope boy dead and the black Picketts seemingly at the center of it—Sandy had been thinking all night about "The Tiger Syndrome," a kind of fable her father had once told her. She remembered her father's words:

"Imagine a tiger at the zoo. Now, he is locked in a very strong and sturdy cage. You have walked by that animal many times, and he has always just stared at you; he sits in the back of his cage with his front paws crossed and his tongue hanging out, panting. In fact, he seems to be smiling with that big pink tongue just a flappin'.

"You've passed that cage ten or twenty times, and sometimes he even cocked his head sideways once or twice as you passed, seeming to recognize you and invite you closer. So, you grow accustomed to his friendliness and, thinking he is just so sweet, one day you stick your whole dumb arm in the cage thinking, 'He'll lick me and I'll get a chance to pet him.'

"Well, that sweet animal tries to tear your arm off at the elbow. I mean, you never heard so much growling and ruckus at one time in your life. Why, that damn tiger acts as if he hates your guts!

"Well, honey, that tiger is 'white folks', and 'black folks' is the visitor at the zoo, so watch out! Don't hate the tiger, by any means, but don't be fooled either. Love it, but pity it also. Love it as much as it seems to hate you."

Sandy would take this parable to the grave with her.

Her father had explained—and even at sixteen she had come to see—that the majority of white people that hated black people were whites that were poor or who had grown up poor. These poor whites were looked down upon by the more fortunate whites who viewed the poor whites as the bitter lees at the bottom of the barrel.

These poor whites, in turn, needed to place someone or something lower than themselves, because, even during slave times, the rich white man's slaves looked down on what they called 'poor white trash'. But, when slavery was abolished, there were blacks wandering around just like poor whites, wondering where the next meal would come from. So, the poor white trash finally had someone lower than themselves—blacks.

With these thoughts in her mind and the prayer that all would remain peaceful in Jesup, Sandy thought maybe she should set her alarm to wake her up about midnight, but it was almost midnight now. She was too excited to take even a short nap, even though she was tired.

"I'm going back now," she resolved. "Now!"

CHAPTER NINE

Charlotte awakened with a start.

It took her a few minutes to remember where she was and why.

Late last night, Teresa had come into the toolshed with a kerosene lamp and, fortified with expensive wine, she tore the beautiful gown from Charlotte's body as she raged about Charlotte's shortcomings and how she would be watching as her naked body would be savaged the next day by the horsewhip.

But as the slave stood there—head bowed and body glistening in the pale yellow light of the lamp—Teresa changed her mind and told Gail, who attended her, to go get one of the girls' old and ugly grey frocks for Charlotte to wear while being whipped. Teresa refused to have another white man look upon this luscious body—at least not until she saw the whip cut it to ribbons!

After putting on the thin frock, Charlotte was left alone, sitting on a bale of hay, for the rest of the night waiting to be taken to the whipping post.

The next morning, from behind some tools, someone whispered Charlotte's name. To the slave's left was Sandy, the 'Black Magic Lady'.

Charlotte was relieved beyond words to see her. She began to sob as she greeted Sandy. "I been prayin' for God t' sen' me some help. Dah las' time a slave girl got whipped, she almost died!"

She fell into soothing arms as Sandy neared her, crying and shaking uncontrollably. Sandy calmed her down and got the whole story from her.

"I'm sorry, Charlotte. It seems I've gotten you into more trouble than done you good." Sandy's eyes grew damp. "I should have known better!"

"Hesh up, gal!" Mammy Tulla's unmistakable voice thundered, breaking the shed's stillness.

Both girls jumped and nearly bolted. Charlotte had asked Mammy to bring her a ball of cotton to insert into her vagina to absorb her monthly flow of blood. Sandy couldn't believe that these women had invented the tampon even before disposable pads!

Sandy learned later that the slave woman often used a tightly rolled ball of cotton during menstruation because she was not given any sort of panty. Even if she had tried to use torn-up linen like her white counterpart, the linen wouldn't have stayed in place; so, out of necessity, the crude but effective tampon was invented.

But now wasn't the time to wonder about that.

With her hand on her hip, Mammy looked ready to have at both of them. "Child, yo was sent heah by de Lord! Ebby slabe on dis plantation is thankful you is heah. We is eatin' betta, and yo sure should see da new dresses we's cuttin' out a dat cloth you gib us. An' dis heah in my hand ain't no cotton boll. Did ya forget? It a new thing. Yo should show her how to do it. Looks ta me like ya do it da same way."

Sandy showed Charlotte how to use the tampon and then sat down next to her.

"Charlotte, I promise you that not one hair on your head will be touched today." The young slave started to cry again.

"How?" Charlotte pleaded. "How are you gon help me if dey cain't see yo?"

Sandy stood up and stood the young slave up next to her. "Listen, damnit, I said I would protect you, and I will!"

The whipping was to take place at noon; the overseer was to do the whipping, and Lady T. stressed that she wanted to be there to direct the number of lashes since Coard may or may not be attending.

Sandy kept Charlotte company and made her laugh. She told her about cars and trains and made her visualize a big iron bird called an airplane that people get in and go from one place to another.

"They eat meals and sleep and even go to rest rooms on these planes."

She told Charlotte about Jello, and, when she finished, Charlotte said she felt like she knew the little girl already. Sandy let Charlotte watch as she wished in a cigarette lighter, a mirror, a bag of chipped ice, six small birthday candles and a polaroid camera and put them in her burlap bag. Sandy had plans—

Voodoo plans, she told Charlotte—to protect her and the other slaves from ever being mistreated again.

Charlotte warily glanced at the foreign objects popping in to the barn out of thin air!

At 12:00 noon, Stoney came to get the 'doomed one'.

When he saw the 'ghost' woman, his eyes grew round. "Sandy, yo cain't help dis girl now. Dat Missy T. aways hated dis girl more din any slave she own. I know you wants ta help, but you cain't."

Sandy walked over to the young man and with tears in her eyes laid her hands on his cheeks. "Stoney, I swear to you that before my deadline is up, I will have done what I've wanted to do all my life—to make life easier for someone in this damned era! Just do what you have to do and I'll do the same."

As Stoney walked out of the barn with Charlotte in tow, Charlotte looked back only once, and she had a smile on her face.

Outside, Sandy watched passively as Stoney chained Charlotte into position.

The spectacle was to be viewed by everyone—by the field workers, by slaves that worked in slave quarters and in the gardens, by the blacksmiths, and by the fancy house slaves with whom Charlotte worked and sometimes lived. The latter were ordered to be there to remind them that they weren't exempt from such harsh punishment.

Mr. Charley, the overseer, took his place.

When Sandy walked out with her bag of tricks, every slave present froze in place. You could hear a gnat pissing on cotton.

Mr. Charley and Lady T. sniffed the air as she passed before them. Sandy was wearing Poison again. Mr. Charley's hand was in position, and Master Coard, who decided to attend, seemed about to nod his head when Sandy walked in front of him with the mirror in his face.

Coard almost swallowed his pipe.

He had been standing there looking so handsome with that mop of hair combed back and wearing a mustard-colored shirt complete with cuffs and links. His ecru riding pants were brushed suede and they fit like a glove.

The slaves that were close to him almost pissed in their pants.

As Coard was regrouping to give the order again, San put a fistful of crushed ice down the back of his shirt, and, as he danced around, she dumped another fistful down the front of his suede riding breeches.

Lady T. and Mr. Charley stared with open horror and fear. It was then that Sandy looked down and saw her own shadow. Not only could the free people smell her and hear her, they could also see her shadow!

Mr. Charley got back on his horse and stood beside Bubba. His eyes were glued between the shadow of a woman on the ground and his boss dancing around and digging in his pants at something that hit the Georgia red clay like hail.

Then Sandy climbed on the horse with Mr. Charley and put the cigarette lighter so close to his nose that the flames singed his lashes and nose hairs. Then she hopped off and out of the way.

This good old boy bucked like a greased stallion with a thumbtack under his saddle!

He jumped back to the ground, spooking his horse, and then bounced around frantically holding on to his nose. After she yelled in his ear, "Don't move!" Sandy then lit two birthday candles and put them one at a time into his pants, one in back and one in front.

But when those candle flames hit his bare behind and burned those pubic hairs, he had to move! He ran helter skelter toward the stream at the back of the slave quarters holding his burning rear end with one hand and his bulbous nose with the other. He rounded the corner of the first slave cabin and stripped to his bare skin.

Sandy turned to Coard again. Reaching into her bag of tricks, she pulled out the already loaded polaroid camera and stood in front of the husband and wife, who, incidentally, huddled together like frightened children. Sandy knew she didn't need to use the flash, but she did. All the Worthinwoods saw was this black contraption the size of two hands floating in the empty space before their eyes.

Sandy was tickled because every move she made with the camera was followed by four terrified eyes.

Lady T. almost fainted when Sandy giggled. And then, FLASH!—the white light sparkled in front of their faces. The next thing the couple saw was a white card slipping out of the machine. To their horror, the solid white card started to change into the very image of themselves. This time Teresa did faint and the mighty Master Coard hauled ass.

As Charlotte cried softly, Sandy told Stoney to untie her great, great grandmother and take her to get some toiletries from the cache so she could shower.

The young slave was clearly in shock.

When she was about to pass Sandy, she freed herself from Stoney and fell to her knees and wrapped her thin arms around Sandy's legs. "Thank yo, thank de Lawd fo his grace."

Sandy untangled Charlotte and stood her up. "I told you not to panic, didn't I?" Sandy whispered.

The other slaves had formed groups and everyone was talking and asking questions. Sandy sent the candles and other 'magic stuff' to the cache with Bubba. She heard commotion behind her and was relieved that Teresa had been revived and was being looked after by Mammy Cinda.

Sandy walked over to see if she could help and was rebuked by Mammy. "Now hesh, chile. Don't go runnin' yo mouth. Lemme get my missus together and back to de house."

Teresa was in a semi-dazed state and looked at Mammy with a furrowed brow. "Mammy, I can't take no more! What's goin' on? I *know* there is a ghost heah. Who is she, Mammy?"

Before Mammy could open her mouth, Sandy piped, "I'm not someone you can see, but

I'm a spirit that will come back for you if you should ever hurt another slave for any reason. Do you hear me?"

Teresa was looking at Mammy's lips while Sandy was speaking. "Mammy, yew wouldn't dare talk to me like this!" she shouted at Cinda. "It wasn't yew, Mammy." Now she was trying to sit up. "Your lips never moved! What in the hell is this, Mammy?" Sandy saw Teresa's face blanch again.

Sandy addressed the Mistress of Worthinwood again. "Teresa, don't be frightened. Unless you hurt someone else or have someone else hurt them, you won't have to worry. I'll be wherever you are, Teresa, always over your shoulder," Sandy said in a soft monotone. Reaching into her big sloppy shirt, she pulled out a tiny, battery-operated tape recorder that she had used to record Teresa's voice earlier. She put it on pause and sat it in Mammy's lap.

"Teresa, I don't want to hurt anyone. The reason I'm here is to prove that black people and white people can be equal. Blacks are slaves, true enough, but not forever. Like other races, we also bleed when we are cut, and the blood is red like yours. We hunger when we fast, again like you, and we hurt when pain is inflicted."

Sandy punched the button, and Teresa's voice seemed to echo in this virgin land where no other apparatus used batteries of any kind.

Listening to her voice on this machine put the icing on the cake.

Still not understanding what was happening, the infamous Teresa put her fists to her mouth and sobbed. Teresa had never even thought of the peons living on Worthinwood Plantation in any way equal to her or any other whites of class, but in its truth, she realized that the only way to keep a slave a slave was to keep him dumb.

Looking down at Sandy's shadow, she sniffed. "I've never believed in this voodoo trash, but I'm not dreaming this, am I Mammy?"

These were niggers talking to her. This was even a nigger witch!

Accepting Mammy's help to get on her feet, she quickly brushed away any attempt at help from the slave. Once she was on her feet, her scurrilous attitude said it all. The metamorphosis was astounding. Teresa brushed the red sand from her clothes, and, with the air of a queen, she followed her nose into the mansion.

Sandy walked across the fine dirt yard to the female slave quarters.

The room had windows, one on each side, but even in the midday sun the dorm was dark, only a few slanting rays of sunshine finding their way into the room.

The fireplace was the focal point of the room; it served as a heater in winter, a light, and a source to cook foods, as was a pot belly stove. Stacked on the hearth was a pole of pots and pans, and on one side of the hearth was a 'potato hole' used to keep yams hard and firm all year long. Straw mats lined the walls.

Gail was kneeling in front of Charlotte as she sat in one of the dorm's two broken and rickety chairs. When Gail wasn't performing her job as a chambermaid or maid in the big house and wasn't made to stay there, she could be found in the dorm or working the gardens—there was always slave work. After working all day long for the masters, she had to come back like any other slave and do her daily chores in the slave quarters. Her mama and two sisters lived there.

As soon as she was old enough to walk, Gail had been sent to the big house.

She was adept at chopping weeds from around the produce, be it corn or tobacco. She learned to sucker the broad-leaved plants, and, when harvest time came, she cut hay and stacked dried cornstalks. The days were long and chores were hard. Sickly children or weak ones were tormented by the overseer's whip.

Only the strong survived, and Gail and Charlotte were survivors.

The blisters on Gail's hands had long ago turned into callouses. Charlotte had been spared the hard, hard labor because of her extraordinary beauty.

Now, having come so close to being dehumanized with a whip, she seemed incapable of comprehending it. Gail kept talking to her and holding her hand and Sandy cleared the distance between the door and the corner Charlotte was sitting in. Again, she felt tears cruise down her face as she looked at Charlotte.

Putting a hand on Gail's shoulder, Charlotte smiled and nodded to Sandy to let her know she was thanked for being there. Sandy smiled through her own tears.

Sandy swallowed around the lump in her throat. "Charlotte I must get going now, the overseer's signal rang long ago, but I wanted to make sure you were taken care of—you know, like a shower, shampoo, and a soft robe and slippers. I saw several women and girls with their empty containers going into the glades to re-stock."

Charlotte squeezed Sandy's hand. "What gone happen to us when you is gone? I be scared, Sandy. All us slabes be scared when you gone. All us!"

Sandy wanted to wrap her in her arms and assuage her fear by telling her that she had to survive this because five years later she would give birth to her first daughter, and she would do so in good health and happiness. Sandy also wanted to tell Charlotte that she was going to live to a ripe old age. But she didn't. She just kept smiling and promised that no harm would come to any of the slaves.

"I'll be back at noon tomorrow." Sandy promised to spend the best part of the day with them.

She bade farewell and arrived home at 8:00 a.m. Exhausted, she peeled her clothes off and crawled in between the smooth pecal sheets and was asleep before her head touched the "Downy" scented pillow. . . .

Richard had arrived at the courthouse to clock in at 7:00 a.m. and stopped in the break room for coffee and to read the daily paper.

The headlines jumped out at him—"Four Killed in Train/Auto Accident." It went on to give the public the names, ages, and addresses of the victims. The paper explained that the three white males were from Hinesville and the young lady was from Jesup. It went on to say that 20 one-gallon milk cartons of moonshine were found in the wreckage.

Richard had been one of the policemen that accompanied Mr. and Mrs. Clifford Pope Sr., Curt Hillson, and Mr. and Mrs. Miller to identify the bodies of their loved ones. All had gone as expected until Clifford Pope Sr. put his fist through a glass pane in the courthouse and swore to avenge his son's death. He had just buried Climmy, and now he was going to repeat the process with another son. Mr. Pope only scratched the skin of his fingers, but he paid for the glass.

Richard was not trying to second guess anything, but he knew that money and territory were somehow responsible for everything happening. It was more than just conjecture on his part. When he discovered that the girl riding with the Pope boys wasn't his daughter, a great weight was lifted from his shoulders, and he found he was able to do his job better.

Richard surmised that the Picketts had a still somewhere in Jesup though it hadn't been found yet. The problem started when the Picketts took over half the Popes' customers. In order to get their customers back, the Popes would have to drop their prices much lower than the Picketts. Driving through Jesup was the only way for the Popes to get to the tiny little towns and sleepy hollows and their customers, but the Picketts weren't having any of that. Many times, the Popes tried coming through Jesup, and they were either cut off by the Picketts, waylaid by the tipped-off highway patrol, or arrived at their appointments only to be told that they were too late and too expensive.

Years ago, when the Popes started making bootleg liquor for sale, their lifestyles changed sharply. They got better cars, trucks, and homes, and they dressed in tailor-made clothes. Now, seemingly out of the blue, they had competition.

Richard theorized that Climmy Pope was spying on the Picketts with someone's help to infiltrate the organization and to get the locations of the stills so they could be destroyed or poisoned. Annette was planted by the Picketts as a spy, uncovered the infiltration of the Pope boy, and he was destroyed. The Picketts probably felt that they had no choice but to kill Clifford Pope once he knew the location of the stills. Annette was used by the Pickett crew to keep them informed about the Popes. Richard was pretty sure that the Popes would have discovered the girl's double-cross and kill her sooner or later.

Throughout the years, the Popes were suspected in several murders, but they were always careful to leave nothing for anyone to trace back to them. Even under the strict scrutiny of a task force, the Pope case had proven to be a tough one to break, but somehow Richard was sure this time that this case could and would be resolved.

By 11:30 a.m. Richard could tell that it was going to be a slow day. But at 2:30 a call came in that put pain and fear in the hearts of almost everyone in Jesup—white and black, old and young, male and female.

Richard was sitting in his patrol car with his radar on waiting to catch a speeder out on Highway 30 when he got the call. He was to go out to 582 West Pine Street. A mother had called to report her five-year-old daughter missing.

Jello had been restless that morning. She played school with her dolls and had a tea party. At 11:30, she took what must have been the world's shortest nap. Thirty minutes after Carolyn put her down, she heard her talking to her dolls. Carolyn took a few minutes to put her daughter on her knee and gave her a big healthy hug and explained that the thesis she was completing had a deadline and in order to get her master's degree, she had to meet it.

Jello put her arms lovingly around her mother and gave her a hug right back. She watched her mother fix her lunch and was satisfied that she had a legitimate reason for being lonesome. She took the sad blue bows from her doll's hair, but kept the lonesome yellow one in. But right in the back under the doll's fat braid in the very back of its head sat a blue bow.

Yelling to her mommy that she was going into the backyard to play, Jello went outside. Carolyn heard the screen door slam and realized Jello hadn't eaten lunch—it was still on the table. But she needn't have worried. Jello dashed back into the kitchen, grabbed her bologna and cheese sandwich and a napkin, and dashed back out.

Jello had sat in her sandbox for a little while. She had wrapped her sandwich up in the napkins after biting into one of the halves and putting it on the picnic table. She sat playing with a set of toy cars and trucks that once belonged to Carnell when he was a tiny tot. They were called "Putt-Putts." She would push one of the little wooden toys along the top of some flat boards she had laid out like roads. She had them laid end to end, but she kept running out of 'roads.' She was too hot to keep running back to move them to the front in leapfrog fashion.

Picking up her doll, she sat down on one of the boards. Reaching into her pocket, she took out some lonesome bows and put two more into the doll's hair. Jello knew she wasn't supposed to go beyond that fence, but she was so lonesome she felt like crying. She looked up at the patio door and wondered if her mom would see her if she left the yard. No sooner had she thought that than her mother came to the back door and asked her if she wanted some lemonade. It was about 12:45. Jello knew this was her mom's way of checking on her.

She ran to the door and got the frosty glass of pink lemonade from Carolyn's outstretched hand.

She asked if she could call Sandy. "Sandy'll come-n-play with me, Mommy. Please?" Carolyn told her she would see Sandy soon enough because Sandy was supposed to sit for Jello at 6:00 p.m.

Carolyn's heart went out to her pretty, perky little cherub, but she had a deadline to meet, and she intended to make it.

Jello gave her mother her 'I'm okay' look and went back to her doll. It was 1:05 before Carolyn went back to the door to check on Jello.

The gate was still locked, so Carolyn assumed her child was on the side of the house or up in the tree house. Carolyn checked and found both places empty.

Jello's doll was gone, the half of the sandwich that wasn't bitten by the child was gone, and the glass of lemonade was empty, the ice melting.

Carolyn began calling Jello. Not getting an answer, she ran through the house and into the rooms calling her. Out the front door and up and down the sidewalk she called and heard no answer.

She called her husband at work and was told to call the police; he was on his way home. After Carolyn was assured that the police were on the way, she called Carnell and he was coming home too.

Sandy had forgotten to unlock her bedroom door, so at 3:30 p.m. she was awakened by several sharp raps at the door. Sandy was in such a deep sleep that she sat straight up in the bed but didn't know what woke her up until she heard the knocking again. Glimpsing the clock, she saw it was 3:30!

Opening her bedroom door, she was face to face with her mother—but there was something else in Olivia's face besides the usual concern about her daughter's whereabouts or her 'withwhoabouts'.

"Mom?" Sandy asked as she stepped forwards and touched her shoulder. She felt a cold chill run down her spine as she watched her mother sit slowly on the bed and pat the space beside her for Sandy to sit too. The fear in Sandy was becoming a living thing and she felt like the air around her was becoming too thin to breathe.

"Sandy, Jello wandered away from her yard today and she hasn't been found yet. Carolyn saw her in the yard at a little before one o'clock, but then she just disappeared!"

Sandy's heart slumped, like a video running in slow motion, she remembered the incident that occurred when she and Julie sat with Jello. Didn't Jello say she had been down by the old barn? Maybe that's where she was now!

Sandy rolled over across the bed and grabbed the phone.

Olivia looked searchingly at her daughter as she dialed the Shaw number. Sandy put her finger to her lips to silence her mom. She relayed the entire incident to Mr. Shaw and told him she was on her way over there. She took a five minute shower as her mother told her what happened from the start. Sandy told her mother all about Jello's trip into the woods and why—sure that Jello had learned her lesson—she hadn't told anyone but Carnell about it.

"Mom," Sandy said as she put her brushed hair into a bun and smeared on some lipstick and eye make-up, "when we find her I'm going to spend more time with her, I promise."

Sandy felt tears sting and well up in her eyes, brushing them angrily away she declared never to be late getting to a sitting job with Anita again. But, Sandy thought, spinning around abruptly, she knew that wherever the little girl was, she was safe. Everyone loved her and she loved everyone.

Suddenly it occurred to Sandy that she could try to use the stick of ivory to wish Jello to safety.

Of course! As she groped for the amulet, the smell of lilacs filled the room and a force—like a gentle but firm hand—prevented Sandy from touching the ivory. "Oh, Grandma Mary, please, please let me help!" But Sandy understood, somehow, that the ivory was not to be used this way. She dropped her hands to her sides in resignation, and the smell of lilacs disappeared.

"Mom, let's go!" she yelled at her mother who had stepped into the hallway.

Olivia grabbed her handbag from the hat tree on the wall and Sandy's from the rack in the foyer. The two women had to walk only four houses down to get to the Shaw house.

The porch was full as was the sidewalk in front of the house and the yard.

There was already one posse that was out looking for Jello, and a posse was forming right then to cover the woods that stretched behind the house.

Mr. Shaw walked up to Sandy as she came into the living room and thanked her for calling them with the bit of info. He had doubts that she was down there because Jello would have called out or heard them calling her. But they were going in there anyway. Mr. Shaw sounded absolutely sure his child was somewhere safe and crying because she was lost. He had an 'it's OK' attitude and a slight smile for Sandy.

Carolyn was reclined on the sofa with her family and close friends.

The next time the Shaws would have that many people over would be at a wake and a funeral. . . .

Jello had been sitting on her big, half-filled beach ball. After she took some invisible bows out of her pocket, she put them in her doll's hair. Then, pausing, she cocked her little head. Tossing her velvety hair out of her face, she put more sad and lonely bows in and placed the happy bows in her pocket.

Picking up her Raggedy Ann doll, she used the wooden fence rails as a balance beam and the doll as a gymnast. Up and down she bounced the doll upside down and backwards. She was so busy balancing her doll that she didn't see the middle-aged white man approach the fence. The section of fence he approached was not visible through the back door or windows.

He hissed and motioned for her to come close.

Jello looked at the man. She was delighted at having someone to talk to. Her face lit up, and she skipped happily towards him. He kept his hands behind his back and asked her name. She replied and asked him his.

He told her his name was Pudding. "Jello Pudding." This made Jello laugh.

The man's face relaxed, and he asked if her Raggedy Ann was her best friend, and she nodded. Jello's eyes danced as she affirmed this. But when the man showed her the Raggedy Andy doll he was hiding, she jumped up and down, making her curls bounce around her face and down her back.

"Can I hold him?"

The man took a step backwards and told her he had to take the doll to doctor's office for a check-up. "Wouldn't you like to go? It's not very far, and the two dolls can meet and talk together!"

Jello looked hard at the boy doll and asked if he were lonely like her and her dolly. It was obvious that this man had done his homework and had found out plenty about Jello and her doll.

Now, looking at her, he replied, "Yes, he is, but he can't play like other dollies until the doctor has checked him out."

Jello ran this through her head. She knew she was not allowed to talk to any strangers, much less leave the house with one. But hadn't she already seen him before? He was the man that was cooking down in the woods by the barn. He wasn't a stranger, but he was a grown-up. She held on to her doll and held out her little arms for him to lift her across the fence. His straw-like hair hid the evil lurking in his eyes as he bent down to pick her up.

"We must go through the woods to get to the doctors and fairies that treat dolls, especially Raggedy Anns and Andys."

Had Jello looked back into his face, even in her innocence, she would have seen the wicked, cold deadness in his eyes.

The man had done evil before. Even his IQ of eighty-nine told him that this was easy, and he wouldn't have to do away with an awkward, bulky body. He put Jello down when the whiskey still was in full view.

When Jello turned around to ask a question, the man's large, sausage-like fingers reached down and picked the little girl up by the neck. Between his index finger and thumb, he lifted her until only the very tips of her tiny Nikes brushed the ground.

Jello's little arms flayed wildly as she struggled to breathe. His intentions were to hang her in this fashion, but he was squeezing too hard and felt her neck snap, so he tossed her little body as far as he could.

Jello landed on her back with blood pouring from her nose and mouth. He knew she would be dead in seconds.

He watched fascinated as Jello brought her left hand up and put her index and middle fingers into her mouth. It was minutes before she shuddered and died.

Kicking leaves and pine straw over her, he picked up the Andy doll from the pile of poison ivy it fell on and left with it hidden under his shirt.

The posse was gone five minutes before the six young men were split to go three ways. Ten minutes later, Patrick Johnson, who was teamed up with Goat, spotted a red hair bow in a pile of oak leaves. Turning it over and over in his hand, he stood in one place and looked out at his surroundings. The barn was visible from where Goat and Pat stood. Pat saw what he hought was another bow under some leaves. Walking closer and bending to pick it up, he saw Jello. A sound close to a wounded animal's yelp came up from the pit of his bowel and tore its way from his mouth. Falling to his knees, Pat brushed the pine straw from the unresponsive face and lifted her into his arms.

Goat went to call the others and led them back to Pat, who was still on his knees holding Jello.

One of the boys ran back to tell the others up at the house that the little girl had been found, but he failed to understand—perhaps subconsciously—that the child was dead. He ran inside to tell the Shaws. When he did, a near deafening shout of joy went up from the crowd as people poured out of the house.

Carnell Sr. grabbed his wife and rushed out of the back door with her. But something was wrong. The happy shouts of joy were dying down and replaced by sobs of "Oh my God!"

Patrick walked through the rear gate with Jello in his arms. Her arms and legs dangled loosely, and her neck was swollen. Her head lolled at a strange angle over his left arm. Pat's tears were falling on Jello as he sobbed silently. Carolyn fainted and was taken back inside.

Carnell Sr. had to be restrained as he screame Jello's name over and over. He dropped to hi knees, and tears streamed down his face. H looked to the heavens, and stretching out hi hands, he begged God to tell him why.

"Oh God, look! Look at my baby! Jesus Lord God, help me!" Carnell Jr. had been i the posse. He had heard the joyful shouts an came running, but before he even reached th gate, he saw his little sister laying in cousi Pat's arms. He heard a roar in his head. H wanted to run to Pat, but at the same time, h didn't think he'd be able to bear it if his littl sister were badly hurt. It seemed to him tha except for his kneeling and praying father wh was sobbing in the yard, everyone was watching him.

His legs shook as he closed the distanc between himself and the boy holding his bab sister.

A deafening noise roared in Carnell's head He didn't feel the hot tears streaming down hi face.

Pat put Jello in Carnell's arms when h reached for her.

Looking down into her face, Carnell smile a tremulous smile and told his sister that sh ıad better wake up and tell him where she put ıis journal. He talked to her and kissed her ıntil the roar in his head stopped. Carnell held ıis head back and screamed his pain at the top •f his lungs.

It was Julie that took the child so that the escue squad could take her. She handed the ·aby to be strapped on the gurney and then .rove the hurting family and another cousin to he hospital to identify the body.

It must've been 8:00 p.m. when a relative rought the three Shaws back from the hospi- al. They had been sedated with Valium and 'embutal. Carolyn's mother identified Jello nd helped get her daughter back into the house nd dressed her for bed; she couldn't get her to at anything, but she did drink some warm ılk. Carolyn's father took care of Carnell Sr. nd Junior. The ER doctors had prescribed xty valium and asked that they use them spar- gly.

Sandy and Olivia stayed over after every- ıe but the immediate family had gone.

Carolyn sat in bed with a blue house dress ı. Tonight, Sandy thought, if Jello were here, e would cheer me up. After all, that was llo's way, always ready with a smile.

Olivia and Sandy were the last ones to leave the Shaws. There were still people standing out on the sidewalks in front of their homes, talking. It was getting late and there was still no breeze to stir the humid heat that lay like a blanket around everything and everyone. Richard, who had left for home earlier, had returned to the Shaws to accompany his wife and daughter home.

There was something ominous about this night. Every mother and father of small children were heavy of heart, and, until something was done to prevent this from happening to another child, they would keep their own children close to them.

Sandy sat at the kitchen table and realized how just having her parents in the same room with her was a treasure. The pain of loosing Jello would've choked her by now if she hadn't had her parents' strength at the beginning to hold on to.

Olivia filled three tumblers with crushed ice and poured freshly made lemonade over them. As long as she lived, she would never let the love she had for Jello grow dim. Understanding how someone as full of love and energy as Jello was could die was a mystery.

This had been a very long day but Sandy knew she wouldn't be able to rest.

She thought about some of the things she and her little God-sister shared. Jello had more love to share with others than they knew what to do with. Until this summer, either Carnell or one of the child's parents was always at her beck and call. Carolyn's decision to work on her masters degree this summer took out a large chunk of time that she normally had spent with her daughter. Carnell had spread himself too thin and had to cut away some of the time he spent with Jello too. Carnell Sr. tried, but he was most often tired when he got home.

Sandy wished she had listened any time that Jello tried to talk to her. She wished she had spoken longer to Carnell that night about everything Jello had told her about the day she slipped off and saw the man that had straw hair; now it was too late.

Olivia and Richard were deep in conversation when the silent tears that kept overflowing and falling down Sandy's face turned into big, chest-heaving sobs. Olivia wasn't surprised. Sandy had been holding back, trying to be everyone's Rock.

"Well, even granite can be broken," Olivia said softly to herself.

She walked around the table and held her daughter until the body-wracking sobs subsided and left only a case of hiccups. Sandy drank a glass of water and felt better.

"Mama, why did this happen? Jello was so soft and innocent."

Sitting beside her daughter on the sofa where she had taken her, Olivia looked deep into Sandy's eyes. "Sandy, only God can answer that question. Look to Him for answers. I've long ago found that the Word is the way."

Without words, Sandy looked at her mother as she continued to speak. Olivia was always speaking to her family about the Word, about Jesus. She always made the bad things better. But, sometimes, her mother's words about Jesus could sting.

Sandy remembered a few months ago how she and Julie were sitting on the couch watching TV. Sandy noted that the white woman modeling swim wear would stick her butt out to make it look as though she had a cute, round behind. The cameraman seemed to have been trained to shoot the flat or low slung behind at a more favorable angle or not to dwell too long on this flaw.

Sandy was sure that when white women were in bathing suits, they all seemed to use

:he same pose with bended knees to poke out :heir behinds—or they wore panty pads made :or bikinis; they must certainly wear panty pads with other attire, Sandy remarked. Their rears ooked OK from behind, but when the women urned sideways, those seemingly round bot- oms flattened out. Sandy and Julie concluded hat, whenever a white woman displayed a gor- geous behind, it just couldn't be hers—just pad- ling!

Well, when Olivia overheard the girls' talk- ng, she came into the room and admonished hem both for sounding like bigots and racists. When she finished with them, the two girls felt ike newly chastised skinheads—like piles of hit!

Sandy and her parents talked for an hour nore before she kissed them and told them she vas retiring for the evening.

Her father stopped her.

"Sandy, are you any closer to ending these fter dark trysts? It's coming to the point where m gong to be asking for an explanation and utting a halt to this."

He was still concerned enough to be afraid or her and he had to voice it to her. He told er about the investigations that the Jesup

Police Department was conducting concerning the illegal liquor trade in Wayne County; and there were still the unsolved burglary cases.

As before, Sandy detected a pleading helplessness in his voice, but, again as before, she explained things to her parents as much as she dared—there was still Grandmother Mary's warning to consider, and Sandy had come too far to throw it all away.

"Trust me, mom and dad. Just trust me."

Her parents watched as she ascended the stairs. A silent terror saturated their spirits. And a real fear gripped Sandy for the first time.

But it was too late to turn back now.

CHAPTER TEN

Sandy left for Worthinwood Plantation at 11:00 p.m.

When she arrived, she walked over to Mammy Tulla's cabin.

The slaves in the fields were pulling up tobacco stalks in what felt like 105 degree heat. Mammy Tulla was sitting in an old rickety chair. Old Henry, a seventy-year-old slave everyone called Uncle Henny, was sitting at her feet with his feet dangling off the porch. He eyed Sandy warily as she approached the cabin. Keeping an eye on Sandy, he spit a fat stream of tobacco juice into the fine sand in the cabin's grassless yard.

He walked away with not even so much as a nod. Sandy had noticed that she wasn't received too warmly by the old man, and was told by Tulla that "Ol' Unca Henny don' have no use ’ ghos' or them haunts."

Mammy Tulla was glad to see Sandy, as usual.

"We's had us quite a day. Ain't seed hide no ha'r of nuttin' from de big house. Charlotte went on ta work dis mornin'. Hettie had a boy dis mornin' and with all de ruckus yestiday, none tol' ya dat Fanny had a girl dat mornin'. She inside tryin' t' get ready to go back to da fiel's. Dey let her rest yestiday, but she hurtin' t'day—she already done been out 'fore noon t'day, but her milk is come-n-fast and she come back here to put some warm campha on dem."

Sandy's knowledge of childbearing carried little beyond what she had been taught in school. She did not hear every word mammy spoke because she was trying to remember what she could do to help. She patted Mammy's hand and went on into the room.

Hettie was asleep, but the baby that lay on her chest with his thumb in his mouth was awake and squirming. Sandy stood there with a big smile on her face. This little boy that she had swooped in her arms needed things.

Grabbing her ivory with her free hand, she chanted in two bassinets, one with pink skirts with a white lace canopy and the other with the African colors—orange, green, black, and brown. Both beds had plenty of blankets, sheets, little satin pillows, and extra sheets.

She chanted in extra long and wide sanitary pads with belts and some nice soft pants and tops for them to work in. She reminded the other girls that the cache in the forest had plenty of women's shower shoes, baby clothes, baby and adult lotions, powders, soaps, cloth diapers, bottles, and pacifiers. All they needed to do was get someone to go get what they needed.

Sandy had not seen Fanny's baby yet, but as she scooped the babe into her arms, she gasped and her arms shook so badly she almost dropped the infant. Sandy laid the child in her new bed and stood staring at it. She didn't hear Fanny asking her what was wrong until Fanny touched her. Regaining her composure, she told her about Jello and that she had been the little girl's God-sister from birth. When Sandy began telling her in short about Jello's death, she couldn't hold back the tears and Fanny listened compassionately. Fanny's baby had a thick head of hair much like Jello's had been.

After Sandy dried her face on a new baby diaper someone gave her, she saw that several girls had sat on the floor around the old chair she had sat in and were looking at her in wide-eyed wonder. One of the women—a thick, dark woman called Cleta May—spoke up; she reminded Sandy of Ceily in *The Color Purple.* "Miz Sandy, we don' know how yo is feelin', but yo's got ebby thang in yo han'. To us, yo is rich. Ya ain' got no massa to beat yo an force hissef own yo. De lil' girl what died sound good enough to be in God's heaven by now. It seem to us dat yo care 'bout us 'n we want ta help ya feel better. Yo has a big heart, Miz Sandy, an' we knows yo is gonna see dat lil' girl gets put away nice 'n proper like. But if yo can come here from da future, it seem likely dat yo ought t' be able to goes to Heaven if yo wants ta."

Even in the midst of her pain, Sandy had to smile at the naivete of these girls.

She explained that getting to Heaven wasn't that simple. There were more than ten girls around her chair now. She needed to do something to keep her mind off Jello, so she told her audience about black people in history who invented great things.

She told them what a traffic light was and that a black man named Garret Morgan invented it. F. M. Jones invented the air conditioner, and she explained how it was used on days just like this to make the weather tolerable to live in. She told them of cars and airplanes, of trucks and subway trains.

"Hey! Why don't we have some sherbet right now!" Sandy explained what sherbet was and watched them squirm with anticipation as she started to chant in the cold confection. Of all the other wonders she had taken pleasure in watching the slaves devour, this one was special—strawberry, pineapple, and lime! Their delight was wonderful. Sandy watched them with much pleasure. Cleta said it was the greatest thing. She decided to put some away for Fanny who had to leave in a hurry because the overseer was coming towards the cabin. Before she left, she had asked Sandy to give her baby a name, and before she realized what she was doing, she named the baby 'Anita J'—the *J* standing for 'Jello'.

Sandy told Fanny to hobble on to the fields and leave Anita in her hands for the day. The delicious frozen lime sherbet they tried to save for Fanny to eat later turned into a slightly cool but creamy delight for her to drink.

Sandy helped the girls and Mammy clean up. They made three trips to the forest cache for Pine-Sol and other cleaning solutions. She could have chanted them to her, but she wanted them to get used to going to get supplies. Sandy became caught up in the moment; she chanted the nice little lacy curtains for the windows, area rugs for the floor, and shelves for the walls for the women to put clothes, books, and other knickknacks.

Smiling at Mammy Tulla, Sandy dusted her hands and folded her arms in front of her chest.

Mammy was grinning broadly when one of the dorm's occupants, a little brown girl called Bunchy with large eyes and very large lips and breasts saw Lady Teresa walking toward the cabin! She was coming across to the quarters with a man that was well known as a slave trader and auctioneer.

Before anyone could panic, Sandy assured everyone that nothing bad would happen to anyone nor would anyone be sold or beaten. When Caleb McCloud and Teresa walked up the newly swept steps, Lady T. noticed the wee button for the door bell chimes; she pushed it and scared the hell out of herself and Mr. Mac! She would've backed off the porch and hurt herself if he weren't there to catch her. He held tightly to her elbow as they entered the dorm.

He noted the absolute cleanliness of the porch and the nice smell. "How is it that this place is fit for quality white folks but is used and kept up by a bunch of nigger slaves?"

Teresa replied that she had forewarned him.

If they were surprised by the outward appearance, they were bowled over by what they saw inside: two white bassinets—one trimmed in pink lace and the other in colors—were sitting on a shiny new linoleum floor. The babes in these beds were clean and lay nestled in the softest, cleanest, fluffiest bed clothes either of them ever saw.

The adult beds were no longer corn shuck burlap mattresses on the floor. They were twin sized cots with real mattresses, and down pillows and sheets flat and fitted.

Hettie had fallen asleep again, but the noise with the door bell woke her up, and, when she saw Teresa, she sat up in the bed and made a feeble attempt to get out of bed but fell back weakly.

Teresa and Mr. Mac walked around with their mouths hanging open. Finally, Mac stopped and stood face to face with Mammy Tulla. There was something strange going on and he wanted to know why and what.

"Some of what I've heard and am seein' is wrong. There ain't no nigger alive got no bizzness wit nottin, like wha' you got righ' now. I'm going to whip every darky in here till I find out what I need to know. I'm even going ta whip Hettie and Fanny!"

A gasp went up from Sandy, and McCloud spun around.

"Wha'? Who said that?"

Hettie was crying softly now. She finally stood and was reaching for the new robe Sandy had given her when instead she turned on Sandy, and in a whisper Sandy told her that they didn't have to worry about getting whipped as long as she were there.

Hettie was unimpressed. "Now ebby one here is jumpy as a cat on a hot tin roof! Why don' yo go 'way! Go back t' yo life an' let us be! We ain't nebba gon ta be free an' all da magic yo do ta conja up deeze fine thangs cain't change us 'n make us free!"

Sandy knew that trouble was at hand and she had to move and move fast!

Before she'd figured out what to do, Mammy Tulla spoke up. "We's been eatin' good food and puttin' clothes on our backs. I nebba thought Ah'd a hear any slabe turn on de notion of a betta life!" The slaves totally forgot about the two whites in their midst.

But Mammy knew she was putting her life on the line, but she went on anyway.

Turning toward Mr. Mac, Mammy squared her plump shoulders and told him she was ready to be the first to be punished because if wanting some comfort in life was a cause for whipping, then so be it!

But Mr. Mac was still looking about trying to find a person that hettie had talked to. Mr. Mac was the first to regain his composure. Teresa forgot her southern etiquette and was hanging on dearly to Mr. Mac's shoulder and clinging to his shirt.

"I told you, Mr. Mac, didn't I? There are invisible deities floating around in this very air! They are protecting these darkies, don't you know! Look at these things in this room. I've never seen the likeness anywhere! Look what these little pickaninnies are nestled in! Look at that window," she said, pointing to the window closest to the door. "How in the world, Mr. McCloud, can this be?!"

Before either of them could speak again, Sandy spoke. She was standing right behind them and felt a warm breeze as Mr. Mac spun around and his arm passed through her invisible body.

"I am an invisible person only to those like you. Your hate has made a complete race of people feel sub-human. It's not just being a slave, Mr. McCloud, but it's how you treat them. You don't give them deodorant but you say they stink. You are afraid to let them learn to read because you know that they would be your equals, although I doubt that you yourself can read. Yet you call them stupid and dumb. They slave all summer in 100 degree weather and you call them 'those dusty black niggers!' There are no products available for the black females so you gather rags for them to cover up the 'wool' on their heads. You put them in chains tethered to a wagon to walk ten miles to be sold because you say they aren't worthy to ride a horse."

By now, Teresa had backed up to the door and was ready to flee.

Sandy walked over to her and told her to stay a little longer because it was going to get better. Hearing Sandy's voice so close again froze her in her steps. Sandy blew in Teresa's face and told her again that she was there to help not to hurt but that it was important for her and Coard to realize that the slaves on the Worthinwood Plantation would not be abused by slave owners, the slave traders, or anyone else anymore because Charlotte was her grandmother many time removed.

As a gasp went up from the slaves in the room, Teresa's knees buckled. . . .

Bright and early the next morning after the dreadful discovery of Jello's lifeless body, Olivia was ready to leave for the Shaw's house.

On her walk to the Shaws, Olivia looked at the fresh clear dew covering the sweet green grass and clover and low-hanging trees. Somewhere she heard a rooster crow. Two dragonflies played mating games in a ray of sunlight that streaked through the canopy of trees hanging over the sidewalk.

Two houses up, she saw Mrs. Myers with her antique pattern canvas purse on the bend of her arm walking briskly to the corner of Maple and Pine Streets to catch her ride to work. Even this early Mrs. Myers had her dip of snuff tucked behind her lip.

The Millers seemed to be getting over their loss pretty quickly because Jeanette was just pulling up to the house from last night. Olivia thought about how hard it would be for her to go on without Sandy or Larry. She had to be strong for Carolyn but it would be hard to tell

Carolyn how she must be strong and to go on with life when she felt like she herself was dying inside. Olivia felt hot tears well up in her eyes but brushed them away and stiffened her back.

Arriving at the Shaws at 6:00 a.m., she found Carnell and his father already dressed and drinking coffee with Carnell's grandfather and Grandmother Ada.

The grandparents had returned after everyone left the night before and stayed over in the guest room. After exchanging greetings with everyone in the kitchen, she went into the master bedroom where Carolyn slept. She said a silent prayer and quietly started laying Carolyn's clothes out for the day.

After she had done what she had set out to do in the bedroom, she was starting toward the kitchen when Carolyn called her name. Olivia turned around and smiled her good morning. She sat on the side of the bed and held her friend's hand. Both women were somber and Olivia felt at a loss for words.

Carolyn's face was still swollen and her eyes were little red slits. For lack of something to say, Olivia asked Carolyn to let her open the blinds and let some sun in. But with a pitiful little wail, Carolyn started sobbing, "No, no, no," over and over, moving her head from side to side on the pillow. "Don't open them, Livia; don't ever open them! How can the sun keep shining and people go on living without Anita to enjoy it?"

She sat up a little and Carolyn's heart went out to her.

Folded in Olivia's arms, Carolyn cried until she was limp with fatigue. Olivia washed her face with a cool washcloth and helped her bathe and put a soft lounger on. While Carolyn brushed her teeth, Olivia freshened the bed and fluffed the pillows. Afterwards, she softly and slowly brushed Carolyn's hair until Carolyn was sleeping once again.

The medicine that she was given the night before in the emergency room was still sedating her. Looking at Carolyn sleep, Olivia began to cry again. She honestly didn't think she would be strong enough for her God sister because she herself hurt, and the hot pain in her chest felt like lead. How? How could she soothe Carolyn when all she wanted was to sleep until this whole thing was over?

When she was sure Carolyn was asleep, she walked into the kitchen where the rest of the family sat. Carnell Jr. had taken another valium and was sleeping fitfully on the sofa now.

"Come on in here, Livia, and sit down for a cup of coffee," Carnell Sr. called to her when he saw her pause in the living room.

Sitting at the table, Olivia was given a cup of steaming coffee by Grandmother Shaw. The old woman had baked a butter cream pecan coffee cake early that morning; it smelled heavenly, but Olivia had no appetite.

Old Mrs. Shaw had always been a giant pillar of strength. She took everything with a firm grip and a steady look in the eye. She reminded Olivia of the serenity prayer: "God, grant me the Serenity to accept the things I cannot change, the Courage to change the things I can, and the Wisdom to know the difference."

There weren't many things that surprised or shocked Ada Shaw, but this thing had her shaky. Her eyes looked tired and tiny lines that Olivia had never seen before were visible in the corners of her eyes. Drawing a deep breath to steady herself, she told Olivia that the preliminary autopsy had shown that Jello had been asphyxiated and suffered a broken neck but the worst of it was that the swelling and bleeding indicated that she had not died immediately. A piece of yellow yarn was found in her right fist. Her black-haired doll was several feet away from where they found her body.

Ada Shaw continued to explain to Olivia. "The police and vice squad from Hinesville and Jesup Police Departments will be working on the case around the clock and have set up a 'hot-line' with a flyer saying: 'The Shaw family offers a $10,000 reward for information leading to the arrest and conviction of the murderer of Anita Shaw'.

"Livia, you are the closest thing next to family that Carolyn has, and you have always been there for her. You were there when Anita was born and you're here now."

Olivia pursed her lips and patted Ada's hand next to hers on the table. "I don't know how much good I'll be, Miss Ada. If I'm strong at all I'll be drawing from a reserve that God has stored for me, and I'll give whatever comfort I can."

After the conversation had petered out, Olivia went back to see about Carolyn while Ada tidied up the kitchen. Carolyn was awake and lying on her back; her eyes met Olivia's when she walked in and she managed a weak smile.

"Do you think you can eat a little something now? It won't have to be anything heavy." As she spoke, Carolyn shook her head, "No." Olivia persisted that she at least let her get her some chicken soup and toast, but Carolyn insisted that she wouldn't be able to keep it down, and she began weeping softly.

Olivia opened the vial of tranquilizers and, giving her a glass of water, she watched her God sister swallow a pill gratefully and lie back on the pillows. It was going to be a long time before Carolyn Shaw would feel anything but pain. . . .

Twenty-eight-year-old Heather Cogdell of Hinesville was taking her hour long lunch break next door to Pac & Save where she worked in the toy department. Hot-N-Hearty, a quaint country cafe where she ate, had a color TV behind the bar next to a homey restaurant eating area. The bartender who was known as Monty stood and talked to her as she ate her lunch and watched the noon news. She heard the newscaster tell of the reward for the capture and conviction of the murder of a five-year-old black girl in Jesup.

Heather thought it was a pity. She didn't have children of her own, but her twin sister,

Clover, had two—a boy and a girl aged four and two. Clover worked at Hinesville Memorial as an LPN in the ER. The news was saying that the little girl was found with a piece of yellow yarn in her hand. The alleged murderer was believed to be a white male with straw-colored hair and around six feet tall.

Heather finished her sandwich and left. At 4:00 p.m., an hour before knock-off time, a man approached her at her check-out counter with a Pac & Save bag and asked about a refund. He told her that he wouldn't be needing the doll after all. She looked the doll over and saw that it was none the worse for wear. There was one problem: since he didn't have a receipt, he would have to fill out a short form, which he did without hesitation.

His name was Todd Pope and he lived right there in Hinesville. As far as Heather could see, the only thing wrong with the doll was that a piece of yellow yarn in the hair was gone and left a little hole in the top of its head.

After taking the information, Heather gave him his refund.

By 6:00 p.m. Heather had been home, taken a shower, ate, and was in the hospital parking lot waiting to pick up her sister. Clover Cogdell

Lee (always known as Clowie) got off at 6:15, but her old piece of car was out of commission again and there was no money to get it fixed let alone to get a new one, so Heather had to be her sister's ride for a while. Clover's husband walked out on her when her first baby, a daughter, was born. The second baby's daddy didn't wait until the baby was born; she came home one day from the vocational school she attended and found him and all of her valuables gone. Today was one of those days that she got off a little earlier than usual.

As Clover walked toward the car, a man came out of the ER exit behind her. He yelled out something to Clover and she looked back and replied.

"What's with him?" Heather asked her as she leaned over and opened the car door for her sister to get in.

"Well," Clover replied, tiredly, "he came to the ER with a rash on his left arm and on the left side of his belly that turned out to be nothing but a mild reaction to poison ivy."

There was something disturbingly familiar about that man, Heather thought; then she remembered—he was the man that returned that rag doll. Clover misunderstood her concern.

"Don't go match makin', Heather! 'Sides, I don't take up wid any man whose hair is yellower or redder than mine! Furthermore, he's kinda slow; his mind ain't quite right."

Heather suddenly remembered something she heard on the afternoon news. The report was on a man that had straw-colored hair. This man had blonde hair that was straw-like in texture. She pressed her tired, bony fingers against her temples and closed her eyes. Yes! The news said a little girl was found dead with a strand of yellow yarn in her hand! Heather put the car in reverse and backed out of the parking lot.

Clover, the homliest of the two redheaded sisters, knew not to ask too many questions, but she needed to know where they were going and for how long because at 6:30 p.m. she had to get the kids at the nursery. Heather was on her way to the police station, but her sister needed to get her children. Maybe it would be a better idea to call the station instead. Clover watched her sister out of the corner of her eye. She was accustomed to Heather's hyper personality and was always curious enough to inadvertently get involved. She just had to know, so she asked. Heather told her about the murder and the events thereafter.

"When he brought the doll back today, Clowey, he had to fill our a form because he lost his receipt but I can't 'member his damn name!"

Clover's little beady eyes sparkled, even as a child she delighted in having something, anything, that her twin sister might not have. "His name is Todd, Todd Pope, but he didn't seem like no murderer; he's just kinda goofy, that's all."

Heather didn't notice that the light had turned green. Todd Pope was the name that he used in Pac & Save! But there was probably no connection to the murder. Heather had begun to doubt that any of her suspicions were true. Her life had been uneventful up to this point. Nothing of importance had ever happened to her or anyone around her. Making up her mind that she was jumping to conclusions, she dismissed the thought.

At 5:00 p.m., Olivia went with Carnell Jr. and his parents to the funeral home to take Jello's favorite outfit. It was a little white jump suit with pink, yellow, and blue lace and flounces on the pockets and neck. Her Grandma Ada brought her prettiest lace hair ornament—a dear pink dish with vanilla ice cream sitting in a bushy nest of frothy irish lace. Her little socks matched her hair bow. They took her little white leather Buster Browns with a strap across the instep.

Jello always liked for Olivia to brush her hair, so Olivia had prepared herself to do just that. She had never done anything like this, and she didn't know the procedures, but Olivia did know that Jello loved it when she got her hair brushed with Sandy's sterling silver natural bristle brush and wide-toothed comb, and she was taking them with her to groom her Goddaughter's hair for the last time.

When Olivia got to the funeral home, she wiped her tears and stiffened her back. Lord, she prayed, only your grace and goodness can pull a mother through something like this. Please give me the strength for Carolyn to draw from and be my shelter in this storm, Father. In Jesus' Name, Amen.

Putting on the 'Armor', she went in with the family and spent an hour dressing and brushing Jello's hair.

In the grooming parlor of Tom Jones Funeral Home, Olivia rubbed Jello's hands, and tears spilled haltingly down her cheeks and onto the still and stony little face. The sickening stench of formaldehyde was strong in her nostrils.

There was a little hole in Anita's neck near the jugular vein left by the tube they had used to force the blood out of her body. The little hole on her heel—where the blood was forced out and which was then patched so that the embalming fluid stayed put—went undetected.

Olivia touched Jello's neck; there wasn't much that Tom could do to eliminate the unsightly disfiguring, but he had done a very good job, and there was nothing more he could do. Olivia kissed Jello for the last time and left the room.

The next day in Hinesville, Heather was rushed as usual because she had to pick up Clover and the kids and take them to the day care. After she'd dropped them all off in the right places, she had punched in ten minutes later than she did the day before but looked the other way when she saw her supervisor watching her. She went over to the refund counter where she'd put the rag doll and pulled it from the basket it was put in while it waited to be re-tagged and put back on the shelf. Taking it from the plastic, she laid it on the counter top, but it was what fell to the floor that froze her in her spot.

Bending over slowly, Heather picked up two small, shriveled leaves. With two fingers, she laid them flat. They were poison ivy!

Heather didn't know what to do. Fighting for control, she forced herself to take a deep breath; next, she took a small Advil bottle from her purse and emptied the pills back into the open purse. Putting the leaves into the empty vial, she closed the top and dropped it back into her purse; next, she took out the cost of the doll and paid for it. Calmer now, she went to her boss and claimed she was ill and needed to go home.

Hours later, Heather left the Police station and started for home just in enough time to pick her sister up from work. She was just about sure she knew that Todd Pope would be their man. . . .

Sandy was exhausted when time came for the field hands to come in. The ladies in the female dorm heard those singing voices grow louder and louder as they drew nearer. The women were beside themselves with anticipation.

After Mr. Mac with Lady T. in tow had taken their leave and Sandy had done what was needed to protect her family, she decided to go home and stay until Jello's funeral was over. Her grief was strong and she would need time to herself to grieve, solitary time. No one knew how badly she hurt; even among so many people, she felt such a vast loneliness.

So Sandy bade her friends and family a hasty goodnight and assured them of her return. She knew she wouldn't be able to make up the days she'd missed, but she could do nothing about it. She needed this time.

She decided to walk back to the kitchen because there was a little mulatto girl named Mandy that Sandy enjoyed talking with. Mandy always knew everything—even gossip Mammy Cinda hadn't heard yet! The little girl was clairvoyant and had a feel for things. But, unfortunately, the girl was thirteen years old, and the rumor was that Coard was grooming her for himself.

She had been orphaned when her mother was sold away for attempting to teach her daughter and some other slaves how to read. Her mother, Yonna, was Cherokee Indian. Mandy lived on an Indian reservation until she was six. Her daddy, Oscar, had been a free man after his master died and gave him his freedom in his will.

Oscar Jackson found that freedom came with a price. After his master was buried, Oscar was asked to leave the plantation and all of his family and friends living and toiling there in the slave quarters. His trade and labor had been in taming and tending horses. His apprentice had been working and training with him for twelve of his seventeen years and knew the job as thoroughly as Oscar.

With the small roll of paper money notes in his pocket growing smaller and smaller, he sold himself out on various plantations around Savanna and in the small neighboring towns, but no one wanted and ex-slave around too long. Finally down to his last two dollars, he inadvertently stumbled across an isolated tribe of Cherokee Indians.

A hard worker and a survivor was welcome. Oscar became like a son to one of the families that took him in. After being there two years, he married a squaw and earned his own tepee. His woman was called Yonna.

She was sixteen moons, but worked as hard as some of the older, married women. In a Cherokee tribe, the unmarried girls didn't do hard labor until they wed. They maintained their smooth, soft hands by doing the little chores around the camp. Yonna was in charge of collecting wild fruit, nuts, and vegetables—anything to add to the communal cook pot. There were old men and women along with young orphans and bachelors like Oscar that depended on the communal cook pot to supply them with two meals a day. That was more than enough to nourish them.

Life for Oscar was good. However, rain always followed sunshine, and, after being married for sixteen months, Yonna finally gave birth to a daughter. Oscar named her Mandy, after his mother.

Mandy was six when pestilence swept through the camp killing at random. On a balmy Indian summer day in September, Oscar took his young wife and daughter and a horse and fled. He took them to the Worthinwood Plantation and left them with the one person he trusted—his mother, Mandy.

Baby Mandy and her mother Yonna were house slaves until Yonna was sold away.

Mandy would sit with Sandy for hours and talk about the days she lived as a free person in the tribal camp. She missed those lazy, hot days in the summer when life was slow and sweet and freedom was born on the wings of the winds.

When Sandy met Mandy and heard her story, she was surprised that Mandy could see her. Wasn't she born free? But Sandy soon learned that, without papers proving you were a free man, you could be enslaved by any white man with guts to lie and stand fast by it. Not only were Yonna and Mandy enslaved, but so was Oscar.

When he first left his family with his mother—a homely slave who, when she was young, lost the four fingers on her right hand for stealing food from the big house—Oscar used to come as often as he could to visit. Again, Oscar found odd jobs and hired himself out as an extra hand around different plantations and stables. Exactly one year to the day that he left Yonna with his mother, he was enslaved again.

He had spent a lazy day lying on a bed of fragrant fresh hay with his daughter. Mandy's job was to carry things from the kitchen to the big house and to run up and down the stairs with various errands. Yonna had a sleeping cot in the kitchen behind the cooking stove. Sandy's face registered pity when she heard that Mandy was now given her mom's work and sleeping arrangements—but not for long.

"I is blessed, Miz Sandy. I stays warm when it cold outside. Summertime, I sleeps in de tater cellar when it get too hot. I's always sleepin' good. I's so blessed."

Sandy pursed her lips and hugged Mandy tight after her little speech. "I knew a little girl whose name was Anita. If she would've lived to be your age, she would've been a lot like you. She always saw good or humor in everyone and in everything. She would've liked you, Mandy."

On one particular day—with the smell of leaves burning and slave children too young to work out picking up pecans that had fallen from the trees—Oscar lost his freedom.

That day, the pecans covered the ground and the kids roasted them on sticks. Someone was baking a sweet potato pie, and the smell was heavenly. Slaves old enough to begin a job were raking the sandy yards around the quarters and burning the leaves and other debris. You could hear the slaves in the distant fields singing as they toiled off in the distance. The sun was playing peek-a-boo with the massive white fluffy clouds that almost covered the blue sky.

Oscar left Worthinwood at dusk and was stopped by the paddy-rollers. With his freedom papers always in his pocket, he wasn't worried any more than usual. He was spotted and tried to explain his reasons for being out unattended at dusk. He knew that just saying he was free wouldn't be enough, so he produced his freedom paper.

The boys had been drinking from a jar of corn squeezin's, and Oscar just happened to be trying to pass at the wrong time. He knew he was in trouble when they told him to get off the horse.

The oldest of the group spoke. "Fine animal for a nigger; he must have some money, too. Nigger, now you better tell us who yew belong to or we gon take you apart."

Oscar was familiar with this type of white folks. They were called white trash, and they were so low on the social scale that it gave them pleasure to be able to low rate a black. They had to have something or someone lower than themselves, even though a black was much better off and was treated better than white trash. If they couldn't find a black to be better than, they chased each other and called it feudin'.

The last thing Oscar remembered was looking up into white faces before he was knocked unconscious and stripped of his clothing. His freedom papers were burned, and he was hogtied and branded as a runaway slave. When he came to, Oscar learned that he had been sold by two paddy rollers to a small farm owned by a poor dirt farmer named Charley Dale Scamper. There were ten other slaves, and although the had purchased two the legal way, he had six that he got the same way he came across Oscar, and two more that he obtained by impregnating the two females he got at an auction. Charley Dee, as he was called, was building his own plantation from the dirt up in his own way—slave by slave. He didn't buy runaways but was always ready to turn a freeman into a slave again. This was called "bootlegging."

Mandy was a beautiful and smart girl. She learned from her grandmother that her father was indeed a free man even as he served as a slave again in this world where things were ugly and unfair. He was free in his heart. Freedom for a black man could only be as fair as a white man said it was or would let it be.

Mandy was the one who told Sandy that the master had decided to sell Charlotte to a sugar cane plantation in Louisiana.

All slaves cringed at the mere thought of being sold down river—it meant certain death. Slaves that worked the cane fields usually lived only five years after they began. Sandy found out that the journey to the slave sale in De Ridder, Louisiana, would start in two days. The average slave sold to the cane fields was a big strapping young man. If a woman was brought to the plantation, her hell was double. She was usually bred to the biggest buck in the lot. After the child was weaned, the mother was sent to the fields and if the child were a boy he was sent to a house on the planation to be raised for the fields. A girl was sent out to be sold.

The nightmare that Charlotte faced was that not in history had any female as delicate as Charlotte lived more than a year in those sugar cane plantations.

Sandy was now certain of one thing: she had to be back in two days or she would lose her beloved Charlotte.

Sandy felt she could do no more here right now; she knew she had to go home, for now she needed to be comforted, and her pain seemed to have permeated every inch of her body.

She walked across the yards slowly, covering the distance between the quarters and the big house and then to the fields where she went into the barn that she first appeared in. She sat on a saw horse for a while before she made up her mind to visit the big house again just to make sure she left nothing undone for the two days that she'd be gone.

Mandy had advised Sandy—the "Good Voodoo Witch"—to talk to the Worthinwoods again just to scare them into being good for a while and buy some more time. She had decided at first that this wasn't necessary, but now she'd changed her mind. Mandy was right—you never could figure out a slave owner.

Sandy entered the mansion through the courtyards and went through the rooms searching for Teresa. She greeted those that could see her and briefly explained why she was there, but she tiptoed around the others so as not to alert them to her presence.

Sandy had gone through most of the rooms when she looked out of an attic window and saw Teresa out in the apple orchard. Chanting on the ivory, she transcended herself down into the orchards.

For a long moment, Sandy just stood watching Lady T. Her steps seemed leisurely but her brow was furrowed in concentration. Sandy wondered as she stood looking at Teresa if she were willing to listen to reason.

Lady T. walked right passed Sandy but one of the little calico kittens that kept the barns and silos free of vermin suddenly jumped up on a low slung tree branch, arched his back, and hissed at Sandy.

Teresa spun around and put her hands over her mouth to stifle a scream. Turning around and around and speaking through her fingers, she started pleading, "I know yew're here. I have done nothing to yew! Who are you and why don't you just leave us alone?" The feisty Lady T. was now blubbering, and her blanched face turned crimson. "Please let us alone. Go away, please!"

Sandy had planned her speech as she was looking for Teresa, but now her mouth had gone painfully dry, and her palms were sweaty. Still, she had to do this.

She drew herself up and took a deep breath, thinking, Here goes nothing!

"Um, Teresa?" Teresa spun dizzily towards the voice speaking to her. Short gasps escaped her mouth and her hands shook violently, but Sandy had no time for pity. "Don't be scared, T. I only want to talk to you. If it's any consolation, T., I'm a little nervous, too. I promise I won't bite!"

At the word *bite* Teresa yipped and began to act as if an animal were nipping at her. She brushed at her arms and legs but would not turn her back to the voice. Sandy's patience snapped.

"Cut the bullshit, Teresa Worthinwood! You can use that fragile malarkey with someone else. I don't buy it!"

T. stopped brushing at herself and stood looking in Sandy's direction. "What is it that yew want?" she asked, affecting a pose of great Southern gentility.

"Now that's more like it, Sandy replied, sitting on a patch of monkey grass. She clapped her hands at the hissing kitty and sent him scampering. The unexpected noise made T. jump.

Sandy mocked her. "I would ask you to sit down . . . ."

Sandy left the sentence unfinished—Teresa wore a pea green watered silk day dress with Swiss lace everywhere. The French chiffon shawl she was clutching was white, frail, and breathtaking.

"T., I know I'm a strange thing to you people, but I came here to lend support to my people. I can't help all the slaves on all the other plantations, but I can help the slaves of Worthinwood." Sandy cocked her head sideways.

"You know, I used to wish I could save everyone in the world who was ever in bondage, but, as I grew older, I realized how dumb that was. I didn't come here to hurt your people; I came to give mine a better life. I don't expect you to help—just stay out of my way!

"The thing is, T., you and Coard and your overseer are always trying to inflict pain on these people. Well, I won't have it, OK? Stay out of my way, T.! I am a very big and mean Voodoo Witch, and if I'm crossed," Sandy's voice grew louder, "I maim! I turn healthy bodies into wasted lumps of torn flesh! But I don't need to remind you of my powers, do I?"

Lady Teresa didn't answer. Sandy, who felt that she had been infallible in building respect and fear in the whites on this plantation, was astounded to see that the peppery mistress of Worthinwood was fast overcoming her trepidation of this Witch.

After all, T. felt as safe as anything or anyone could be. Wasn't she a Southern Belle—a precious slip of pink wrapped in a soft but tangible white cloud? "Why, this witch thinks she is invincible," Teresa thought aloud.

Sandy thought, I'll have to use my trump card earlier than I thought. She squared her shoulders and again appealed to Teresa. "T., you don't' think our dear Mister Coard knows about your little liaison with one of your young slave boys, do you? I think he's called 'Stoney'."

Before Sandy could say more, Teresa—who looked like she couldn't breathe—blurted out, "How did you find that out? I swear it's a lie! Don't' you dare say another word. It's all made up by some nasty slave, that's all. Nobody is gonna believe yew. I'm white! No one's gonna believe that a white lady would consort with a . . . a . . . nigga!"

She had squared her jaw, and, though she was nervous, T. almost had Sandy convinced that she believed she could get away with it.

Sandy knew that this tryst only happened two times until Kate found out and threatened to go to Coard who would have killed his wife and his slave, not caring if it were his wife who raped him or not. But if Teresa thought she had trumped Sandy's king, she had another think coming! Sandy landed that joker and knocked T.'s ace to hell!

"T., do you remember the day of the whipping . . . or, rather, the day you were *going* to have Charlotte whipped?" T. blinked and stepped backward. Sandy grinned impishly.

"Yeah, you remember! Well, I believe I replayed your voice and the voices of some others that day. Remember?"

T. staggered, but she wasn't down. "I . . . if you tell that, I might die, b-but *he* definitely will."

"No!" Sandy thundered. "I," she said, slapping her chest, "me! I'm going to protect him! I have the power to send him into another century. I promise you, you southern slu . . . tramp!" Sandy was proud of the way she'd cleaned up her language lately, and she was determined not to let T. make her lose too much ground.

Teresa was floored. She stood with her shawl clutched in her tight white fists and her mouth moved wordlessly.

Sandy continued. "I mean what I'm saying. Please don't make me get nasty, because if you do, I promise not only to replay your voice that day when you told him to 'fuck me or I'll scream rape," but to torture you by replaying it for the entire city of Savannah!"

By the look on Lady T.'s face, Sandy knew that she had won this round. She knew that her people would be safe until she came back from Jello's funeral. She felt triumphant and couldn't keep it out of her voice.

"I see I finally got through to you. Just see to it that this plantation's slaves stay the way they are today, or else!"

Sandy walked out of the shaded apple orchard and into the sun.

She stood blinking in the sun before she crossed the lush planation lawn and onto the fine sand in the yards of the slave quarters.

Little children came running up to her, playfully pushing each other. When she entered Mammy Tulla's dorm the slaves were surprised to see her still among them. She explained that she had forgotten to take care of some unfinished business; now, she needed to speak to them.

She dispatched Stoney to run to the forest and fetch Val and Renee. She sent other children to gather other slaves to Tulla's dorm. There were five new babies now in the dorm, so mothers were asked to keep them quiet.

When everyone—with the exception of some house slaves that couldn't come—was gathered around Sandy, she spoke. "Before I leave, I'm going to order a feast and you can eat while I talk." The crowd forgot they were to be quiet and began cheering at the mention of one of Sandy's feasts.

After hushing them again, Sandy had them bow their heads as she chanted in Big Macs, Bacon Cheeseburgers, fries, onion rings, large Cokes, and hot apple turnovers. She couldn't help getting caught up in the excitement.

With the first aromas of food, eyes flew open, mouths filled with water, and the people could hardly contain their glee. Sandy watched and helped out as the food was distributed.

Little children were set on red-and-white checkered tablecloths that she had popped in. Mother's spread little legs and set fries and colas within their children's reach. There was giggling as the bubbles from the soft drinks tickled little noses. Eyes sparkled with the happiness of it all.

Sandy loved it. Tears filled her eyes as she thanked God for this chance.

While the last of the food was munched, Sandy told them all that she would be gone for two days; she told them of her meeting and conversation with Lady Teresa. At the mention of his Mistress' name, Stoney's smile petered out, and he clinched his teeth.

Sandy reached for his hand and squeezed it. "It will never happen again, Stoney," she whispered into his ear. Charlotte—who was sitting near them—pursed her lips in a smile of love and understanding.

Sandy finished by telling them all to work hard at taking care of themselves, and when she returned she expected to see every male slave with a haircut and shave and every female without a head rag and with her hair dressed. "Use the cache in the glades. Be ready when I return."

With that, tearfully, she was gone.

CHAPTER ELEVEN

Sandy showered immediately upon arriving home.

After she had slept about four hours, she was awakened by the sound of her mother moving around down the hall in her room.

Sandy lay in bed with her arms behind her head, reflecting.

Olivia had always been Sandy's rock, but now she wondered if this time her mother would need her shoulder to cry on. They both loved Jello, but Olivia had been there with Carolyn when Jello was just an embryo deep in the core of her mother's body.

A rap on the door startled Sandy, and she sat straight up. "San?" Her mother's voice sounded from the other side of the door. "May I come in?"

Sandy got up and unlocked the door and gave her mother a hug.

The two women sat on the bed and talked; Sandy found out that the wake would be tomorrow evening at 8:00 p.m. and the funeral would be the day after at 2:00.

After all was said, Olivia still sat pensively at the foot of Sandy's bed. "San, I wanted to tell you that they've arrested a man."

Olivia went into the hall and came back with the morning Jesup Journal and gave it to Sandy. On the front page in bold letters the headline read: "HINESVILLE MAN ARRESTED IN GIRL'S DEATH." Sandy read on: "Wayne County police arrested Todd Edward Pope in the strangulation death of five-year-old Jesup girl Anita Faye Shaw. The girl was found at 6:00 p.m. Monday in the woods behind her family's home. A spokeswoman at Savanna County Medical Examiner's Office said an autopsy showed that the child died of asphyxiation and a broken neck. Pope, 38, was apprehended early Wednesday morning near his home. After being questioned he was arrested and charged with first degree kidnapping and first degree murder. Police said that the child appeared to have been kidnapped by Pope from behind the Shaw home and taken into the woods where she was slain. Authorities believe that the alleged murderer worked alone. No other arrests have been made or are expected."

Sandy finished reading the article and slowly folded the paper and absentmindedly gave it back to her mother.

Sandy knew that her mother was still worried about her, but she didn't have any new words or anything to say to make it any better than she had before. Sandy felt that her mom needed reassuring again; and she was right.

"San, Jello was killed in broad *daylight* behind her *home*." Olivia paused, hoping her words would have their intended effect on Sandy. "Please," she begged, "If you haven't considered yourself, think about your daddy and me. We are *worried* . . . ."

"Mama, please!" Sandy stood up abruptly. "I've said all I can say to let you know I'm in no danger. I took a chance that the funeral would be within two days, and I need these days, mom; we need each other, please?"

Olivia didn't know if she understood Sandy's plea or not, but they did need each other to get through this. She went over to Sandy and pulled her into her arms. "When you want to tell us, honey, we'll be here."

The streets of Jesup had been packed the night following Todd Pope's arrest—or, at least, the west side of Jesup, the black side. Sidewalks served as informal meeting places for small groups of people. Porches held gossiping cliques, and homes and stores buzzed like bee hives. No one could believe that a white man from Hinesville could steal into Jesup's black side and take one of its most precious gems. The people were angry and had it not been for the calming influence of the black churches, there most certainly would have been a riot.

Todd Pope was questioned and arrested by the Hinesville Police, but he had been taken to the Jesup Police station where he freely confessed to the crime. Near imbecile that he was, Pope believed his biggest problem was the corn liquor still the authorities were sure to find beside the make-shift cabin in the woods: to him, the death of Jello was an inconsequential evil—'just a nosey little nigger kid'.

Jesup's small population quickly became aware of Pope's attitude about the girl's death—and the news hit the streets hard.

There were six men in the city jail now, all of whom were black. The Rhodamine red and pink prison suits rarely covered the bodies of more than three white men a month. The night Pope was booked and thrown into the bull pen, he was scared, being the only white man there. The first thing he did was to ask the jailer if he had to share this cell with "these stinkin' niggers."

The fat pink jailer chuckled around a plump wad of tobacco lodged between his bottom lip and his teeth. "Todd, ol' boy, a sure-footed dog like you what killed a li'l black youngun deserves to be put over there with those coons." Fatso chuckled again and slapped Pope sharply on his back, like it was all a big joke. "I know you killed that little black girl. Didn't ya?"

Pope looked at the jailer—who he had grown up with—and grimaced. "Boy, I never touched even a hair on the dog's nappy black head!"

Odie Moutry, the jailer, had grown up with the Pope boys, lived two miles from them in a little place five miles south of Hinesville called Pigs Holler. Unlike the Popes' relatively fashionable home, the Moutry's ragged, unpainted, tar-papered house was home to six girls and Odie.

Odie's sisters were all younger, except one, Mary Lee, ten months her brother's senior. Odie and Mary Lee practically raised the younger girls, probably loved them more than their overworked father and submissive mother ever could. Lacy Moultry would still be barefoot and pregnant if her husband hadn't worked himself into a near fatal heart attack leaving him with a condition that required blood pressure medication—one side effect of which was impotence.

Growing up, the Pope boys were no strangers to the KKK. By ages ten or eleven, they had been taught to use guns and other weapons. While Lacy was delivering the last of her tow-headed daughters (Ray Lynn, now fifteen), Odie was out bootlegging whisky and testing the results of those hard-working stills.

One night, long ago, he and Clifford Pope and another, older boy were coming from Ludowici after dropping off the standard twenty gallons when they encountered a black teenaged couple coming back from a date. The pair were later identified as sixteen-year-olds Carolyn Norwood and Ronald Robinson. Having been well-juiced with corn squeezin's, the three boys decide to play a game of chicken with their prey.

Clifford was driving his daddy's old, beat up pickup.

Ronald was a Baptist preacher's only child and Carolyn was Ronald's first real girlfriend.

Odie and his gang decided to run the couple off the road since they wouldn't stop when they were told. The game quickly became the white boys' effort to inflict pain, any kind of pain. The racial slurs being hurled at the couple were ignored, so the three boys decided to do something that the couple couldn't ignore.

Two large oncoming lights signaled the approach of an eighteen-wheeler. With cheers of support by his passengers, Clifford Pope drove onto the shoulder of the road next to the passenger's side of the Ronald's car. Ronald tried speeding up, but Clifford stayed with him. Ronald slowed down, but so did the boys.

The blasting horn's wail prophesied the truck's unswerving approach.

Just as the semi was upon them, the couple was forced into the oncoming lane.

The impact was deafening.

The two innocent kids were smashed and torn by the metal, rubber, and asphalt. Odie remembered feeling nothing but fear. He feared what the other boys feared—getting caught!

Four days after the closed-casket funeral, the truck driver (who was white) stepped forward and told authorities what he had seen. The driver, forty-two-year-old David Atwater—the only unbiased witness to the accident—disappeared and was never found. It was rumored that the KKK had a hand in his disappearance.

Now, as he shuffled into his cell, Todd Pope turned to Odie and said, "Ya don' think the good ol' K will lend a hand, do you Odie?"

Odie chuckled again and cocked his head sideways in mock contemplation. "Well, ol' boy, it ain't like it was back in the olden times. They's got laws to protect blacks, Jews, and spics these days. If'n the Klan's done anything 'tall lately, I ain't heard of it yet."

The slamming of the iron door echoed in the cell and caused Pope to flinch. He looked around at the other men and wiped his thin, flat lips with the back of his hand. How long, he wondered, would he have to stay in here? He'd have to get out soon. He desperately needed a drink.

Following Jello's wake, tempers ran hot and deadly as the family and friends met back at the house after leaving the funeral home and viewing the body. The yards, porch, and sidewalks at and around the Shaw house were packed. The elder Shaws and older people sat inside and talked church, dipped snuff, and reminisced about the good ol' days.

Everyone brought covered dishes. There was barbecue ribs falling off the bone, chicken and dumplin's, potato salads, macaroni salad, baked beans, creamy and cheesy macaroni and cheese, collard greens cooked with smoked neckbones, turnip greens with dumplin's, mustard greens cooked with ham hocks, corn bread and cracklin' bread, tender yellow corn cobs swimming in rich butter, sour dough yeast rolls, rice and red rice, cornbread dressing, and giblet gravy. On makeshift tables sat every kind of cake, pie, cobbler, and tart known to the South.

The younger people were all hanging around in large and small crowds, laughing and talking. There was beer in ice chests in half of the young peoples' car trunks. Some of the older crowd also had a stash of liquor. Music was booming on car stereos and on different boom boxes. The little kids played games. Later, there were street lights, and from the windows came the filtered house lights.

Sandy was standing in a crowd of about ten kids. Most of the Shaw family relatives were up from Florida.

Sandy, Julie, and Robin had become acquainted with sixteen-year-old twins Doris and Dottie and seventeen-year-old Reesha Uma. They talked about boys mostly, but it wasn't long before unthinkable news surged through the crowds of people: Todd Pope's bail was set, and he was on his way home.

This news came like a slap in the family's face. The consoled older people at the wake became somber at the news, but the young and more lively crowd reacted to the wounding news with rage. The instinct to retaliate was overpowering.

Goat's little gang had shown up to give Carnell their support and were responsible for much of the white liquor floating from car to car. The boys in this crowd were really helpful when it came to the black community, so helpful, in fact, that they sometimes went overboard. Tonight was one of those times.

They decided to go down to the police station and ask some questions. Carnell reasoned that, if nothing else, the whisky on their breaths would get them into trouble.

"Trouble? Trouble was already stinkin'," Goat said. "When those crazy fools set a bond that low for murder, you can bet it's a white killing a black!"

The older people and parents begged and pleaded for them to "stop talking foolish." Little kids clung to their parents. Some cried as the frenzy grew.

Later, Goat was the first one arrested.

They had been in front of the county jail talking loud and making empty threats for ten minutes. He was knocked around pretty damn good by a thick-necked, ham-fisted policeman with hair the color of a carrot and a face almost solid brown with freckles. By 6:00 a.m. the next morning, all of the boys had been arrested except three. These three kids got together and got their unfortunate 'brothers' out of jail in time to go to the funeral.

Sandy and her parents walked into the church last with the Shaws.

The church was so full that people were packed in every available nook and cranny. The ones that couldn't get in were standing around outside waiting to view the body, some for the second time.

Sandy's face was swollen from crying even before she got to the church. She had been coaxed to sip hot cocoa for breakfast so that she wouldn't get sick.

The small, silver and pink coffin sat up at the front of the church's middle aisle.

Sandy sat on the second row from the front; on either side of her sat her mother and father. Directly in front of her sat Carnell and his parents. Carolyn was covered from top to bottom in black crepe. Even so, you could almost touch the grief under her veil. Carnell's shoulders were slumped and his father seemed to be trying to bear the weight of the whole family on his shoulders. When the organ stopped playing, you could hear sniffling coming from different locations in the church.

Shawnkia Chestnutt stood up and sang Jello's favorite song, *There is a Shadow*. Sandy didn't try to hold back the tears that started all over again. That song was Jello's favorite. Everybody that belonged to Bennet Union Baptist Church always associated *Shadow* with Jello.

Sandy narrowed her eyes and took in the beautiful flowers that shrouded Jello's tiny coffin. There was one flower arrangement in particular that caught her attention. They were rare pink orchids in the shape of a harp. She knew that Jello had never seen a live orchid but had often said that when she was all grown up, she would fill her house with pink orchids. She fell in love with the flowers when she saw them in a movie. Sandy had sent daisies shaped like a sun bonnet and many sent assortments of flowers shaped like Raggedy Ann. All of the flowers were beautiful and she knew Jello would have loved them.

The minister was starting the eulogy.

Now muffled sobs could be heard coming from different locations in the church.

Despite the overwhelming grief, the service was beautiful; the funeral went on smoothly until the last opening of the coffin.

As the church stood with the back pews starting around to view the body, the cries and screams became very painful sounds to Sandy from where she sat.

She could see Jello's still little button nose over the rim of the coffin. Sandy broke down completely as her row went around to view the body. She grabbed Jello's little hands that used to pet Sandy's cheeks in mock admonitions, little hands that used to make Sandy roar with laughter. Clinging to her mother, she was led back to her seat, but, before she could sit down, Sandy heard an animal-like grunt rise in the midst of the mourners—a sound that caused almost the entire church to cry and sob in unison.

Carolyn was standing at the coffin flanked by her husband and her son; she began sobbing, "Oh, God, my baby, my sweet girl baby. Why did you give her to me? Why? You gave her to me and you've taken her back, Lord. I only had her a little while and she's gone, Lord."

Carolyn's grief overrode her good Christian faith. At any other time, she would have known that you don't question God. In her heart, she knew that God hadn't taken her baby. She was a good and firm believer, and her faith would gradually pull her through.

She made another lunge for the coffin but was grabbed by her husband who lifted her and carried her from the church leaving Carnell to stare down at his little sister's remains.

It seemed as though time stood still as Carnell slowly lowered his face to kiss Jello. "Bye, Squirt; I'm so proud of you; no one but you could have lived and died with so much dignity."

He reached under his suit coat and pulled out Jello's Raggedy Ann doll and placed it on her chest.

As he slowly turned around to walk away, the whole church went crazy. Shawnika led the choir in *Wind Beneath My Wings.* Sandy felt as if her heart would come through her chest. Strange thing was, when she left the church, there was a smile dancing on her lips, and *Shadow* flitted through her head. She knew Jello would smile again. . . .

It had rained a couple of hours before Sandy got back to the plantation.

She was pleased to see the slave children clean with their hair dressed and no head rags. The cabins smelled of Pine-Sol, the yards were swept clean, and even the old ladies were looking good with their curled or straightened hair.

The slaves had been in from the fields about an hour, and Sandy's heart sang when she saw the line of slaves with clean clothes over their arms waiting for their turn at the showers. They looked so dusty and tired, but they had a light in their eyes that wasn't there before. She had been able to help them and teach them about basic life beyond slavery. Smiling widely, she half skipped and half ran to Mammy Tulla's cabin.

Her joy was short lived when she burst through the door and saw the fear in Mammy Tulla's face.

As soon as Mammy saw Sandy, she drew the girl into the dorm and threw herself into her arms.

"Sandy, Sandy, we is got problems! I is sho glad you is back. Deese fools 'round here ain't got sense 'nough to see we is in danger!" Sandy had a time, but she finally got Mammy Tulla calm enough to get the whole story out of her.

It seemed that the whites on the plantation had been secretly watching certain slaves and had begun following them into the forest to see where they were getting the clothes and supplies that they were coming up with. Well, they found nothing in the forest. Baffled, the sentries organized and carried out a raid on the slave quarters. The raid wasn't without confusion. The things found in the quarters were without question some of the most amazing things the slave owner ever laid eyes on. Mammy Tulla heard Missy Katie say that some things that were found were fit for royalty. They took her breath away. Where in the hell did this stuff come from? Never in the history of slaves has any slave owned such property, and Coard promised to search until he found the source even if he had to maim or kill every slave on his plantation.

After seeing certain things take place, he was almost convinced it was Voodoo. Someone on his plantation was doing witchcraft.

Mammy Tulla took a deep breath and wiped her face. "Sandy, chile, de has been white folks comin' and goin', even de sheriff and his debatees came lookin'. Deese white folks is comin' lookin' at us all de time and deese neggars 'round here ain't worried 'bout nuttin'; they says they works too hard to care an' they has found some thing in dis world to look forward to after dem fields and de boot blackin' and black smithin' and de big house cleanin'. They say they die before they gib up anything!"

Sandy reached over and smoothed Mammy's newly curled hair and pursed her lips as Mammy went on to tell her how Lady T. had been just as mean as ever but that she hadn't touched Charlotte. Just as Sandy thought Mammy had told her everything, the portly slave remembered another important fact.

"Lordy, Sandy, Worthinwood gettin' fit t' go t' Great Oak Lawn Plantation for Missy Peggy Murch'son and Massa Leon Hair's 'gagement cel'brations 'morrow at noon. De massa an' all of dem in dah big house is goin' and so is a bunch of slaves in 'tendance."

Turning solemn and fearful eyes to Sandy, she shook her head.

"What gonna happen chile? What gonna happen?"

Sandy reassured her friend that she would never let anyone harm them. "Remember, I've got the power to protect my people and Mammy I promise you that I'll use it if I have to!" Sandy felt angry as the adrenalin rushed through her body.

For the rest of the day, Sandy walked around and visited with friends until enough of them had talked her into chanting in some new food for them. Sandy loved it.

She had them close their eyes as she chanted in hoagies and chili dogs. As an afterthought, she added large grape sodas with lots of crushed ice and red candy apples on the side.

After the food was eaten and the 'mmmmmm's' and 'ahhhhhhhh's' died down, Sandy jumped in and helped the slaves that had to go to the celebration prepare themselves for the next day after they completed their daily tasks for their owners. Sandy took the dresses they had almost finished for themselves and substituted the muslin for silk and satin Liz Clarborn and Gucci gowns. She chanted in ballet slippers and had the girls cover them with the same materials and colors the dresses were made of.

There was much ado as the correct sizes were matched with the correct feet, and then hose were chanted in.

It never occurred to Sandy that simple pantyhose could bring such joy. It so awed her that she sent a pair to Lady T. and had them laid out with her outfit in the place of her ordinary stockings. Of course, this was done with no knowledge on Lady T.'s part.

Sandy found out later that the pantyhose did more than amaze Lady T. It baffled and charmed her almost beyond sanity. Curious T. did try the pantyhose on after agonizing about how they got there, what they were, and how to get them on. She locked her personal maid out of the room as she dressed, but not before the girl saw her frantic fight with the nylon hose. Dripping with perspiration, but sporting a sleek and amazingly unfrazzled pair of pantyhose, Lady T. had thrown open her bedroom door and, breathing deeply, ordered her maid back into the room to lace up her stays. The day after the wedding, gossip was that Lady T. had been seen at the festivities peep-ing slyly under her slave's gowns when she thought there wasn't a white person looking. She really knew where those stockings came from: they were true nigger voodoo products, as far as she was concerned, but they were the most luscious things she had ever felt against her skin!

Sandy did the four children's outfits last, so it was dark as they helped put the last bit of fabric on the little girl's slippers and hung up the last little silk gowns.

Charlotte and Sandy argued about head rags. Sandy wouldn't hear of making new silk ones to go with the new gowns. "No way! I don't care if I never see another head rag," Sandy insisted. "Look, you guys have the right products for your hair now, and everyone's hair is looking great these days." And it was.

Even some of the girls whose hair wasn't an inch long when they started and who believed they would never grow any now had lush hair growing even in so short a time. There were still a few diehards that wouldn't put that Voodoo stinky stuff on their heads, but they were becoming few and very fast.

"Really, Charlotte, I want to hear you promise never to wear another one, and don't let anyone else wear one in your presence, OK?"

Charlotte complied and Sandy was content as she began her chant home.

At 4:00 a.m. the next morning, the plantation was a-buzz with excitement. The attending slaves in the big house finished packing wagons with things that had to be packed last.

There were two wagons—one for the many gowns, hats, and gifts; the other for the transportation of the attending slaves and their clothes. The two shiny black, lacy two-steed drawn buggies were for transporting the whites.

Great Oaks was only six miles away, but the socially accepted way of the southern elite called for long visits, twenty-four hours at the least—and plenty of gossip! The overseers would be the only whites left on Worthinwood. The six whites in the big house each took personal valets plus drivers, three nannies, their own seamstresses, a wet nurse, and four children for various reasons— like carrying large ecru-colored ostrich feathers around to fan their masters with.

When Sandy chanted back in, they all had been gone about eight hours. She got details together and chanted herself over to the other plantation. Attired in what Sandy called a *Gone With the Wind* evening gown, She popped into a plantation much like Worthinwood, so finding her way around was a snap!

There was much activity going on. The morning festivities were over and most attending slaves had their young female charges gathered in a very large room and were getting them out of their first day dresses and onto cots and feather mattresses to rest until it was time for the next party.

Charlotte attended DeeDee, and Misty was attended by Gail.

There were many girls with their own attending slaves from many different plantations. Each plantation tried to outshine the next in every way, but this year—much to the residents' chagrin—the female slaves from Worthinwood were so extremely well-dressed that their gowns and other accoutrements outdid even their mistresses'.

The place was afire with gossip. People were staring and pointing out the beauty and elegance of the gowns worn by the Worthinwood slaves. To the attendant slaves from other plantations who could see Sandy, she appeared to be just another of the lucky Worthinwood slaves.

"Why would they dress their slaves almost as well as they dress themselves?" Sandy overheard one of the party guests ask.

"Did you see the slaves from Worthinwood?" asked another.

Sandy decided to try to get Charlotte's attention without causing any confusion. She had already gotten Gail in trouble for appearing to be talking to herself when she was really talking to Sandy.

Just as she saw a way to get her alone, she turned a corner and walked right through some teenaged boys; for some reason, this encounter left her a bit lightheaded: could the ivory's magic be wearing off? Naw! She had lots of time left. However, she didn't miss what they were talking about.

These boys had never seen so many pretty 'nigra girls'.

One little red-haired boy with ears like palmetto fronds and a bulbous nose kept repeating, "Just look at them, look at them! I have never seen so many pretty slaves, David."

He spoke to another youth of about sixteen that just had to be his brother.

"Look at all that black hair glistening in the sun! Why have they been wearing head rags?

And look, David, even the men have shiny, curly hair, look!"

The boy was trying to keep his voice down but it still carried; besides, David was staring at a young slave girl that had just passed them on her way to speak to a group of Great Oak slaves. The perfume she wore was still in his nostrils. This was nineteen-year-old Sudie Ray.

Sudie was responsible for ironing and keeping the gowns fresh and doing any last minute touch-ups in tailoring. Before Sandy came, Sudie was what most Southern whites would call plain 'niggerish'. Her beauty had never been obvious in the traditional sense. Although she had thick ropes of shoulder-length hair, she had never been seen in anything but head rags, so her hair stayed matted, dry, and brittle. Her skin was the color of pecan flesh, and, because the sun and other elements had it chapped most of the time, it was hard to make it look anything but dull.

Sandy'd fixed all that and more, with pleasure!

She had first permed Sudie's hair into heavy, ripply waves; then she showed the girl how to apply natural subtle makeup; she arched her brows. Sandy had pierced Sudie's and every other female slave's ears and inserted little 14 kt. gold loops. They all had three gold bangle bracelets and an ankle chain.

Sudie was stunning. The toning and vanishing creams that the slaves had been given to use to smooth and to lighten skin that was damaged by the sun was working! These creams on their sun-cooked skins had done their jobs well!

Sudie's skin was radiant and her eyes sparkled like diamonds. The gown she wore was one of the most stunning at the function. The creamy, peach-colored gown had yards and yards of colored lace and lots of little green velvet bows. The bodice was cut low to show plenty of cleavage, and the billowy sleeves came to just below her elbows and were fastened with pearl buttons.

Sandy was proud of her people and her handiwork, but as the day wore on, things got hairy.

The young belles and the older women noticed more and more that the slave girls were every bit as alluring as the young white girls. The whites from Worthinwood were also perplexed but had to keep up the pretence of having planned to have their slaves so well dressed, but, in actuality, they had trouble keeping smiles on their faces. Coard and Teresa felt damned.

People gathered in groups to gossip and whisper; if they hadn't heard about the strange goings on at the Worthinwood Plantation, they saw with their own eyes now! The men gawked or scowled. The slaves from Great Oak and other plantations quietly asked questions and were basically told the truth.

"Come on over for a li'l visit," they were told. "Come on over t'see our things." The Worthinwood slaves were on a pink cloud.

For the most part, the other slaves were jealous or incredulous. The Worthinwood slaves seemed to be on public display, but this pleased Sandy and all of the slaves as well. Didn't this just prove it all, Sandy thought? If we had been given the same care that everyone else had, it would have been different from the start!

She was so caught up with her handiwork that she didn't see the ugliness brewing.

When Sandy left that evening, four or five different plantations had numerous slaves anxious to visit Worthinwood.

CHAPTER TWELVE

Sandy returned to her room about 8:00 a.m. and slept until 11:00. Before she got up, she just lay on her back with her hands clasped behind her head and stared absentmindedly at the ceiling.

There was a tap on her door and abruptly Sandy's bedroom door was pushed open by two strange men; these men, a woman stranger, and her father walked in. She didn't have time to think before her father's weary-pinched face and red-rimmed eyes backed out of the room, and the two men and the woman restrained Sandy and read her her rights!

As she was led out of her house handcuffed, she realized that she was still wearing the muslin evening dress she had conjured up!

At the juvenile section of the county jail, Sandy was told that she was being charged with breaking and entering and larceny. She was being charged with burglarizing Q Mooney's Department Store, Pac & Save, two bridal shops, and the McPherson Museum.

Sandy offered no explanation when she was asked to take off the dress she was wearing and hand it over for evidence. She asked if her parents were in the building and was told they were but they weren't available to her yet. By sitting calmly and listening intently she found that her father had decided to turn her in for her own good. He was convinced that she was part of the gang that was breaking into the different businesses. He'd decided to turn his only daughter in when he learned that some of the store owners were arming themselves and sleeping in their stores so they could catch the thieves. Upon hearing this, Richard had taken this up with Olivia, and together they set up a vigil to observe their child's comings and goings.

Olivia had approached her daughter again, but, again, she received no clear answers, just, "Ah, mom, don't worry about me." Both Olivia and Richard agreed it would behoove them to turn Sandy in; they agreed that they would rather see their daughter locked up than dead.

Richard wasn't very far down the corridor from the room Sandy was in when he heard her cry out. A part of him wanted to run back to his child and take her home. But another part of him knew that she was in good hands. She would be OK and he knew it. He was doing this for *her* own good.

Sandy sat slouched over in a straight back chair. Her hands were hanging uselessly on either side of her. Her ivory and chain had been taken from her and put in lock-up with her rings and watch. In the excitement of the moment, she had placed the ivory in their hands with her other things, despite the fact that the ivory was invisible to all but her. How was she going to help her people now! They needed her now more than ever! She was the cause of their new self-confidence—their sassiness, according to their owners. If her people kept that attitude too long without her there to protect them, it could lead to a massacre!

She was told that her jewelry would be returned to her after ten days and that any aggression on her part during this time would earn her a shot of thorazine. With no options, Sandy let herself be led to her room, a room shared with one other girl who was dressed in a grey T-shirt and black pants, just like every other inmate.

Sandy was given a list of do's and don't's and a hygiene package. To her relief, she was left alone. She dropped to her knees and prayed like she'd never prayed before. . . .

The Worthinwood occupants—both black and white—returned home from Great Oaks exhausted.

This had been the wedding of the century and everybody who was anybody had been there. The attending slaves, valets, nannies, coachmen, and maids bustled around getting their masters and mistresses settled down at home again. Only a few slaves noticed what appeared to be the sheriff and other horsemen visiting with Master Coard. After situating their charges, the slaves—particularly Charlotte—were tickled pink when the slaves from neighboring plantations started making appearances the very next day! They wanted what the Worthinwood slaves had, and they wanted it badly!

They were taken to the glades to see the cache and they were each given supplies. They were shown how to perm and care for their hair and how to care for their skin. They read books to show off their first grade reading skills, basically the alphabets, but they were a proud bunch!

"Oh, I wish Sandy was here! She pops food in here you ain't nebber heard of!" Charlotte gushed.

By the time the slaves were home from the fields, the slaves that didn't work the fields had what looked like a regular flea market going on. What they didn't know was that they were being watched—closely!

Coard had made a decision to get to the bottom of this problem. He would, too, he thought—even if it meant sacrificing some slaves, and slaves were expensive. . . .

Sandy slept fitfully that night. She knew her people were looking for her and wondering if she'd abandoned them. Morning came slowly. The juveniles were awakened at 6:30 a.m. to make up their own beds, shower, and be at breakfast by 7:15.

Sandy's roommate turned out to be very friendly; her name was Joyce, and she was part Navaho Indian. At breakfast she introduced Sandy to most of the other girls and told her which one of the girls and counselors to stay clear of.

"What are you in for?" Sandy asked her.

"I helped my father rob an all night diner two months ago."

"Your father?"

"Yeah. And he's my real dad, too."

Sandy shrugged her shoulders. "Shi . . . I, I mean, shucks; it takes all types, I guess." Sandy's resolve to clean up her vocabulary was a serious resolution. She sort of patted herself on the back for this one. "How did you get caught?"

Joyce sat on the edge of her chair and looked at Sandy for a long time before answering. "The damn fool went and told his stupid brother; that's how we got nabbed." Crossing one leg over the other, Joyce tied her shoelaces. "Now he's gonna serve time for armed robbery." In a quiet voice she continued. "I don't know what's gonna happen to me yet."

Sandy felt sorry for her roommate; Joyce was a cute girl, and her pep and smile made her even cuter.

After breakfast, they went from one recreational group to another until lunch. Sandy didn't mind because it kept her from thinking too much.

After lunch, they went to art, music, and more groups; the last group met at 6:00 p.m.

and ended two hours later. The rest of the evening was free until lights out at 11:00.

"Uh, what are you in here for, Sandy?" Joyce finally asked.

Sandy flinched but answered. "They think I have something to do with the robberies of some of the businesses around here."

"You mean that was *you*! Did you steal the copper from the museum too? Wow, that's cool! Fuck, it's good to meet you, friend. Hey, girl, the cops think some black guy robbed the museum." Joyce was gushing but it only annoyed Sandy.

"Listen, roommate, don't go broadcasting this to the other girls, OK? First off, I didn't say I did it—I said they're *accusing* me of doing it!" With this, Sandy sat down. But Joyce wasn't done yet.

"Oh, come on, roomy! I'm not tellin' anybody else! It'll be our secret, OK? Details! Gimme details!" She threw herself belly first on her bed.

Sandy wasn't having any of it. She turned her back on Joyce and stood staring out of the window until she heard the girl get up from her bed and leave the room.

For the two days she was there, Sandy found her roommate incorrigible but decided to tolerate her by only speaking when she had to. She could tell that Joyce had told everyone that she was the person responsible for the robberies. Most of the girls didn't believe it, anyway; how could this sixteen-year-old be responsible for such daring and successful robberies? Besides, on the second day she was there, they let Sandy go home. The authorities must have realized this too—and she got her ivory back!

Olivia and Richard had communicated with her off and on for the two days. On the morning of the day she was released to go home, her father and her counselor—an Archie Bunker look-alike—sat her down in the jail's little chapel and talked to her for two hours.

It seemed that Richard and a small task force he obtained permission to assemble had been working around the clock before and after Sandy was apprehended. It wasn't until later on that day that she was arrested that their work started paying off. The story began to unfold.

The thieves that broke into the museum made a full legal confession, clearing Sandy. The culprits were the Pickett boys and the copper and other metals stolen were used to make their illegal stills. By coincidence that same day, the Jesup Police received a wire from—of all places—Sydney, Australia: some international organization was clearing out warehouses and stores and not leaving so much as an eyelash for evidence. They did leave sales tags and hangers strewn everywhere, though. And, just like the robberies in and around Jesup, there was never anything like diamonds or money taken.

In this age of global telecommunications, it is information and know-how about committing crimes that, unfortunately, moves around the fastest. Some local criminals were simply mimicking their Australian cousins, Richard and his task force reasoned.

It was more than clear to everyone knowing this story that Sandy Tucker was not likely involved in an international string of robberies!

Although the complexity of the case still had the authorities baffled and would take a perspicacious and compliant mind to break—it would, in fact, remain an open file—Richard and Olivia knew by now that their sixteen-year-old could not possibly be involved.

As Richard held Sandy's hand, he told her that Jello's case, too, had unfolded.

Todd Pope confessed to killing Jello because he believed she had spotted him trying to poison a Pickett still in the woods behind her home. Todd thought that his brother Clifford Pope had been caught doing the same thing to another Picket still and was forced at gunpoint to drink some of the tainted whisky. He wasn't about to face the same fate, so, in his simple-mindedness, he would simply eliminate the only witness.

But that wasn't the end of the story, Richard explained, holding Sandy's hands now. "Todd Pope was murdered last night."

Pat Johnson, the cousin that found Jello in the woods, left a note confessing to shooting Pope—before going into the same woods where he found Jello and then putting a bullet through his own head.

Sandy started to cry now, and her dad held her close.

"We still don't know all of the details yet; but you just hold tight, and your mom and me will be back after lunch to get you out of here."

Sandy knew that her parents loved her and that concern for her safety was uppermost in their minds.

Sandy tried to smile at her parents when she saw that the haggard look on their faces was replaced with novel concern—they still wanted answers. Sandy was given her personal items back and couldn't wait to put them back on. She beamed at the counselor as he gave her the package including—unseen by him and the others—her stick of ivory.

Her mother brought her jeans and a shirt to put on, and she explained that the authorities had her dress and wouldn't return it until the case was solved.

After settling down at home, Sandy wrote Larry and told him she couldn't wait for him to get home. Boy, this'll throw him for a loop, she thought. Imagine me missing that little twerp!

Late that day, she really sat down to dinner for the first time since this thing started. Her parents were thrilled. Her mother bubbled over as she sat salisbury steak, rice, gravy, and turnip greens on the table.

But, of course, it couldn't last.

Sandy was restless and, soon enough, Richard and Olivia noticed. When Sandy couldn't sit still for another moment, she told her parents that she had to finish what she'd started.

Tears began to gather in Sandy's eyes; she didn't want them to have to go through this hell again, but, she explained, she had no choice.

As hard as it was, Sandy knew that, if her parents discovered her powers, her work would be aborted. No! She had to stay silent about it. There were only a few days left now, anyway, before the ivory lost its power.

"Mom and Dad," she said, putting her dessert spoon down, "I have to do this. I have to! But I promise you that I'll tell you all as soon as I can. Look," she stood up; "I'm not in danger. Just trust me a little longer."

With that, she ran to her room.

Olivia and Richard sat at the kitchen table staring at their half-empty plates until Olivia forcefully cleared her throat and stood up.

"Well, I better get these dishes washed, huh?"

They both knew that more words were useless.

Sandy was thinking in her room. Before I leave today, she thought, I've got to get through to Grandma Mary. She took her ivory in both hands and closed her eyes tightly. "Help me, grandma," she prayed, concentrating fervently. "Come to me, please. I need you this day!" Beads of sweat popped out on her forehead.

Suddenly, the room was bathed in the familiar bluish-white glow—and the smell of lilacs.

"Oh, grandmother," she nearly choked. "I called you because I need to ask you something terribly important."

"Yes, honey," her grandmother smiled more than spoke in reply; "what can I do for you? But, Sandy, before you answer, I want you to know how proud I am of you, my baby. Now, what is it?"

Sandy asked if she could save one of the few days she had left and use it at Christmas.

"Is that all, child? Yes, of course, my dear."

Sandy jumped up, and, clapping her hands, she thanked her grandmother. After speaking briefly with her grandmother, Sandy saw the light grow dim, the lilacs fade, and Mary vanish.

As soon as the last of the light was gone, Sandy grabbed her ivory and went to the aid of her people.

Quickly, Olivia had stacked the dishwasher, but she had put off cleaning the kitchen until after she comforted her child. When she reached Sandy's room, she heard voices. Thinking it was the TV, she peaked into the cracked door. For the rest of her life, Olivia would remember what she saw in that room.

When she thought she had seen it all, she then saw her daughter vanish into thin air. She hadn't meant to ease drop, and this was too much for her—she fainted straight away, for the first time in her life! . . .

Sandy's premonition was right.

She landed on the outside of the whipping posts. She stood up and ran to Mammy Tulla's dorms. Mammy was sitting on the porch rocking and singing tearfully. When she saw Sandy, she jumped up and grasped the girl's arms. She started praying and telling Sandy in fast, rambling sentences what was going on.

"Missy," she started, trying to steady herself, "Massa Coard done come down here wit some mens and declared we was doin' Voodoo in dis slabe yard. All de slabes from de other plantations been warned not to come here no mo'. They done gib us til tomorrow night to hand over de guilty witches and to show dem where de stuff is hid in da woods. They know it's out dere 'cause they been watchin' us bring stuff out. Some of de slabes from some other plantation got scared and took de master an' some law mens back to de glades, but they couldn't find nuthin'. Sandy, they means b'ness 'cause they hung one of dem slabes as an example. They got Charlotte locked up in de barn again and they's gon hang her and Stoney t'mara if nobody come fo'ward. Some of de slabes from 'Forks of Cypress' done said they de ones dat tole on Charlotte-n-Stoney and dat they gots to look out for theyselfs. They done tol' eberything, Sandy! They done tol' eberything!"

Tulla's sobbing had abated while she spoke; now, she was sobbing again. For no apparent reason, Sandy's eyes caught Tulla's hands. Why, I never noticed how old her hands looked, Sandy thought.

"OK," she said to Mammy, "you've got to get a hold of yourself and we've got to put together a plan and then execute it."

Two hours later, the women had an elaborate plan put together. First thing was for Sandy to go to the barn and untie Charlotte and Stoney and feed them.

"We knowed you was comin'," Stoney gushed as he dug into the hot meatball and cheese sub.

Charlotte had little to say but Sandy saw a deep vacancy in her eyes, a fear that was echoed in her soul like carving on granite. Sandy felt as if her heart was in her throat. Taking Charlotte's hand in hers, she assured her that she wouldn't be hurt.

"I'm taking charge now, so you're safe. I won't let anyone hurt you ever again. I promise." Sandy's tears mixed with Charlotte's as they clung to each other. Before leaving the two slaves, she loosely tied them up again, reassuring them again that no harm would come to them.

Sandy went up to the big house and into the parlor where Coard and three law enforcement officers were discussing their plan to execute the two slaves in the barn to make some of the other slaves come forth. If not, they would kill two more and so on until someone told them what they wanted to know. Coard expressed his disdain at killing expensive slaves, especially his own.

"Let's not get 'kill happy' here now, Sheriff Luckus. I paid close to $500.00 for my female slaves not born on this plantation, and I can get $600.00 for the ones born heah."

Sheriff Luckus looked at Coard and frowned but said nothing.

Coard continued. "A healthy young male brings $1,000.00 and more." Coard stopped talking; the other men in the room weren't slave owners. They stood glaring at him.

"We are here to help yew find which one of those thievin' niggers is stealing and from where. If yew don't wont our he'p, we'll leave ya to yaself!" The orator spat a glob of snuff into a spittoon.

Coard threw up his hands and sat down on the black horse hair sofa and gave them the go ahead. It was that serious to him.

They were going to kill Stoney, Charlotte, and two new babies. The punishment would start the next day at noon. No slaves would go to the fields that day. They were not even allowed out of their cabins until they were called out. Sandy hurried out of the room. The house slaves knew what was happening. Mammy Cinda was in a fix. She knew she would be spared. But Cinda had three children that lived in the slave quarters.

It was the house slaves that kept the cabin and field slaves caught up with the latest big house news. Sandy reached the slaves' cabins and burst through Mammy Tulla's door.

"We've got to start getting out of here." She panted, out of breath. "Those law men are going to kill babies tomorrow, too." Tulla's eyes were as bleak as a sunless day.

Sandy grabbed her shoulders and shook her. "Mammy, you can't give up on me now; I need you!" As the woman came out of her trance-like state, she nodded her head to show Sandy she was ready. "We've got to get news to the other plantation slaves that were at the party and give them a chance to come with us. Who can do it, Mammy?"

Mammy told her she could send Luther, a twenty-one-year-old field slave that was swift on his feet. But Tulla was reluctant. "Lawd, Missy, yo is gonna get us all kill'. Dem other plantation slaves is de ones what tole on us. 'Sides, they been two oberseers on guard ebby night and de pattyrolla's. How we gone get outta here?"

Sandy looked at the woman with disbelief and said, "Have you forgotten that I'm the one who saved Charlotte from being whipped? Remember the other things I've done, too, Mammy Tulla." Sandy was angry now. "I can get everyone out of here that wants to go. Now, send for Luther and five other able-bodied young men; right now, damnit!"

With that, Sandy slammed out of the door and went to find Faye and Bubba. Together, the three crept into the woods and Sandy chanted the caches away. She assured them there would be another cache at their new home.

Next, Sandy found a large clearing at the edge of the woods and chanted in two large

Greyhound buses with full tanks of gas! Then she chanted in twenty five large, flat pieces of steel and metal nails.

"What da hell . . . ." Bubba began; his eyes nearly popped from their sockets as he took a step backwards; but Sandy had to grab Faye to keep her from running away. She explained that the monsters they were looking at were called buses, "a sort of mechanical coach that doesn't need horses" and admonished herself for not warning them first.

The two really trusted Sandy and calmed down but they walked around and around the buses touching them before they went inside.

"Listen," Sandy told them, "only slaves can see these buses unless slaves are inside. Remember that."

The three left the forest in time to see a group of white men leave Worthinwood on horses. Sandy directed Faye and Bubba to spread the news and to have everyone who wanted to leave with them to meet in the woods at midnight.

"Tell them to bring nothing but their most valuable possessions. Leave everything else. Tell them to be here on time or be left behind." Digging her fingers into Bubba's arm, she said,

"Bubba, if that grapevine *ever* worked, you *make* it work this night!"

Dusk fell as Sandy made her way back to the barn and Charlotte and Stoney. She chanted in chicken sandwiches for everyone, but she didn't want a picnic atmosphere; she had the slaves stay in their cabins, and she had the food popped in at each hut.

Sandy was aware of the two sentries at their lookout points. Usually only one overseer was posted in his own little hut. His job was to keep slaves from running away and to stop fights among them, but, until now, there hadn't been a reason for him to do anything after the slaves came in from the fields, so the two guards were very conspicuous.

She went back to Tulla's dorm and told her to send the five men to the woods where the bus was. Sandy walked in the shadows slowly towards the bus. Tears welled up in her eyes blinding her; her throat ached with fear. Dropping to her knees, Sandy gave way to her fears. Sobbing, she tucked her chin to her chest.

"Almighty God in heaven, please hear our cry tonight. We're down here in the hands of slaveowners that haven't a whit of compassion. Remember us, Lord; only You know what will happen."

Her chest heaved with anxiety. Looking up at the darkened, starlit sky, she prayed on.

"And, Lord," she sniffled, "Lord, I'm afraid. We are all your babies and . . . we need you this night to protect us; don't let us die, Lord, please. I'm only human, and if these people are killed, it will be all my fault! Help us to make our way. I thank you and I love you, Lord. In Jesus' Name."

Sandy sighed deeply.

"Amen."

She stood up feeling drained but somehow reassured. The five men that Sandy had asked for crept into the forest one at a time. After talking to the Lord, Sandy felt strong again. No matter what happened, she had no doubt that God was watching over them. Her actions had been sometimes adventurous, but no more. With her trust in God through Jesus, she surged forward.

The first thing she did was to explain to the five men what the buses were about. She assuaged their unspoken fears and took them inside.

The men were filing out of the bus when Luther showed up, breathing hard. "Sandy, I was foll'd by da oberseer; tell the men to get down on the ground!" His whisper was loud and the men sought refuge but not before the overseer with a torch in his hand saw the buses before the last slave could get off.

The overseer couldn't believe what he'd seen. Thinking all sorts of evil, he probably thought he was looking at some sort of voodoo monster. But when the bus vanished before his very eyes, he fell to his knees. He saw the slaves taking shelter behind trees and felled logs. But his flight or fight instinct took over, and, in a flash, he aimed his gun at Luther and shot him in the chest.

Sandy put her fist to her mouth and stifled a scream. The overseer got back to his feet and stumbled backwards out of the forest, dropping his gun before he turned and ran. Rocking and cradling Luther, Sandy told the other men that he was dead.

"We can't help Luther now; he's gone." The trembling slaves were glued to the ground in shock. "Get up and listen to me! We've got to move, fast!" They got to their feet. "That overseer is going to alert everyone! Let's move it!"

Sandy's orders were concise and direct.

"Go to every cabin. Make sure everyone is in the bed, or at least acting normal. They will be coming, and soon! Let's be ready. Tell them . . . . Tell my people to pray."

She had already gotten word by Luther to warn the slaves from the other plantations to be careful and to take cover in the woods where the caches used to be.

It was only two hours later when she heard the horsemen approaching.

There were ten of them next to Coard and the frightened overseer. Sandy walked right beside them as they checked each cabin. Every slave was in place.

"Well, I'll be damned!" the sheriff's deputy said. This was his first time in the 'redecorated' slave quarters. Spitting his snuff on the floor, he continued. "I ain't never seed the likes a this! These niggers got it better then most decent, God-fearing white folks. Look at these heah clothes and furnishin's!"

The Worthinwood men had already heard this too many times. The white men, with their kerosene lamps ablaze, kicked more doors in. The deputy kept spitting snuff on the clean linoleum floors. Other lawmen bent to touch tiled floors or carpets. Sometimes the occupants were awakened and sat straight up in their beds.

"I say we pull those pickaninnies outta them cribs and make a point tonight! If we wake these niggers and make'em watch us cut up a coupla live babies, somebody gon start singin' like a bird to spare their babies." This man who spoke was called Tipper. He was a tall, big-bellied redneck that needed this type of thing to make his own lean life exciting.

But as Coard struggled to agree, Sandy spoke threw clenched teeth. "You put so much as one finger on any of these people, and I'll send your hatin' ass straight to hell, Tipper!"

Tipper's face registered shock, and the other men, including Coard, made a beeline for the door.

"Who said that?" Tipper asked as Sandy stood toe to toe with him. She took his lamp and slapped his face. The fat man paled; then, as if a devil were on his heels, he ran also. He left his horse as he ran toward the big house. Sandy knew that they would be back with more men, drinking liquid courage. Just like cowards, Sandy thought. With a streak of meanness, she hit his horse on the flanks and sent it scampering in the opposite direction.

Gathering her men, she headed quickly back to the woods. Sandy worked fast; she and the men used the steel sheets to turn the two buses into gauntlets. All of the windows were covered in this fashion and the gas tanks and tires were shielded too. There were two small holes left in the windshields for her and the other driver to see where they were going and several small cracks in places for the other look-outs to peep from.

Next, she gathered the slaves. Women and children got on first. Mammy Cinda was among them as were many of the house slaves.

It saddened Sandy that not every slave wanted to go. Some of the very old slaves and a few house slaves that had it 'real good' stayed. But she didn't dwell on that long. Bubba, who would be driving the other bus, approached with Charlotte and Stoney. Sandy had given Bubba a crash course in driving the bus; she didn't, however, use the term 'crash' when she instructed him!

Sandy hugged Charlotte and Stoney before they boarded. Then the other slaves from Worthinwood and some from a few surrounding plantations boarded both buses. Sandy started the engine in her bus, and Bubba followed suite in his. The slaves were flabbergasted and ill at ease when the air conditioners were turned on, 'high'. Sandy stood beside the driver's seat and began to speak. She assured them that everyone would be fine.

"I don't know how long it'll take and I don't know exactly where we're going, but God does, and He will lead us. Put your trust in Him, not in me." She assured them that wherever God took them, they would arrive there fat and well even if they were packed like sardines in a can. Sandy could only imagine how the packed slave ships had been.

Valery and Renee decided to stay behind, but Buddy, their houseboy, came along. Buddy, like Mandy, could read. They would be able to teach the others more than just their ABC's one day. This gladdened Sandy's heart. Mandy reminded Sandy so much of Jello. She hugged the young girl as she entered the bus. "Don't be afraid," Sandy whispered to her.

The bus had cooled off inside, and everyone was comfy when, suddenly, Sandy heard horses—many horses.

She had instructed Bubba simply to follow her and do nothing more until informed. One of the men yelled that they should have guns.

"No," Sandy said. "We don't fight fire with fire. Remember our prayers, people. Just hold on, and you will see!"

The first bullets pinged off the steel-encased buses. Sandy and Bubba remained calm and steered carefully but deliberately onto the dry dirt road. She knew the roads weren't designed for autos yet, but she had faith that God would provide a way.

The bullets came steady now, and one of the young men told her that he counted fifteen horsemen.

The women on the bus started praying aloud and singing good, old-fashioned hymns. But in between verses they heard the bullets and shouts from the horsemen, filling them with fear.

Wanting to keep them calm, Sandy began telling them about Martin Luther King, Jr. Everyone became calm as she spoke. Not even a baby stirred. Some asked questions; others hummed softly with their eyes open wide, showing Sandy they were still listening to her.

By the time Sandy was through, most of the kids were asleep, and the grown-up were softly but resolutely singing a song Sandy had taught them:

"We shall overcome. Deep in my heart, I do believe, we shall overcome, someday . . . ."

CHAPTER THIRTEEN

At 8:00 a.m. the next morning, the freedom-bound buses came to a stop.

Sandy chanted in hot eggs, bacon, grits, toast, milk and coffee for everyone on both buses. They all heard the men outside beating on the buses to get inside, but their efforts were in vain. Sandy and Bubba's gauntlet was secure!

The people dozed off while the men on the outside swore these metal machines were giant devils straight from hell and that they had swallowed up the slaves! To the horsemen, they looked like trains, but *where* were the tracks!

Sandy was so excited that she had to force herself to eat. When she started moving again, the men crawling on top of the buses were flung to the ground. Someone had tried to torch the buses, but to no avail.

By noon, the people on board were hungry again, and babies needed to be changed and cleaned up. Sandy chanted in cheeseburgers, fries, and iced water. She also popped in a fresh change of clothes for everyone. She had shown the women the bathrooms and how to use them after breakfast.

All day long, they rode on. The horsemen kept up their attacks.

Through every town or small city, people ran from homes and businesses to stare in obvious shock but Sandy and her people were calm. One horseman stationed himself in front of the bus thinking Sandy wouldn't hit him, but she closed her eyes and pressed on. Fortunately, he got out of the way just in time.

It was growing dark again and Sandy was faced with a challenge.

They were approaching a river, a deep river, and she had no idea how they would cross it . . . or even if they should!

The ruck of horsemen following them now numbered thirty, and there were still astonished onlookers at every town they passed through even as it grew dark. Peeking through cracks in the steel, the slaves kept Sandy informed about what was going on outside that she couldn't see from the vantage point of driver.

Men, women, and children stood aghast as they rolled into town after town. In each town, more horsemen swelled the ranks of the slave owners hot in pursuit. Women fainted, children hid and cried, men swore by everything holy that the end of the world was nigh, but, still, the buses rolled on. The bright headlights of the buses must have seemed like dragon fire to the people in these towns.

By the time they reached the river, Sandy knew what she had to do.

She stopped the buses with instructions for Faye to close the door immediately after Sandy disembarked. She took Stoney with her. She chanted that, as long as she held his trembling hand, the horsemen couldn't see him or her. The horsemen stopped too, of course. Only, this time, they kept their distance. They kept plenty of space between themselves and these Monsters from Hell!

Sandy stood looking at them in the distance but decided against addressing them to warn them off. The next sight they saw would probably do the trick, anyway.

She stood on the river bank and chanted in a cruise ship!

Some of the horsemen fled immediately, others cursed then left, and Sandy bid the ones that left a fond farewell.

The staff on board the luxury liner—who had been preparing to receive passengers for a trip to Bermuda—were a bit dumbfounded by their having appeared on the Savannah River, but these people from her own time could see Sandy! And the befuddled captain wanted an explanation . . . . Now!

The few remaining horsemen—include Coard Worthinwood—watched in amazement as the doors of the buses opened as if by magic; they could hear the slaves leaving the buses and boarding the ship, but they could see nothing: Sandy was leading her people on board by having each of them hold hands in a long chain!

As the last of the slaves boarded the ship, the busses disappeared and along with them Coard and the last of the horsemen. Worthinwood Plantation would never be the same!

The captain of the ship, a tall, stern Italian man, was concerned about his ship's whereabouts. He demanded that Sandy tell him where he was.

"We are on the Savannah River, sir. And the year is 1821."

The captain shook his head and muttered to himself that it was definitely time to stop drinking.

His navigational aids confirmed his location, and, in a stupor, he commanded his crew to follow Sandy's orders, convinced that he was dreaming and that his alarm would soon wake him up.

The crew did as Sandy asked and went about their normal duties and served these new passengers as if they were on a normal cruise. Polite and courteous to all of the slaves who boarded, the crew, too, were sure this was a dream.

And, as for the slaves, they thought for sure they had all died and gone to Slave Heaven! They couldn't believe that these white folks were saying 'Yes, Sir' and 'No, Sir' and 'Yes, Ma'm' and 'No, Ma'm' to them! They were being served hand and foot!

For two days, Sandy's people were served, dressed in beautiful gowns and suits, and fed like royalty.

The crew watched the people dance and dine in the ballrooms, served drinks to them and heard the people call *them* master; they heard babies cry in the night with their mothers crooning beautiful melodies to them. Never had the crew served a more gracious and appreciative group of passengers!

Up in the 1900's, however, things were a bit less harmonious.

The World News at 6:00 p.m. reported the astounding news of the disappearance of a cruise ship—just as it prepared to board its passengers! The U.S. Government was in an uproar. Were terrorists responsible? Was a hostile government to blame? The world's attention was focused on this bizarre event.

Even the Shaws forgot their grief for a time while these strange events unfolded.

Newscasters from around the world reported the story. Even the soaps were interrupted for news updates. How could a luxury liner just disappear without a trace?

Meanwhile, the Jesup news still reported its own similarly bizarre set of disappearances: several employees from different local stores had reported merchandise vanishing from under their very noses. It took one loudmouthed clerk to admit it, and everyone else admitted it too. Most stores had either fired their black employees or had them under close surveillance, despite the news from Sydney about the international thefts.

Before, the blacks of Jesup had been outraged; now, they wanted apologies.

It became festive in the black community, especially for the younger folks. Most swore that white organized crime was responsible for all the strange happenings. If it had been black folks, wouldn't the blacks in Jesup have known?

The robberies continued even after the black employees were fired or closely watched. The media tried to link the disappearance of the cruise ship with what had happened and what was continuing to happen in Jesup.

Olivia tried to pretend all was normal and, strangely enough, no one asked where Sandy was. Richard went to work and came home as always, but he, of course, would ask Olivia if Sandy had returned yet.

The ship now headed for the open water of the Atlantic; Sandy depended on the ship's captain—with Grandma Mary's guiding hand to help—to carry the slaves to a place of safety: Sandy put it all in God's hands.

During the time of their passage, Sandy gathered her people around her under the clear, unpolluted skies of the Atlantic Ocean, —the skies that witnessed other ships' passage from Africa not long ago—and she spoke to them some more about the very special man who would come to play such a vital role in the lives of their great, great grandchildren.

Explaining the word segregation, Sandy went on to tell them about the life and death of Martin Luther King, Jr. Dr. King's voice was like many waterfalls; it was mighty, but Sandy's Bible said that Jesus' voice rang majestic like thunder. Imagine!

"He was like Moses, whom the Lord used to bring the Jews out of bondage. You all have heard of Moses, haven't you?"

Many heads nodded and voices chorused, "Yes, Sandy."

"Well," she continued, "Dr. King was used by the Lord in much the same way the Lord used Moses." She told them of the many struggles that King endured, being spit on and being beaten, stabbed, and jailed. "I mentioned him to you briefly before, but tonight I'm going to talk about him even more; and, more than that, you yourselves will <u>hear</u> his voice. I will make that possible."

Looking around the crowd, Sandy saw confusion on many faces, fear in others. Even though they had witnessed Sandy's 'miracles' before, they were still unaccustomed to them.

"King's fight for justice was totally without violence on his part and on his followers' parts. God put him on earth in the twentieth century, and thirty-nine years after his birth the Lord allowed a man named James Earl Ray to take Dr. King's earthly life away. But his legacy of non-violence continues to live in the hearts and souls of millions. He had done the job the Lord sent him to do."

Sandy paused again. Each little family was huddled together. Mothers held their babies on their laps, and fathers held on to the older children, and the teens sat together in little cliques. Grandparents and older people sat closest to Sandy, along with the orphans and young single men and women.

"Dr. Martin Luther King Jr. left behind his beautiful and faithful wife, Coretta, and four little children—two boys and two girls—who Coretta had to raise alone; but she did an exceptional job.

"Now," Sandy said, after she surreptitiously chanted in a cassette player and a tape of one of Dr. King's most famous speeches, "Now, my people, listen to the future."

As the people anticipated hearing King's voice, they were not so much in shock as in awe.

After all, Sandy had shown them many strange things before, hadn't she? Stoney, who was sitting right beside Sandy, looked on intently as she put the tape into the slot and pushed the 'play' button.

The people froze as King began his "We Shall Overcome" speech. For minutes it seemed liked time stood still. Not even an infant whimpered.

King talked about loving one another and about non-violence. His voice was dynamic, and Sandy had the bass and volume turned high. He spoke about winning the victory so that all of God's children—black, white, Jew and gentile—could live and work together in peace. There was a battle to be fought, but it must be fought by not raising a hand against the abuser.

King's voice went on: "Before the battle is won, some of us will have to be thrown in jail some more but . . . We shall overcome!"

Sandy looked out at her people as the tape rolled on: "Before the battle is won, some of us will have to face physical death. But if physical death is the price that some must pay to free their children from a permanent physiological death, then nothing will be more redemptive . . . . We shall overcome!"

As the speaker's continued, his voice seemed to fill every molecule in the air. He went on to say that some negroes will be called bad names and dismissed as rabble rousers.

"But we shall overcome! I'll tell you why, because the Ark of the moral universe is long but it bends towards justice . . . . No lie can live forever! We shall overcome because truth crushed to earth will rise again . . . . We shall overcome because the Bible is right. You shall *reap* what you sow. Deep in my heart I do believe we shall overcome. With this faith we will go out and adjourn the councils of despair and bring new light into the dark chambers of pessimism."

His mighty voice poured out like rain in the desert as Sandy's people listened, thirsty for the wellspring of hope in his words.

"And we will be able to rise from the fatigue of despair to the buoyancy of hope. And *this* will be a greater America and *We* will be the participants in making it so! And so as I leave you this evening I say, 'Walk *together*, chillin', don't ya get weary! There's a great camp meeting in the Promised Land!"

As Dr. King's voice soared and thundered to the end of his speech, sobs and cries of "Oh,

Mighty God!" sounded through the tearful crowd of listeners. The young children were the only dry-eyed people in the bunch.

Sandy had heard this speech many, many times and it still moved her in a way she couldn't explain. On this evening so many decades before she was born, she sat in the midst of her people and her tears flowed as easily as theirs. No words were necessary. No one stood to move or talk for many minutes.

Families held each other. Husbands and wives seemed to stare out and into that 'greater tomorrow' that Dr. King had promised. Finally , she clicked the tape button to 'off' and looked around at the faces surrounding her. Some had the same question in their eyes as they looked back at her: Had Dr. King's prophecy been right? Had the negroes made a difference? Had Sandy been telling the truth? Were the negroes really treated as normal people in her time?

Sandy acknowledged their questions, but, searching her mind, she could come up with no definitive answer. If she said 'yes' she wouldn't be lying, but she wouldn't be telling the truth either. Taking a deep breath, Sandy took a few seconds to explain what they were about to see and why. This would, to a certain extent, answer their questions.

Chanting, Sandy popped in a wide screen TV and a VCR. The tape that appeared in her hand was one of *Oprah*. The guests on this particular show were several young black men. One guest was the late Martin Luther King, Jr.'s son, Dexter.

The show was about the hidden discrimination still present in America. The film had more than one reason for Sandy's choosing it. The people were absolutely shocked, of course, to watch TV. Many were frightened. But to see Oprah Winfrey, a young black woman, in control of the show with so many white people in her audience clearly adoring her—seemingly fawning over her—had to mean something special to Sandy's people. The respect the audience showed this beautiful, vibrant black woman was simply astounding!

"Oprah has a deep love for people of all colors," Sandy explained. "And there are adverse personalities she finds hard to tolerate in persons of any color."

The show about hidden discrimination in America—as heartbreaking as it might have been to some of its twentieth century viewers—was something out of a beautiful dream for Sandy's people: A white woman openly embracing a black man made them gasp and some choked. "What was the problem?" they all seemed to ask.

Sandy explained it as simply as she could before whisking away the TV and standing to try and end the questions she couldn't seem to find adequate answers for.

At supper, everyone was unusually quiet except for the children. Sandy sat with Charlotte and both girls merely picked at their food. Sandy felt that the reason for the silence was her inability to supply sufficient answers to her people to make them understand the position of the black race in the twentieth century. She felt that maybe they were quiet because they thought she was selfish.

In their eyes, Sandy led an ideal life. And from what they had just seen on film, many of them would give anything to live like that and be treated half that good. So how could she possibly make them understand that justice sat on a full platter and only a fourth had been served to people of color? The rest was reserved for the so-called 'superior' race—the white race!

She was deep in thought when Charlotte spoke. "You know, Sandy," she said with a sigh, "Seein' da way de times is gon change so, so long from now is gon make it so hard for some of us to die. Eben if things in yo time is still so far from being what Dr. King wanted, it still is *so* much better din now. Us alive now is gon be dead long before our Dr. King grandmammy eben get born. Do yo think dat some o dat hidden unfairness gon get right while you live?"

Sandy, who had begun staring at Charlotte as her speech unfolded now abruptly stood up with an audible gasp. "You did understand, Charlotte; you did!" With that, she grabbed Charlotte in a bear hug and pulled her to her feet also. "Oh, Charlotte, my precious Charlotte! You won't die. You'll sleep, and while you sleep, we, your children and our children's children and on and on will live on because of your love and your life."

The other grownups that had previously been so silent now gathered around the two girls. They had all heard everything that had been said and the majority agreed. There were quite a few of the older people that didn't and wouldn't see anything but magic and miracles in what they'd seen on the film and emotionally they would not be moved.

But one old lady with a prominent lower jaw and a lot of spunk called Rose spoke up: "I ain' seed nothin' but a good new life in dat TB thang. I ain' worryin' 'bout dyin' now 'cause I know thangs gwine get like dey 'pose ta be. I hopes my children have a lot mo' children now so they can see de promise land for me. Lord, We is gwine be blessed by de Lord God Awmighty." She threw her head back and wept with joy as most of the other elderly people joined in with shouts and tears of their own.

Irene looked at the young women and giggled. "I thought de only freedom niggers was gon see was gon be in da North like New York."

Gail guffawed back. "And we all knows dat slabes dat gets ta run up North and gets caught comes back skin and bones. Dey don't like niggers there neither."

Rose sputtered, "Naw! If de whites won't give them no jobs, how's dey gwine get somethin' to eat? Dem North white folks kin tell a runner. Dey gots a nose for it."

Everyone had a say and tried to speak at once, each louder than the next.

Sandy held up her hands to get their attention. "Shhhh!" She hissed as loud as she could. "Listen to me, people. After this trip, we are never, I mean *never*, going to use the word *nigger* again when we speak of our race. We are black people, now and forever more. I mean this. Never call another black person a 'nigger' ever again. Do I make myself plain and clear?"

Loud choruses of "Yes" and "Yes, Ma'm" went up around the dining hall, accompanied by beaming smiles of pride.

"Now," Sandy continued, "go to your cabins and sleep well tonight, for tomorrow we arrive at your new home. And remember, God will provide!"

Applause rang out amid shouts of joy and tears.

Early the next morning, a still exhausted Sandy was awakened by the captain's first officer who took her to the ship's bridge.
Sandy had already determined that the ship had anchored off shore of land, but she didn't know where. The ship's Captain informed her that they were off the coast of South Carolina, anchored off an uncharted and, as far as he knew, uninhabited island a score of miles due east of Edisto Island.

The captain was at a loss to explain why or even how he had steered the ship to this location, but Sandy understood. "Thank you, Heavenly Father, for guiding your people home. I love You."

Sandy named the place 'Tucker Island'. Here, generation after generation, her people would live out their lives in freedom.

The crew helped her people disembark, small boat loads at a time, and, when they were all safe on shore, they turned to wave goodbye to the ship's crew. As they waved and gave thanks, the ship's whistle blew loud and then slowly faded, along with the ship, back to the twentieth century, the crew still believing it was in a dream.

Tucker Island was perfect!

There was game to hunt, fresh water, plenty of forests, and, best of all, it was deserted: no one had claims on the island—it was all theirs.

Sandy chanted in a wonderful breakfast to celebrate their first day of freedom. However, this time she chanted in uncooked food, and she and several of the men and women would do the cooking. "No male or female duties here," Sandy admonished. "I'll show you how to do it right!"

She chanted in pots and pans, made a fire, and they prepared omelets and fried bacon.

While they drank coffee, Sandy discussed her plan for them to stay on this island and how she would go about doing it. She knew the building materials and other equipment she would have to chant in would cause another mess at home but, she reasoned, I have to do this one last time.

She looked at the contented faces around her and realized that these people had put their lives in her hands.

Jimmy Lee was lying languidly on his mother's lap. He was a peaceful child and had asked Faye quite a few times if his friend Misty was going to come to visit them. Fanny's own baby would grow fat now that the child wasn't sharing its mother's milk. These were all good thoughts, but now Sandy had no time to waste. She had a full day ahead of her, and she could not stay away from home too much longer.

Clapping her hands, she asked the people if they were ready to make this island into their home and got a chorus of "yeah's" and "uh hum's" and broad, toothy smiles. The first order of the day was to appoint Dorsey and four other teenagers to take care of the children and keep them quiet.

"I guess the first building I'll chant in will be a school." And Sandy gave the responsibility to tutor the people, young and old, to Mandy and Buddy. Buddy smiled wide and stuck out his chest at the news. Sandy grinned back at him. "I'm going to be chanting in some pretty large buildings here today, so don't be alarmed, OK?"

Closing her eyes, Sandy popped in the very first building, an oblong structure with everything a school needed—blackboards, desks, books, pencils and paper, maps, even two old-fashioned toilets that Stoney and Bubba hooked up.

There were shouts of praise to God from all the people.

"Now, this is where Dorsey will take the children today while we work and, other times, when day care is needed."

Next, Sandy chanted in a small, white clapboard church with a bell and high steeple. The cheers were deafening. She chanted in one large community Bible and stood back, proudly grinning like a Cheshire Cat.

Now she asked that each family stand by itself. She counted twenty families, and in four rows she placed each family in little white houses complete with picket fences and a large piece of land in the back for gardens.

Sandy could have made it easy for her people by using her powers to plant the gardens, but she didn't. She chanted in tons of seeds—tomato, cucumber, potato eyes, corn, and much, much more.

Several people asked her to chant in some sugar cane—"We knows how to make sugar, Miss Sandy." She was proud of them.

The biggest test yet was to chant in caches with enough supplies to last for decades, and she didn't think of the uproar she would cause as she chanted in a large building filled with dry goods, canned goods, and other things that don't perish.

The applause and cheers from Sandy's people was the loudest yet. Some cried; others threw their hands in the air and praised God, but all were happy.

"Oh, First Aid!" She popped those things into the church in a special room.

Next, Sandy chanted needles, pins, sewing machines, and yards and yards and bolt after bolt of cloth. Then the order of the day was livestock. Each family received two cows and one bull, ten laying hens and one rooster, three sows and a boar, and a mare and a stallion. The horses were placed in a communal stable in the heart of the little town, and ten ewe and one ram per family were placed together in a meadow that the men would clear by cutting trees and fencing it in.

Sandy didn't want to make them lazy; they knew how to make moccasins, quilts, and rugs. The whitewash and paint brushes were chanted in by the tons along with paint thinner. By the time Sandy had the beauty aids tucked in their own cache, she was exhausted. The very last thing she did was to chant in some waterproof canisters to store matches in.

At that moment, she couldn't think of one thing she wouldn't do for her people. But she knew that they would have to do the rest on their own, with no more gifts from her except tools and nails. They would have to build their own lives here now, and she knew they were willing and able.

When Sandy was done, the people hugged her and the men picked her up and carried her above their heads. Sandy felt jubilant. She had put her fingers in her ears to drown out the cheers. This had been a day that she and her people would never forget.

Later in the day, Sandy rang the church bell for the first time. When the people gathered around, Sandy chanted in a large clock that sat inside the steeple on the front of the church.

Next, they went into the church and she gave them calendars for the next ten years and stacked them in order in the pastor's study.

"Now we gon know when Christmas come," Said Fanny.

Sandy explained, in fact, that when she left this time, she wouldn't return until Christmas, and then only for one day. She then called Charlotte from the crowd and put her arms around her.

"There is something I want to tell you, Charlotte, and I want the rest of you to hear also." She looked at Charlotte. "Charlotte is my grandmother, many times removed. Charlotte, you will live to be almost 100 years old. Five years from now, you'll have your first baby, a girl. But your husband isn't here yet. He is an Indian." To Sandy's surprise, the crowd applauded. Nothing could surprise them now.

Charlotte looked at Sandy in disbelief, and asked simply, "How you know?" Others nodded their desire to understand the mystery, too.

"In my time," Sandy began, "we trace our ancestry through libraries and records in the court house. Back in this time, your masters keep records of slaves' births and deaths. And you, my people, must remember to tell your children and grandchildren the stories of each of your family trees."

She turned again to Charlotte.

"You are going to have one daughter and three sons. One of the boys will be my great, great granddad. It goes down like that, generation after generation." Sandy tried to keep it short; she knew it was time for her to leave, but her heart was growing heavy and she did not want tears.

Sandy glanced down at her watch.

"Hey, time is flying, people! I'm going to walk around the town and make sure I'm not forgetting anything. I'm open to suggestions: if anyone thinks of something, yell it out, OK?"

As they walked around the little village, someone yelled that they needed a well. Sandy slapped her forehead with the palm of her hand. "How could I forget the well? I'll do better than that!"

Grabbing her ivory, she popped in a communal well in the middle of the village, complete with buckets. Next, she put old-fashioned water pumps in the back of each cabin.

"Now you'll never be without fresh, cold water. Oh," Sandy exclaimed, "We have to have a spring house to keep things cold and for ice, right?"

The crowd nodded gaily. Sandy popped in four large spring houses. She had read in history class how the first ice was made. Water was put out during a winter freeze and when it was frozen solid, it was taken in blocks down deep into the belly of the spring house to stay frozen even in the hottest weather. Milk, butter, and other perishables were preserved in this manner.

Sandy told the men that it was very important that they get busy right now doing things that would turn this perfect little village into their home. She had already supplied them with every kind of tool they needed. Every man was given a shotgun for hunting and protection against intruders and wild animals. She filled numerous 100 gallon drums with ammunition.

Sandy stood back and looked at her handiwork. Her people were happy and they had no fears. They loved her and trusted her. She said a short prayer of thanks to God through Jesus. Just then, Sandy remembered! Throwing up her hands, she got everyone's attention. "Guys! How are you going to make music in the church?"

Herb stepped forward. "Miz Sandy, we knows how to make instruments-n-stuff. I brought some rawhides dat I hid under my shirt." He spit and moved his snuff around in his mouth, but he wasn't finished. "I heard ya say to bring nuttin' but I jus' couldn' leave my hides behin'. Point is, I can work dis here piece o' hide and make tabereens-n-drums wid it. What ya need t' gib us is some terbacky!"

Everyone started laughing. Irene put her arms around her husband and said, "I think dis man o' mine tryin' ta tell yo dat he almos' out a snuff!"

Now Sandy was laughing too. She looked at Herb. "OK, good buddy, I'll give you enough snuff to last you till you sow and reap your own crop of tobacco."

He grinned and told Sandy that, as a way of thanking her, he wanted her to have a silver dollar—his prize possession. Sandy hugged him as he pressed the coin into her palm.

She knew that her people could make it on their own now.

Until she came again for Christmas, this would be her last day here for a while. Tears flooded her eyes and started to overflow. She turned her back to the crowd so they wouldn't see her crying, but they did. Earlier she had told them that she wanted to see each family in their own houses, so she waved them away.

"I'll be around to see you in a minute," she said, trying to control the sobbing in her voice. Everyone slowly drifted off in small clusters.

Today, when Sandy scrutinized the people, she liked what she saw. They didn't look like slaves anymore. Gone were the head rags and dirty fingernails. Most of the women wore clear nail polish. They were clean inside and out. The caches that she had chanted in for cosmetics and hair products were huge. The women and men had perfumes and colognes. The babies had diapers with rubber pants, plus cradles, cribs or bassinets, and the older children had plenty of blocks and games to play with.

Sandy smiled through her tears. She remembered what happened when she chanted in a bike for Jimmy Lee before they left Worthinwood. The boy ran when he saw it, and Faye had to talk to him for hours trying to calm him. After a while, he timidly let his mother take him back into the front yard. Soon, Jimmy Lee let Sandy teach him how to ride, and he became a teacher to the other kids that got bikes.

Sandy entered the first house and looked for anything that would aide in making the new homeowners comfortable. Each house held smiling, proud people—sweet smelling babies and a lot of love. In one house she chanted in an area rug; in every house she put in screens for the windows; some house plants here; a painting there. But, again, in every house were the basics: dinner table and chairs, beds, wash-boards, cleansers, dishes, and flatware.

Sandy prayed that she wasn't forgetting anything. Kerosene lamps? Yes. Candles? Yes. She ticked off a list, followed by "yes's."

Satisfied, she said her goodbyes and prepared to leave for home. She told her people that Indians were somewhere close by because she saw arrowheads, but she told her people that they would be friendly Indians, so they shouldn't be afraid. She winked at Charlotte. She explained that blacks and Indians usually got along just fine: it was the white man they should fear, but be fair to and love anyway.

Sandy had often said that when it was time to leave she would be able to do so because she would have accomplished her mission. The very last thing she did was to chant a family Bible in to each house. Then she stood in the middle of the compound, waving goodbye to everyone. She closed her eyes with a picture of smiling faces before her. And she faded away. . . .

The first thing she noticed when she returned was that her door was wide open!

Then, Olivia stepped in.

Her mother looked calm but determined. "I saw you talking to my mama, Sandy. And, if I live to be a hundred, I'll never forget what I saw—I almost had a heart attack!" Olivia wasn't wasting time with small talk.

Sandy had never seen her mother so calm and resolute. Mother and daughter reached out for each other and embraced. Sandy was again crying softly.

"Mom, if I tell you, will you believe me?"

Olivia pulled back and looked into her daughter's big, brown eyes. "If I saw you vanish into thin air, Sandy, I think I might just believe anything you say, honey! What I won't believe is that you're a thief."

She dried Sandy's face with a Kleenex and then dried her own.

Sandy showed her mother the ivory—which had become visible to her—and then told her the whole story. Olivia shook her head and looked incredulous from time to time. One thing she knew was that Sandy wouldn't lie to her. At one point, she grabbed Sandy and just embraced her again. The story floored Olivia, but she knew that it was true—in fact, she didn't know how Sandy could have made some of the story up!

Olivia had grown up knowing about her great, great Grandmother Charlotte. But she couldn't have been part white; she was part Indian; at least, that's the way it appeared to be. Olivia had heard stories about one of Charlotte's sons who lived like an Indian and wore his hair to his waist. Sandy explained how it happened. She told her mother that the island was home to a friendly band of Indians. She knew this because her history book told her that no savage Indians lived in South Carolina during this era. Charlotte married and bore three sons and a daughter; that was her family's link to their Indian ancestors.

Olivia told Sandy that, when the time came to tell Richard about all of this, Sandy should let her do all the talking. "One thing I've never done is to lie to him. He'll just have to believe me, so just let me take care of daddy." She paused. "Sandy, sweetheart, I just can't believe it! You've met my great, great grandmamma Charlotte!"

When they went downstairs, they watched the evening news report the re-appearance of the cruise ship and the bizarre disappearance of more items. An anonymous but reliable source reported that a young black girl from Jesup participated in the strange events. But the mayor of Savannah was emphatic. "No way could one girl or 2000 girls, for that matter, execute such heists." A Wayne County reporter said that the ship's captain had suffered a near nervous breakdown and was in the hospital. The first officer wouldn't talk to anyone, and the rest of the crew attributed the events to mass hypnosis or hysteria, the reporter said. The crew spoke of feeding ghosts and watching people pop in and out of thin air. One crew member interviewed on the news said that, according to the way people were dressed, he was sure that they were from the Civil War era. Then he laughed and said he was just teasing when he saw the way people were staring at him—but the look in his eyes betrayed him; he believed what he said.

Another man, in a slow, Georgia drawl, said he heard negro voices for two days while they were hijacked. "They played with the elevators and escalators. Sometimes you could see them, sometimes not, but the voices were always heard! But one thing for sure—we were there!"

Later, the news reported that pre-fab homes and double-wide trailers had disappeared, and not only in Jesup but in Hinesville, Savannah—even Atlanta.

Sandy saw her mother frown, and she asked her mother why.

"Something's wrong, Sandy." Putting a hand to her throat was a bad habit Olivia had when she thought Sandy had bungled things. Her mother's next words were totally unexpected. "Sandy, honey, how can you go back at Christmas after you've told me everything?"

Olivia looked crushed for Sandy, but Sandy quickly put her mother at ease, patting her mother's hand. "Mom, don't worry. I can go back. Grandma Mary said it was OK. But, mom, there is one condition that she gave me."

"What's that, Sandy."

"Well, you and daddy and Larry will have to come with me!"

Olivia sat dumbfounded, wondering how she would explain all this to Richard so that he wouldn't call the funny farm to cart her away!

. . .

After Thanksgiving dinner, Sandy helped her mom clear the table.

"Mom, I know what I'm going to give them."

"Give who, honey."

"Charlotte and the others, Mom. Have you forgotten? When we go back, I'm going to give them ledgers so that they can record births and deaths. And I want them to see a real plane. And I want to give the kids cotton candy. They are so happy with simple things, things we take for granted."

She put her hands into her pocket and cracked a nail on something hard—her good luck piece, the silver dollar Herb had given her! "I'm going to make a long list, Mom. Let's see: Christmas candy and popcorn; pretty black dolls with carriages and tea sets for the young girls; Barbie dolls and dream houses for the older ones; a star for everyone's Christmas trees; wrapping paper for their gifts for each other.

"But the best gift of all will be a battery-operated cassette player, a big one, for the whole town," Sandy babbled on as Olivia looked on, smiling. "Not only will they get to hear beautiful Christmas Carols, but, most important, they will be able to listen to Dr. King's speeches, especially 'I've Been to the Mountain Top', the greatest speech of all. And they can listen to the Ten Commandments and the Holy Bible."

Sandy smiled at her Mom as Olivia put the tape in the player she kept on the kitchen counter. Dr. King's voice filled Sandy's head. In her mind's eye she stared into space and saw Tucker Island. She listened:

". . . . He's allowed me to go to the mountain top, and I've seen the promised land. I might not get there with you, but I want you to know tonight that we as a people will get to the Promised Land."

The smile on Sandy's face danced with love.

From God's Truth Sandy was born again.

ABOUT THE AUTHOR

Sachincko Parker Tucker graduated from Cameron University in Oklahoma with a Degree in medicine. A Registered Nurse turned author she's on her way to becoming one of America's popular and respected authors. She became interested in writing after a near fatal automobile accident. Stick of Ivory was birthed between one of the ten surgeries it took to correct her injuries. With still one major surgery left to be done she presses on to complete her forthcoming novels Donna's Lies and The Other Side of Vanilla. She resides in North Carolina with her husband and two birds.